Lucy,

go

see.

Marianne Maili

CHEZ SOI PRESS

Chicago   Los Angeles   Barcelona   Paris

Marianne Maili/Chez Soi Press
info@chezsoipress.org
www.chezsoipress.org

Book Layout © 2017 BookDesignTemplates.com

Font: Iowan Old Style

Lucy, go see./Marianne Maili. **REVISED** edition, **2023**
Chez Soi Press
Paperback ISBN 978-0-9996631-2-7
Hardcover ISBN 978-0-9996631-0-3
Ebook ISBN 978-0-9996631-1-0

With gratitude for my mom, grandmothers, and all the ancestresses alive in me.

IF YOU'RE LUCKY ENOUGH TO FIND A WAY OF LIFE
YOU LOVE, YOU HAVE TO FIND THE COURAGE TO *LIVE*
IT.

—Owen Meany

This novel is the alchemy of some years of life lived and the lead of that experience turned into gold using an elixir of imagination and joy. It has gone through many transformations. At its genesis, it was titled *The Beautiful Chaos of Camels and Gold,* and concentrated on a love story between strangers that I eventually saw was essentially part of a greater love story with life itself. Chaos, camels, and gold were some of the signs and symbols, some of the *prima materia,* along the path of a young woman's adventure out into the world, her going and seeing.

Though *Lucy, go see.* is the story of how a young girl from rural Iowa becomes an international model and the trouble she gets into and out of, and how she learns about the powerful autonomy of her sexual desire, it is also a deeper story of how integrity is formed while carrying an unvoiced, unrecognized wound. It tells of an ambitious young woman whose instincts, curiosity, and principles are her guides on a quest simply to be herself in a world where she is repeatedly challenged by male privilege.

The story is also a vision of how a powerful mother's voice can aid a young woman in that journey.

Ultimately, like the turtle in search of home while carrying it, this is a story that asks where home is and finds it within. As we all can, and hopefully, do. As you travel through the novel, please keep in mind and heart that joy is what holds it.

Marianne Maili
The Gold Coast, Chicago
November 2017
Los Angeles
January 2023

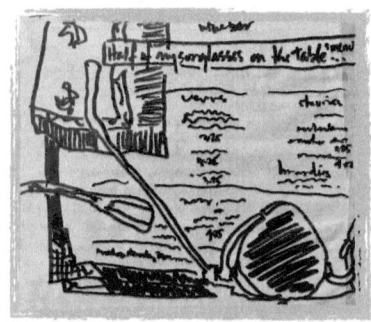

These are the things she knew. Joy was a house to be lived in with laughter as its guardian. Sorrow and anger visited but Lucy would not let them stay. It was a mobile home, her house of joy. Its walls were her skin. She knew she was different, that she was born with desires no one around her seemed to have, and because she was just one sapling in a massive forest of relatives, rooted and thriving where they were, it seemed the problem surely lay with her—and she became nervous as what she knew did not fit with what she saw—was she in the wrong place? She knew, too, that nature knew the way to be—she knew the solace of trees, the openness of pastures and meadows—the enthusiasm of brooks, rivers, and streams—the beauty of growth in all stages—the triumph of flowering, the following decay. The warmth of the sun, the strength of the wind, the cleansing rain, the pristine nature of snow, the color of fall. She saw there was pain and she saw love eased it. She knew she was pretty and she knew she was smart and it seemed that almost everyone wanted her to think she was not that pretty or that smart. She wanted to prove to the world and herself that all she knew was true. She wanted to go and see what lay beyond the rolling green hills of the Upper Mississippi Valley and she wished she could take all those she loved with her, which she did, for she was made of them. Lucy wanted to sculpt her life in much the same way she shaped the earth after rain as a girl. For her life was to be play and her work to be play—earnest, serious play. If there was a god he or she was a benevolent one, she knew that, too, and the only thing she saw right in the church was the singing. She saw death left behind the shell of a body, that mobile home discarded, it was obvious the spirit fled it, though she didn't know where it went, yet, she could feel her pioneering ancestors both around and inside of her. She listened more to the voice inside than the multitude hawking their wares, out.

She knew, too, that what most people called love was not, and that love was uneasy. And she knew that desire was something altogether different, too. She had a feeling that sex was much more important than anyone seemed to realize, much more sacred than anyone would like to believe, and even more powerful than anyone had already imagined. She sensed it was at the base of creation, not to be messed with, without messing up the whole system. And she knew early that something in the system was very messed up.

I. The Manner of Her Setting Out

The first inkling of a way out came via envelope, handed off by a departing spectator after the Twins/Astros game in St. Paul. A breeze cut through the heat in the shaded seats of the stands. It smelled like spilled pop and cool cement. Lucy's two brothers and dad were in the dugout visiting her uncle and meeting the players. Her two sisters were back in Iowa. Viola Pilgrim looked over her daughter's shoulder. "What's that?" Lucy showed her mother the Miss Teen-Age America application she had just unfolded. Viola wrinkled up her nose, then darted her eyes around. "Who gave you that?"

Lucy lifted her chin toward a balding man exiting the stadium. "Him."

Viola glanced, already shaking her head in rapid disapproval. "Throw it away. That's all you need is to be getting yourself mixed up with characters like that."

Lucy was engrossed in the fine print at the bottom of the page. The guy had looked as normal as any other to her. She thought her mother was a suspicious woman who would do what she could to keep her captive, like a sort of Cinderella in a tower, only letting her out for chores or family activities. Yet, she was surprised—and not—that someone considered her Miss Something or Other material. She believed she was good-looking but as scarcely anyone else mentioned it—"You clean up real nice, Lulu" was the biggest compliment doled out, and that by her dad—she had begun to doubt. Now here was proof of some kind of attractiveness, though she had already read that she was unable to compete for the prize, which was just as well, she told herself because there was no way anyone would get her in sequins twirling batons, a talent she associated with such competitions.

Her brothers, Blaze and Eze, bounded up the stairs ahead of their dad carrying freshly autographed baseballs like prized gems. Lucy raised her eyes, and then slid the application toward her father's firm, round stomach saying, "Look."

Tom Pilgrim glanced at the title. "You're not a teenager yet, are you, babe?"

"I will be in November. Anyway, it's only for Minnesota residents."

He waved it away and looked out over the empty ball diamond. "Then just forget about it. There's no sense in thinking about what you can't have or can't do."

Lucy saw his point though she was looking for some acknowledgment of this recognition of her beauty, or her appeal, whatever it was that had caught this man's eye. She wondered why her dad did not say more. She watched his eyes for any arrow of sadness, always curious if he regretted giving up on professional baseball to raise a family, and if it was painful for him to now watch his younger brother on the field. All she ever saw was his joy and pride in his younger brother, and right then, a longing for the field and the play. She admired what she imagined as a lack of envy and a sacrifice of one desire for a greater one, even though his choice was difficult for her to understand. Giving up professional baseball to live in a small city in Iowa and raise five children sounded boring to her, yet she imagined she would not be alive without it, so she had to be grateful for it. She wished he had done both, and she could have had the exciting, glamorous life of being a daughter of a professional baseball player. She also liked the way home, family, and friends were more important to him. Lucy wanted an exciting life, though, that was certain. How could she do it? She folded and rolled the application, then slid it into the front pocket of her jean shorts like a bullet. Like ammunition ready to aim at future naysayers. As if it were proof of some sort of power.

Lying in the back of the station wagon watching the puffy clouds fly by on the ride home, she wondered if what inspired that man to consider her a contestant could be her ticket out of the cornfields. Could the way she looked, alone, be enough to take her to places she wanted to go?

*

For the time being, her life in Iowa was junior high in the city, and home in the country. Lucy kept to herself, mostly, in both places, because she felt misunderstood in both places. She was at once bold and shy, and her budding self-consciousness was gnawing at her self-esteem. She loved to spend afternoons wandering in the woods with the squirrels, sitting by the streams molding the silt, or lying flat on her back on the hills watching birds, butterflies, and clouds. Evenings she walked across the yard to her grandparents' house to help Grandma Pilgrim bathe and prepare for bed.

Lucy emptied and then cleaned her grandmother's bedpan, as she often had, looking at the color, taking in the smell, thinking about the cow pies in the pasture, and feeling grateful that humans used toilets. When Marie Pilgrim said, "Honey, you should work in a nursing home," Lucy turned toward the tub where her grandmother was pouring warm water over her drooping, tired breasts and shook her head.

It was hard for her to look at her grandmother's naked body very long, yet she did long enough. She would wonder later in her life if seeing her grandmother's naked, tired, and arthritic body had taught her early that focusing only on physical beauty was unwise.

"I do this for *you*, Grandma," Lucy said as she helped her grandmother out of the bath and to her bed.

This was the woman who taught Lucy to read when she was four, who stuffed butterscotch drops and dollar bills in her hand when she brought her the daily paper from across the road, who told her the family history, whose eyes glistened with both joy and a sort of sadness when Lucy offered bouquets of hand-picked violets. Lucy enjoyed the nightly ritual of carrying her a small plate of Club crackers, a pitcher of iced water, and painkillers for her arthritis. After Marie swallowed them, she rocked back and forth on her bed. Lucy caressed her back. She wanted her grandmother to know what she wanted to do so she told her. "I'm going to see the world, Grandma, that is what I am going to do."

Marie smiled wistfully. "I'd just like to go somewhere." Lucy noticed the emphasis on the last word and wondered if her grandmother had had a happy life. "Ask your mother if she goes into town tomorrow if I can go along, even if it's just to sit in the car."

Lucy nodded. It struck her then that her grandmother did not even know how to drive. Lucy looked out the window to the pasture. "Grandma, did you ever want to see the world?"

Grandma Pilgrim sighed as if to say oh, honey, if you only knew how much then spoke. "Lucy, I could get on a bus and ride, and ride, and never come back." Lucy wondered what her grandmother wanted to get away from, and what had kept her there, just up the hill from where she started her life, all her life. Lucy had yet to see how difficult it would be, and was, for a woman to move in the world.

*

"She looks so pretty, so at peace, she looks so good, Ernst," some offered with condolences at Grandma Pilgrim's wake. Lucy, now fourteen, watched her grandfather stare at his wife's lifeless head on the coffin's ivory silk pillow, how he looked like a horse struggling with a bit and how he winced. She wanted to scream–What the hell is the matter with you people? Pretty? Good? She's dead.

Lucy was kneeling in front of her grandmother's body, trying to figure out if her lips were glued shut. Viola, who was standing behind her, put her hand on Lucy's shoulder and whispered, "Touch her, if you want." Lucy was shocked by the cold hardness of the body but didn't flinch. The touch only confirmed for her that her grandmother wasn't in there. She stood up and wandered through the funeral parlor, a Victorian mansion formerly owned by one of the city's pioneer industrialists. She poked her head into a den off the viewing room, where the closest family members gathered, and smiled as she asked, "Isn't it funny that they lay dead bodies out in what was once someone's living room?" Nobody laughed. Lucy sighed and wished, yet again, to be understood.

Graveside, it became clear to her that her grandfather was in trouble. She had never seen emotion in him, and he was overcome. She watched Ernst palm one corner of the casket and not let go, and then was both horrified and awestruck by her father's ability to lift his father's hand so that his mother's body could be lowered into the ground. She gazed at her grandfather's face, bathed and dripping in tears. He did not attempt to brush them away. She cased his movements as he climbed down into the grave and walked around every corner of the casket, ensuring it was sealed and secured as if he were tucking his wife into bed for a long, deep rest. Lucy froze watching his grief. She stood with the taste of salt in her mouth, perspiring, then stared at her scarred, trembling knees, smiling a smidge when she noticed the reflection of the tall cedars and blue sky in the silver buckles on her red patent leather shoes. She liked to think her grandma made her look.

*

Out of a sense of duty and a need to fill the hole left by Marie's passing, Lucy slipped into her grandparents' house at night like a cat. She sat on the floor in front of her grandfather's recliner as he watched the news. If he was downstairs, she alit on a stool in his workshop. Watching the way he could make any broken thing work—simply by taking it apart, studying it, and putting it back together—made her believe she could, too.

She would come to apply that approach to everything in her life.

When Ernst was working in the garden or pasture, she waved and then took the opportunity to go inside alone, and sit on her grandmother's bed and remember. She touched the pillow, polished the silver monogrammed hand mirror, or fingered the cut glass doorknob where her cane still hung, opened her closet, and smelled her clothes. She was glad that Ernst did not let her aunts take the robes, house dresses, Sunday, party, and card club dresses to Goodwill as they wanted to. Marie's passing was the first hole made in Lucy's life. Touching what her grandmother had touched eased the rip of death. Her grandmother's passing made her think about her own and she felt shorn and did not want to die, to vanish, to never see all those she loved again.

Even though she went to Methodist Sunday service with Ernst, and the Congregationalists with her mom's mom, Grandma Bighart, in town on Saturday nights, her parents still insisted she attends the Catholic mass. "I don't think God cares which church I go to," Lucy protested, "or even if I go for that matter. All I do is sit there and think about everything else."

Her father lifted his hands. "Then it's good for that." Lucy saw his point but she would have preferred an empty church in which to be alone with her supposed Maker, rather than one crowded with hypocrites. She saw that most people who called themselves Christian did not act like Christ.

*

As she grew, her grandfather often passed his large hand along her thigh and then slapped it, saying, "You've got legs just like your grandmother's. You're built just like her." This petrified Lucy but she told herself that it was harmless, even though it didn't feel that way. She felt a certain quivering around her leg, like a thick plasma spreading and fixing itself into a transparent sort of shield. Not wanting to believe what she felt, the wrongness of it, she blinked it into impossibility, shook it off, willed numbness onto it. She sat or stood a little farther away when talking to Ernst but always hugged him good night. He needed a hug good night was the way she saw it. One evening, when she opened her arms and wrapped them around him, he slipped his hand between their bodies and kneaded her breast. He had strong hands the size of dinner plates. It hurt her. She had no idea what to do but she felt what he was doing was a betrayal.

She teetered back and he let go. Her breast felt like it was scarred by a wrench, never to be the same again. That was the first time anyone other than herself had touched her there. With her glistening eyes down, she decided to pretend it hadn't happened, and she walked to the door as normally as she always did, and then walked home, stunned, her heart both breaking and aching.

She began a terrible gauging of degrees, thinking of horror stories she had heard about girls' fathers coming to their beds at night and asking or forcing them to do unspeakable, unthinkable things. In comparing Ernst's abuse to those fathers, Lucy worked at exonerating her grandfather. She was ignorant of the massive weight she was accepting to carry by her silence. He wanted to touch a breast, she guessed, and there had been hers in front of him. That, at least, seemed the best-case scenario, and the only thing to do, it seemed to fourteen-year-old Lucy, was dust it off and find a way to carry on. The thought of telling her parents—if she told anyone, it would be them—only brought images of pain. The thought of her grandmother knowing about this stopped her breath. Shame scattered throughout her body. She could not imagine being able to speak the words rising in her: Grandpa squeezed my breast hard and acted like it was normal and didn't even say he was sorry. Speaking that, telling anyone about this, she knew, would officially ruin her idyllic illusion of their relationship.

She loved her grandfather the way she loved her whole family, like a task. She knew love was not a feeling, it was work. It was what one did, how one lived, and it was easier with some people than others. Being close to her grandfather made her feel special in a world where she often felt overlooked. She wanted one of those tender relationships—between a strong, wise, caring grandfather and a curious, smart, brave granddaughter—that she had read about and seen in movies. In her determination to make one, Lucy kept showing up for the job and darting, dashing, or ducking when need be. When she did hug him, she covered her breasts with one arm and wrapped the other around him. She hoped he would get the hint. Mostly he did. Yet, a certain sickness lingered inside of her whenever she thought about what she was hiding to be close to him. That felt wrong, too, and made her feel dirty somehow, but her successful shielding of herself made her feel less shame.

At fifteen, and five feet nine inches tall, she was six inches taller than her petite and curvy mother but still four inches shy of her broad father and grandfather. With the money she made babysitting, she subscribed to the fashion magazines she'd seen while waiting for her mother at the beauty parlor. She was confused why they didn't appear in the mailbox until she found them hidden in the hall closet. She stormed up to her mother waving them in the air. "Why are you hiding these?"

Viola turned from the African violet she was watering on the kitchen windowsill. "That's a waste of money on useless crap. How many times do I already have to tell you to get your nose out of some book and do something?"

Lucy, who knew "something" meant either setting the table for seven, peeling and chopping vegetables, vacuuming, dusting, scrubbing, cleaning toilets, and mirrors, shining silver, or ironing, went livid. "I'll mow the lawn, I'll shovel snow, I'll walk the garbage across the road, let them come inside and do what I do." She was talking about her brothers, of course, but she may as well have been talking to the apple trees in the backyard for the response she received. She let the screen door slam behind her as she walked out on her mother.

Leafing through the magazines down in the pasture, Lucy saw modeling as a fabulous ticket out. What enticed her was how happy, independent, and cosmopolitan the young women looked; that, and the fast piles of cash she heard they made. She, too, wanted to stand in the middle of busy sidewalks in

Tokyo, take Japanese baths, walk with elephants in Kenya–all while wearing fabulous clothes and getting paid for it. She looked up at the house, seething at her mother for trying to keep her from all she wanted, then marched back up the hill and slipped inside, taking care that the screen door did not slam notice of her return. Upstairs in the kids' bathroom, she stood in front of the mirror comparing the magazine models' faces and bodies with hers. She saw no reason why she could not be among them. She thought of the Miss application she still kept in her drawer. Her older sister, Ruby, looked in, then rolled her eyes. "Don't you have anything better to do than stand around staring at yourself in the mirror?"

Lucy shrugged. "Not at this moment, no."

*

After Lucy saw a feature with Candice—a tall and very pretty girl from New York who had just transferred to her high school—in the fashion section of the local paper, she waited until Candice was alone in front of her locker, and then handed her the paper asking, "How did you do that?"

"I'm taking modeling classes and the woman who teaches arranged the job."

Lucy looked the woman up in the phone book that afternoon. Viola was on her way out the door to the grocery store and was surprised by Lucy's offer to go along to help. Afterward, as they were leaving the parking lot, Lucy pointed to a building nearby. "Would you stop there for a minute? I'd like to get some information about a school."

"What kind of school?"

Lucy braced herself. She knew her mother would disapprove. "It's about self-improvement and beauty. And they give modeling classes."

Viola glared. "Would you just forget about all that phony bullshit?"

"Mom, please, I just want to talk with them. By myself. It'll only take a minute."

Viola parked. "I'm not waiting here forever."

Lucy sprung from the car.

The front walls and door of the agency were glass. A well-dressed woman talking on the phone behind a desk motioned for Lucy to come in, then pointed to the brochures at the desk. As Lucy waited, the door swung open again and the most un-Iowan woman she had ever seen, with cropped red hair and flawless skin, sashayed in with a briefcase, knocking her knuckles on her left breast saying, "These things are hilarious." She looked at Lucy, who was wondering where she could get a set, and answered the question in her eyes. "I'm breastfeeding. They're breast cups." The woman circled Lucy then, smiling and nodding, not missing a beat. "You must be here for the modeling course."

Lucy—standing there looking down at her jeans, button-down shirt, yellow rain slicker, and plastic boots—didn't know how much these women knew about fashion and modeling but she could see they looked more sophisticated than she did. She glanced at the clock, then moved toward the door waving the brochures in her hand. "I have all the information here. Excuse me but I have to go. My mom is waiting."

The woman's eyes widened. "She didn't come with you?"

Lucy wanted to tell the woman it was best her mom had not popped in to tell them what phony bullshit their business was but decided to just smile and perhaps leave that for another time.

Viola was no longer in the parking lot. Lucy didn't care. She was glad to have gotten where she wanted to go. As she contemplated calling her father, Viola charged in, the white Toyota Corolla splashing through puddles. Her mother stared straight ahead as Lucy slunk into the car, shut the door, and heard for the umpteenth time, "Don't you think I have anything better to do than chauffeur you around?"

"Why don't you let me drive by myself then?" Lucy knew her mom would not answer that. She watched the headlights of the approaching cars blur and refract through the rain and waited until they were further down the road to say, "I would like to take this modeling course."

There was a moment's silence as if Viola were considering it, then Lucy watched the veto happen in her mother's brain. "I don't know why you need to go to school for such a thing. With all the brains you're supposed to have, why don't you use them?"

"Supposed?" Lucy asked.

As Lucy thought about how many times her mother had declared that letting her be put a year ahead in school had been a big mistake, Viola proclaimed, "I'm not paying for it."

Lucy shrugged. "I will." She promised herself she would find a way. She could not understand her mother's disdain for modeling and did not ask because Lucy was afraid of her mother, specifically of her mother's anger. She did what she could to avoid it but she would not let it rule her life. It hurt her, but she knew her mother would just tell her to get over it or get used to it if she talked about it. "You're fiery, like your mother," Lucy's dad told her, but Lucy sensed that her mother's flames burned hotter.

*

Lucy's first modeling job was a television commercial for a trucking company. In jeans, cowboy boots, and hat, she climbed into a semi-truck's cab, tossed off a few lines, and then pulled the horn with a big smile. Her father shouted, "It's Lulu!" every time it came on. Her mother shook her head rapidly as if things were all headed in the wrong direction fast. The rest of the family seemingly paid no attention. Lucy happily took the check to the bank. Next, the local newspaper booked her for a fashion shoot on the Delta Queen, then a furrier paid her to stand in a fur coat next to a limousine, and after that furniture companies paid her to stand next to couches. It was so easy and fun and gloriously paid compared to her new part-time job at the department store. But she had to agree with her mother that not much of her brain was involved. At that point, she didn't care. She enjoyed walking the runway for mall fashion shows, and smiling down at all those she figured had not voted for her for class president, and certainly had not invited her to their parties or cliques. Why didn't they like her? Lucy did not know. It made her feel insecure so she increased her bravado.

*

On Mondays at school, she often heard girls talking near their lockers about their weekend sexual experiences in words that disgusted her, telling and asking each other if they had "been porked." Although Lucy could not imagine why pigs were involved in their metaphor for penetration, she was curious as to what all the whispers and giggling were covering. Not just at school but everywhere. Sex seemed so delinquent and important at the same time. Her mother had told her it was for babies alone but all the hullabaloo and desperation surrounding it told Lucy there was more than propagation involved. She decided to approach it as an equation and set about deducing its unknown values.

She looked around and found the most handsome young man, an athlete a couple of years older than her, and set her sights on him. She waited until it seemed like he loved her, and since love was a task she could perform with whomever she chose, she found it fitting enough that he was clean, pleasant, and fun. Sex, she found, or penetration, more precisely, was rather boring and painful at first. "That's it?" did not seem the best thing to say to her boyfriend.

She was ill-equipped to connect her lack of pleasure to her heartless algebraic approach. Lucy was organizing love and sex like divisions of labor. Even though she imagined they'd fit best in the same department, she was wary of putting them together. Yet, she did her best to apply love to sex through romantic gestures she learned on television, in movies, and in novels.

Could her grandfather's abuse have had something to do with her separation of love and sex? She was unaware. Whenever she thought of it, she would find herself humming, "One of these things is not like the other, one of these things just doesn't belong."

She continued to approach sex as research on the pleasure of touch. The rest of her time she worked on preparing her dreams to become reality, and she felt it was good to have a fun jock of a boyfriend while doing so. Until she found out her bed was not the only one he shared. The months of lies not a teeny aside, it was also a combination of hygienic and practical issues that killed the attraction for her, and there was even chemistry involved; Lucy sensed that two essences required a closed vessel to do their best work together. It took her a while to let go of the relationship, but she did. After that disappointment, she slipped another coat of armor over the first.

She noticed how deep pleasures rippled in her groin when she was in nature, or in her nature: feeling good in her skin, happy and working on something exciting, sculpting or drawing, or even reading. A party scene in a novel in which a woman, dressed in a tuxedo, was flirting with the woman next to her turned Lucy on so much she read it again and again. As did another scene in another novel where a married mother blisses out during a secret summer affair with a young man. The daring play across borders and limits thrilled her. Yet it scared Lucy to realize she was attracted to women; society certainly made it uneasy to explore that, she thought. When her modeling teacher joked, "God, imagine how exhausting it is to be bisexual, everybody turns you on," Lucy sighed and wondered what kind of exhausting life awaited her as it seemed to her that it was life itself that turned her on.

Such arousal seemed too volatile and unheard of to be trusted. Lucy wondered why people had to label their sexuality, why they couldn't just live it. She deferred the rushes and vibrations mounting in her because she had never heard of sex talked about in the way it seemed to be coming alive in her, and she wondered if there was something wrong with her. She found she was attracted to authorities, teachers, managers, professors–people she wanted to be, who had qualities she wanted to develop in herself. Some let her close to them even at the risk of arrest. One recent divorcé twenty-five years her senior initiated her to the arts of non-reproductive lovemaking. He cared for her, too, it must be said, but he had to drop her. One might say Lucy slanted all of her experiments toward proving her hypothesis that men would only hurt her.

Males could be her friends, she noticed, until the inevitable question of sex appeared. However she answered, it changed the relationship. She was always grateful for reprieves from that pressure. She wondered, too, if sex really was all that most males were looking for from females because it seemed their behavior became less respectful once they either had it or were denied it. It seemed she would have to choose between love and sex, and she felt safer not loving. In the span of a couple of years, Lucy concluded that desire was more enjoyable than consummation, and the best she could do was carry a good shield.

What she couldn't understand, though, was why boys her age did not ask her out. Her brother, Blaze, suggested a possible reason. "If you didn't talk, they would." This only puzzled her more. Lucy generally thought what she had to say was funny or interesting or important.

*

The summer after she graduated from high school she begged her mother to let her visit Candice, who was modeling in Chicago. Viola yelled, "You're only seventeen years old. Do you have any idea what can happen to you in a city that size?"

When Lucy said, "I'm your daughter, what could happen that I can't handle?" Viola let her go.

After looking through a pile of Candice's portfolio pictures in that apartment on Grand Avenue, Lucy was wistful, wondering again if modeling could give her the worldly life she was dreaming about. It seemed like such a risk. She also thought about the acceptance letter she had received from the University of Iowa. She wanted to travel and she wanted a college education. She could feel Candice's eyes on her profile as she heard her kind voice. "You could make a good living doing this, you know?"

Lucy turned her focus from the fire escape outside the window. "You think so?"

"Yeah, you just need pictures and an agent. You have a great nose."

"Hmm, a nose model?" They both laughed. "But I want to go to college, and tuition to any university in Chicago is out of the question."

*

Her mother and Grandma Bighart were waiting on lawn chairs in the August sun, watching Lucy load the trunk. The air was humid, which made Lucy irritable on top of eager to get to college. She dangled the keys as if she were calling guests to supper and said, "I'll drive."

Viola stood and smoothed her white pants. "*I* am driving my daughter to college."

Lucy thought she was being helpful when she said, "You can just drop me at the dorms."

Viola's blue eyes sliced into Lucy's. "Did you ever think that it might mean something to your mother and grandmother to take you out to lunch and spend a little time with you when we take you off to college for the first time?"

Grandma Bighart, who, like Grandma Pilgrim, had never had a driver's license, raised her index finger in the air. "I only finished the eighth grade, honey. My mother made me quit school to stay home and help her take care of my six brothers and sisters. The proudest days of my life were when I saw my daughter graduate from high school, and when I saw her driving a car. Now, look at you going off to college. You think maybe we could have lunch?"

Lucy lifted her arms in a truce, then glanced at Viola, who days before had called Lucy her problem child. "I thought you'd be happy to get rid of me."

Viola shook her head and rolled her eyes as she opened the door. "You really get some damn dumb ideas in your head."

Lucy smiled but her mother could not see it. They missed each other sometimes like that, each declaring affection and attention in a way that surprised the other.

*

During lunch, while Viola was in the ladies' room, Lucy asked her grandmother what she had been wondering throughout the ride. Lucy was picturing her grandmother as a young girl, torn away from school and forced into domestic drudgery. "When did you leave home? How long did you have to take care of everyone?"

Willa Bighart sipped her iced tea, and Lucy watched a sad sigh lift and lower her breasts as she set her glass back on the table. "I was nineteen. I'd been taking care of my brothers and sisters since I was thirteen. We lived out in the boonies. I know it's not kind to bad-talk the dead, but my mother was not a kind woman. One day your grandpa was coming to pick me up, and I was wearing what we called knickers then, short pants just below the knees, which were the fashion. My mother told me I wasn't going anywhere in those. Your grandpa drove up in his jalopy and I got in and rode into town with him. Never looked back, never went back."

Lucy was speechless. That was the first time she saw her grandmother as a young and feisty woman instead of a gentle, resigned old one.

2

That fall, just to see, Lucy sent pictures of herself to the top modeling agencies in New York City. One week later, she found a note in her roommate's handwriting telling her to return a call to Vanity Fair agency. When she did, a woman named Apollyona invited her to come to New York to meet the owner of the agency, and told her to keep in touch with Serena, her assistant.

It was the first time Lucy had ever flown, and she loved being in the clouds. She stared out the window most of the way. In the cab to the city, too, following the line of skyscrapers.

The driver pulled to the curb in front of the Blackstone Hotel, a narrow, fifteen-story brick building on 58th Street. As Lucy walked into the lobby, the stout, balding concierge smiled from his wood-framed window, lifted the key off the wall, and nodded toward the elevator. Lucy felt like she was being given a pass to adulthood, which also made her feel like an impostor, as if someone might stop her anywhere along the way and ask her who the hell she thought she was and where the hell she thought she was going.

The suite was empty and dark. The carpet, bedspreads, curtains, walls, and towels were all teal, making Lucy think of a theatrical blue room, as if she were in the waiting room, just about to go on stage. She opened the curtains and looked down to the street. Two blocks to the west she could make out parts of the Plaza Hotel and Central Park. She turned on the radio to a man's voice giving a Manhattan traffic report. As she changed clothes, she had the feeling of stepping through space into a different dimension that had always been there, yet not, as if she were in a sort of real dream world.

The phone rang. It was her mother checking to make sure she'd arrived. "So what kind of cathouse do they have you in out there?"

Lucy did not catch the reference because she did not know what it meant. She did not even know that her mother thought of models as prostitutes. She was still thinking of them as she did years before—worldly, traveling, beautiful women. "What do you mean, cathouse?"

Her mother sighed. "Oh, never mind." So Lucy did not.

*

Vanity Fair was on the 25th floor of a mirrored skyscraper on 57th Street. As Lucy waited for the elevator, a woman she recognized from an Ivory soap commercial walked in and stood next to her. She looked like a street-wise Snow White in jeans, a white t-shirt, and leather jacket. When they reached the agency's floor, Lucy hung back, letting the already-working girl walk through the glass doors ahead of her.

A trim pointy-breasted woman with red curly hair piled on top of her head sat erectly at the reception desk. Her voice was soft and rich with a lilting Swedish accent as she spoke through a headset on the sound system, "Serena, Lucy Pilgrim is here to see you," then pushed the microphone away from her mouth and nodded toward the black leather couch with a smile, "Please, have a seat."

The walls were lined with magazine covers featuring Vanity Fair models and Lucy's favorite, Julie Nancy, was on many. She probably sat right here, too, Lucy told herself, as two tall men in silk suits strutted down the hallway toward her, ending a meeting, planning another, looking self-satisfied and sophisticated. Lucy recognized Bill Zabub from pictures. He was a tall, portly handsome man with dark hair parted on the side and falling over half his forehead, and he had an aquiline nose, olive skin, a fine set of lips, and a little dimple in his chin. As he and his colleague stood in front of Lucy talking in smoky voices, wearing what smelled like matching musky perfume, Bill reached into his pocket, pulled out a pink lacy bra and panties, then dangled them in the air as if they were just-caught big fish. "Now where did these come from?" As he chuckled, Lucy was glad her mother was not there, knowing she would already be dragging her out the door.

An elf-like woman with black curly hair, brown doe eyes, and red painted lips wearing high heels, a white lace body suit, and a black miniskirt skittered down the hallway on the other side of the desk. When Serena held out her tiny white hand and introduced herself, Lucy recognized her voice. Serena looked Lucy up and down, then scratched her head in a way that made Lucy worry she didn't look the way they thought she would. Serena paused her gum chewing to say, "Follow me."

They turned at the end of the corridor and entered a large open office space with a round table in the middle. Serena alighted onto her chair and spun a circle of files in the center of the table as if she were playing roulette. She came to Lucy's name, extracted what she had on her: the photos, the letter, a record of their phone conversations. "I need your birth date, telephone, and social security number." She penciled them in as Lucy recited them. "Now we just need to weigh and measure you."

Lucy calculated how many pounds her clothes alone added up to–wool pants, thick cotton long-sleeve shirt, wool sweater, corduroy jacket, suede boots. She stood on the scale against the wall, her nose twitching from Serena's powdery perfume, and watched Serena's gold-laden manicured fingers and long red finger nails fidget with the balance. One hundred and forty-seven pounds. Having read that models weighed no more than one hundred twenty-five, Lucy thought she would not get farther than this.

But Serena went on. The height was easy, painless. Five-foot ten. Then came the unfurling of the yellow tape measure. As Serena wrapped it around Lucy's bust, waist, then hips, Lucy thought about fairy tales with small elves circling tall girls, and withstood the temptation to blurt, "But my clothes are heavy and thick, and isn't that a little loose, here let me pull it a tad tighter." Her suffering could have been relieved if she knew then what she would come to learn: every model's card lied about measurements.

37-26-38, Serena wrote carefully in big loopy numbers. Lucy thought about the so-called perfect measurements for a woman's body, 36-24-36, and considered the trip wasted even further. Serena swiveled around in her chair, and dropped her teeny feet to the floor and looked toward a nearby desk. "This is Apollyona."

The gaunt thirty-something woman who had been quiet at the desk in the corner moved one side of her long, straight, black hair behind her ear, and with it, motioned to the chair across from her. "Come and sit here in front of me."

Lucy could tell that this woman did not like her, or somehow did not quite approve, and Lucy noticed the way she crossed her arms on the desk in front of her, putting up a wall between them.

"I am the head of the New Faces division," she said as Lucy sat. "In this department, we introduce you to photographers and help you put together a book of pictures to show to clients. Then we send you on "go-sees," to go and see prospective clients. We also dispatch you on castings to meet clients who already have a specific job in mind. But before we talk anymore, I want you to meet the agency's owner, Bill Zabub. He is the one who liked your pictures and is interested in you."

That last piece of information hit Lucy like a small dart. She followed Apollyona through the adjacent department, pausing to look at the piles of well-known models' composites stacked on the shelves against the wall, imagining her own among them. When she looked up, she saw Apollyona across the hallway, through an open door, talking in front of what she assumed was Bill's desk. Lucy glanced at a glimmer of vulnerability in her there, embers of kindness that seemed nearly burnt out. Apollyona turned, and as quickly as she motioned Lucy into Bill's office, the glimmer was gone.

Bill was on the telephone speaking French, running his hand through his hair. He nodded toward two brown leather armchairs and gestured for Lucy to sit. As she did, she saw the photos she had sent from Iowa lined up in front of him on his maple desk. After he hung up the phone, he stretched his arms like a bird in mating season and then dropped his elbows at the edges of Lucy's pictures. That made her chuckle silently. Bill joined his hands, rested his chin on top of them, then gazed into her eyes. "Why do you want to be a model?"

She could see he was playing some sort of game. She stayed at the edge of it. "It looks like an interesting way to travel and make money."

He smiled. "I can give you a tour of the world." Lucy wondered how many times he may have said that to young women, and if that was what put bras or panties in his pocket. "I have agencies everywhere. And you have everything you need to become a star. All you need to do is lose a little weight."

Stardom seemed the least interesting prospect to Lucy as she scanned the Manhattan skyline through the wall of windows behind Bill. It was the world she wanted, not fame. She imagined herself hanging out in international capitals and exotic locales, being photographed in studios and on locations, and being paid a lot for it. She saw herself exploring cities and countries, sipping coffee and wine at outdoor cafés with foreign friends, walking boulevards and country roads, and crossing deserts and ancient bridges. She would see wonders, stroll narrow, cobblestone streets—all the while with the wind blowing through her hair and a wistful smile on her face. Then she thought about weight, diets, deprivation, exercise. This made her hungry and tired. "How much?"

Bill reclined. "Do you know who Julie Nancy is?" Lucy nodded. Bill went on. "You remind me of her. When I met her she was waiting tables. I told her that if she lost twenty pounds I would get her a five-page spread in Vogue. She did it in three weeks. Lose twenty pounds and you will be perfect. Run every day until you lose weight. Eat only salads—that is what she did. She set aside her pre-law studies and you can see the successful career she has made for herself."

But Lucy wanted it all: studies, modeling, and traveling. "I would like, at least, to finish this semester of college."

Bill leaned forward. "Drop the weight and come in January then. Nineteen is already getting old for this business. I like to get girls around sixteen, before they have a mind of their own and I can't do anything with them."

At that moment, Lucy considered it an unwise career move to ask Bill if he'd always been an asshole or exactly what had triggered the development of this attitude. She decided to do what she often did, to disagree silently and carry on. She loaded her eyes with the information that he was already too late with her as they shook on the deal. Then she walked out of the building under a cloudless sky and headed for the park.

The Brandenburg Concertos and the smell of roasting chestnuts floated in the air as Lucy strolled north. She liked the music so much she stopped and bought a cassette tape from the vendor, then continued along, a lilt in her step. An uncomfortable feeling moved through her as she saw a man standing alone in the field she was approaching. The waist of his pants was around his knees and he was pumping something with his hand. Lucy thought no, not here, he can't be jerking off in the middle of the park, but she saw he was, yes. She picked up her pace to pass quickly by. He bellowed, drawing out each vowel as long as each breath would allow. "Suuuuuuck myyyyyy diiiiick!" She sensed it had nothing to do with her; rather, he was asking the world for this favor.

Did life boil down only to that for men? Lucy wondered, couldn't believe it, and didn't want to. Some men, maybe, she thought. Maybe even most, if she ventured. Some women, too, for all she knew. "They only want one thing and don't give it to them." "Why buy the cow when you can get the milk for free?" She'd heard these things back in Iowa and thought moo? Me? Do I moo? I think not. Am I for sale? I think not. But suppose it for a split second; what milk? Ah, so that was the magnet in her breast.

Her back now to the misery that hung in the air like a swarming cloud of flies around the jerk-off, Lucy scurried toward the crowds. As her breathing slowed and deepened, she looked into the faces of the people who passed, wondering about their dreams, wanting to tell them how far she'd come toward hers. She imagined screaming out, as that man had, Hey, listen, I am just a little girl from Iowa who wanted to see the world, and I picked up a magazine and saw some models in interesting places, and compared their looks with mine, and thought I could do that, too, and look here I am in New York City and the owner of one of the best agencies in the world just offered to give me a chance. He is not exactly the nicest guy in the world, but, hey, how many are?

Then she walked downtown, imagining a life of her own in the city. This was, after all, something she had been longing for—to be in a place where she could meet people from all over the planet all wanting to do something interesting with their lives. She wanted to be one of the cool people of the world. Yet, not knowing any cool people, she dined alone in Greenwich Village. It could be lonely, she thought, as she looked around at others in animated conversation, but the prospect of merging with all this was so exciting to her.

*

When Lucy was back in Iowa City, Apollyona called. "It is important that we have some pictures when you arrive in January. Could you come to New York during your Thanksgiving break for some photo sessions? We will forward the cost of the photos and hotel expenses and deduct it when you work."

Not wanting to say, "No, I am still too fat by your standards," Lucy ate as little and ran as much as she could, without fainting, for the next ten days. She told her parents that she was using savings for the ticket and then forged her father's signature to receive a short-term loan.

*

The city was dark, gray, and cold this time. The morning Lucy arrived, Apollyona sent her to a studio in a former slaughterhouse on 20th Street. The stairwell was rough cement, the elevator was wide enough to fit at least five cows. She knocked on a steel door, and a short, long-haired man with a scarred face opened it. "I am Hyde." Lucy thought he looked like an ogre or a troll, and it made her step back. She had not known what to expect yet expected something more glamorous. She followed, thinking how it made sense that a man who looked like Hyde might want to create portraits of beauty.

He led her into the musty loft and she took in the faces of the two other teenaged models, a makeup artist, a hair stylist, and a couple of technical assistants eating at a long makeshift table under opaque windows. Lucy swallowed her hunger looking at the mound of thick deli sandwiches and the collection of soft drinks. She looked toward the bright lights and a backdrop on the other side of the loft and wondered what she was going to do once on the set. She declined Hyde's offer of a sandwich. How dare you? she thought but did not say as she sat under the window with a glass of water and a magazine, reading while everyone else ate until she was directed to the hair and makeup area with the two other girls. They were each rail thin, and Lucy wondered how they could eat hero sandwiches and look like that. They didn't talk to each other, or Lucy, and she didn't speak to them.

It was strange this silence; all seemed wary of being friendly.

After the tiny goth makeup artist finished working on her, Lucy was startled by her reflection. The rose blush on her cheeks looked like war paint, and it appeared she had a new mouth with huge fake lips—lines drawn above and below her lips were filled in with pink lipstick. Lucy scrunched them up and around. The makeup artist patted her on the back. "You're ready for the hair chair."

The smell of hair spray and cigarette smoke made Lucy dizzy. She half-smiled into the mirror at the reflection of the skinny, dark-haired man in a tight black t-shirt and jeans standing behind her who placed his hands on her shoulders. "And what shall we do with you?"

Thinking all these New Yorkers must know better than her, she shrugged and smiled. The young wan man pulled her hair painfully tight behind her head, then let it fall, sprayed it with water, blew it dry, added gel to immobilize it, then curled it up at the ends. Lucy hated it and thought she looked ridiculous. Yet she remained silent, squashing her unspoken words into more tension inside of her.

The other two girls rummaged through the boxes of clothes. Lucy wished she did not have to dress herself; she thought a stylist did that. She wondered if it was okay to say so, but her silence was going deeper and deeper, her voice getting farther and farther away from her, as she stared at the collection of leotards, shirts, tights, and belts, and thought about how she did not want to dress like that. She heard the shutter clicking and walked toward the set to watch one model, then the other, posing, laughing, smiling—in leotards, tights, and boots–looking like grounded Tinker Bells without wings. It seemed so easy to them, so carefree. Lucy wondered how they could do it without feeling silly. Hyde raised his voice to be heard across the set, "Now jump," and the blonde model ran, and then jumped through the air, turned, and smiled at him. Maybe they had been cheerleaders, Lucy told herself, maybe that made it easier. Hyde turned to Lucy and nodded toward the trunks. "Help yourself to some clothes."

Lucy pointed to her hair and makeup. "I don't know what to wear with this."

Hyde scuffed over to the box in his new white sneakers, and Lucy liked how clean they were; they seemed the freshest, brightest things in the room. He reached in, tossed her purple tights, a purple bodysuit, and a thick black belt. "Try this with your boots."

Lucy thought she looked like a cross between a Concord grape and Robin Hood. Her thighs trembled as she approached the set and heard, "Run, then look at me as you leap across the set." Lucy gathered her courage, ran, and leaped. At least twenty times. Feeling gangly, heavy, and silly. When she heard, "We've got it," she thought, we do?

Then he tossed her turquoise tights, a turquoise body suit. "Put these on and go to the hair chair." Lucy closed her eyes as the chain smoker sectioned off half of her hair, then added more gel to stiffen it so it stuck straight out on one side. He gathered the other half into a tight bun at her nape. Now she thought she looked like a blue cockatoo stuck in a nightmare that had started as a dream. On the set, Hyde peered around the camera. "Just stand there and look at me." Lucy did. "Now move."

"Where?"

"Just move. I will shoot when it looks good." Lucy wondered what could look good about her at this point, and she hated this part of being told to just move, she always would. She thought of the pictures that had first attracted her to modeling and how they were all natural, outside, in the movement of life. Not in studios, stuck on a set. She took a deep breath and lifted an arm. Moved a leg. Crossed them. Stood profile. Flinched with every click of the shutter. Hyde waved her off. "Okay, back to the chairs."

Her nerves were somewhat soothed when her hair was let down and combed through. Hyde passed behind the chair, rested his hand on her shoulder, and looked at the makeup artist. "The close-up is next. Accentuate her eyes." Then he looked in the mirror at Lucy, and gently said, "You know you have amazingly beautiful eyes." His sincerity jarred her. She had not expected this kindness and wondered, then, if anyone had ever said this to her. As another glob of gel hit her head, she closed her eyes and savored the recognition.

Her hair was slicked tight against her head and twisted into a ponytail, twirled around and painfully stuck with bobby pins. She slipped on the clothes he'd given her and then sat on the set. When he zoomed in on her face, she relaxed and peered into the lens, knowing he appreciated her eyes. This being-seen changed everything in her confidence, and those would be the only salvageable shots of the session.

Walking out of the studio that chilly evening, the smell of corner fires and exhaust mingling in the air, Lucy asked herself how long she could survive weeks of days like that—working with people like that, jumping through the air in ridiculous hair, makeup, and clothing. The only part she liked was peering into the lens as if into a rabbit hole.

*

The next morning a pretty photographer opened the door upon which Lucy knocked. Dove's studio was clean and organized, a bright loft with crystal clear windows looking out onto the sparkling Hudson River. The wood floors smelled as if they had just been polished with a lemony scent and they, too, were reflecting the morning sun. Dove appeared so happy and comfortable with herself that Lucy thought she might prefer her job.

When she edged closer to Lucy on the couch, Lucy loved the way she smelled like orange blossoms. As she glanced into Lucy's eyes, then scrutinized the features and angles of Lucy's face as if holding an interesting and precious object up to the light, Dove smiled and softly said, "We are going to shoot beauty this morning." Lucy wondered what she would do if Dove kissed her. She was that close, and her touch so tender, her eyes admiring. "Focusing on face, hair, and skin," Dove added as she caressed Lucy's cheek. "You have lovely skin." Then she backed away to survey Lucy from more of a distance. "How long is your hair?"

Lucy released the bauble on her ponytail. Dove ran her fingers through Lucy's hair. "To feel the texture," she said when Lucy stiffened. The door buzzed. Two women, one tall and one short, each with pixie haircuts, both wearing black, and carrying metal cases, walked in. After introductions, they directed Lucy to a small paneled room off to the side, instructed her to sit on the red vinyl barbershop chair, then swiveled her around considering angles and discussing plans on what to do with her. Dove poked her head in to say, "Curl her hair, do some soft natural makeup, pinks, to start," then left to set up the camera, backdrop, and lights.

As they did her hair and makeup, Lucy felt like a real-life Barbie which she both liked and didn't. She liked the pampering but not the talking about her like a mannequin, inhuman. She closed her eyes until the woman patted her on the shoulder. "Time for makeup."

Lucy loved the fluffy white towel wrapped around her neck that smelled like pine, and the rosemary moisturizer delicately caressed into her face and neck with the same spiral-like movements used for the application of foundation. A light powdering was followed by swift brush kisses of blush. The touches on her temples whenever she was to open her eyes, followed by the commands, "Open. Close. Look up. Look down," put Lucy into a quasi-hypnotic state.

And this time, once finished, she loved her reflection. Her features were enhanced, not altered. The hairstylist removed the curlers and brushed and styled Lucy's hair with her fingers. Dove peeked in, "Ready?" she asked as she handed a blouse the color of morning glories to Lucy. "Put this on, then come to me."

Lucy moved across the room as if on a red carpet, then perched herself on the tall wooden stool in front of the camera. Dove carried a fan over to the edge of the backdrop, aimed it at her, and then turned it on. A light wind blew steadily through her hair. "Just relax and be yourself. Smile, but not every time," Dove advised. "Play with the camera, and leave the rest to me." Lucy gazed into the camera lens and imagined someone she loved and trusted there. Dove shot a couple of Polaroids to test the light. She shook them as she waited for them to expose, looking at Lucy's face as if perceiving something uncommon she'd missed before. Then she ripped off the coating, moving closer so that Lucy could also see the Polaroids. Lucy thought the images looked like magazine covers. Dove loaded the film and shot a roll of thirty-six photos. And then another. The first smile was easier for Lucy than the fiftieth. Imagining a beloved there could only work for so long. Summoning a genuine smile repeatedly made her think one might only have so many to give.

*

That afternoon, in another studio, in another loft in Greenwich Village, the photographer, a tall man in his thirties with a beard and nimble hands, placed tiny model cars all over the set around Lucy. "Play with them. Look surprised about how small they are." Lucy stood over the cars in a short skirt, polka-dot body suit, and high heels, with one hand on her cheek, and her mouth in a big O, attempting variations on the theme for three rolls of film.

She ended the day with a sense of longing. Despite the morning's sensual pleasure, being prepared for and posing for photographs felt too passive and out of her control, and there was a vague uneasiness coupled with the delight of being pampered. Beauty alone seemed a not-important-enough offering to the world. She could only see the silliness of what she had been doing. Yet, the possibility of cosmopolitan adventure through this use of her beauty still glimmered like a lodestar. She wanted to learn to make the most of her inherited features, and she thought modeling could teach her that, as well as take her places she wanted to go. As she exited the old factory, she lifted the collar of her jacket around her neck. The trees, where she spotted them, were bare, and the sky felt to her like a vacant, gray stare. Pollution coagulated in the cold air. Men in fingerless gloves warmed their hands above fires on the corner of Broadway and 20th. People passed, Lucy looked for connection through faces, but all heads were down, protecting themselves from the wind, perhaps from the world.

*

The Monday after Thanksgiving Lucy was dressing a mannequin in the clothing boutique where she worked when an associate called her to the phone. It was Apollyona. "After looking at the slides it seems that you still haven't lost enough weight, and we no longer feel prepared to represent you."

Lucy took a few steps back into the small office and slid the door shut. "I am sure I can lose the weight by January as was originally planned."

"In our experience the girls who really want it lose the weight right away. If it is difficult for you, that is not a good sign."

"I went slowly because I thought I had more time. I didn't say no to you, but I should have. Just give me until January as originally planned."

There was a pause. "Okay, but I am not promising you anything."

"I am not asking for promises." After she hung up, she called back and asked for Serena. "Could you send me those slides that Apollyona just called me about?"

"First thing tomorrow."

Lucy slid open the door, then smiled at the nosy associate lingering nearby. She went back to the display window and slipped the red wool skirt slung over her arm onto the mannequin. She never told anyone about the phone call.

*

The slides arrived within a week. Lucy waited until she was home alone during Christmas break to look at them closely. Up in her warm paneled room, she turned the key in the ceramic lantern on her desk and then held each slide above it to look at them again through a loupe. The first ones she saw were the leotard shots. They were so awkward and awful she wondered if Hyde had intended sabotage. The others stunned Lucy with their beauty.

One-by-one she cracked the slides she didn't like in half then threw them away. She carried the worst into the bathroom and put a match to them above the toilet basin, watching the awful images of her curl, melt, and fall into the water. Then she scooped them out, wrapped them in paper towels, and went downstairs. It was nearly midnight, she paused to take in the full moon glistening on rolling blankets of snow outside the picture window in the den. Her mother was in bed watching television, and the smell of pork chops and apple sauce lingered. The house was quiet, save for the sound of her father shaking peanuts over a bowl of vanilla ice cream and chocolate syrup. When Lucy passed through the kitchen, he glanced at the contents in her hand and asked, "What the hell you got there?"

"Just some slides from the shoot in New York that I don't need." She opened the door and carried them to the wastebasket in the garage, lifted the lid, and pushed them to the bottom of the bag. Once back inside, she sat down at the table. She wanted to talk about what she was feeling but she was afraid of her dream being misunderstood or belittled or dismissed.

Her father examined her face. "I don't understand why you want to pursue such a career. I have to say I envision much more for you."

"I want to see the world, Dad. I see modeling as a means, not an end. Why not try if I have the chance?"

Tom Pilgrim raised and opened his hands as if holding the possible emptiness of the decision. "Why not wait and go in the summer? That way if you don't like it, you won't have lost any school."

*

The next morning, Lucy called Apollyona. "I've been thinking it would be smarter for me to finish the school year. Would you still be willing to see me in May?"

"I told you I won't make any promises, Lucy, but you can stay in the models' apartment when you come, and, yes, I will see you."

Her dad was reading the paper when she came downstairs. Her mom was griddling pancakes. "I called New York this morning," she announced as if everyone had been waiting to know. Then Lucy stood behind her father, massaging his broad, tight shoulders as she looked out over the snow-covered valley. "I told them I will come in May."

He cocked his head. "Now that makes a hell of a lot more sense."

Lucy patted his shoulders. "Dollars, Dad, think dollars."

Lucy watched her mother's back as she poured a batter into the electric frying pan, without a word.

*

Lucy lost weight gradually and sent weekly postcards to Apollyona to report her progress. By May she weighed 130 pounds. A friend did a double-take when he saw her walking down Clinton Street on a windy day at the end of April. "You are going to blow away if you get any thinner."

She played "New York, New York" and sang along repeatedly at her goodbye party. She was sure this was the beginning of her new, exciting life.

3

Apollyona looked up from her desk when Lucy walked in. "You are a persistent girl. Let me take a look at you." She smiled while circling and scanning Lucy from head to toe, then said, "You have definitely lost weight. Let's put you on the scale." Lucy stepped up, hating it all the while. "136, hmm," Apollyona then turned to Serena, "Measure her." Serena unfurled the tape and Lucy winced.

Apollyona looked over the numbers. "It's a definite improvement. But you still need to lose another six or seven pounds. We will arrange a weekly weigh-in to monitor your progress but we can start some photo sessions now. Just keep exercising and watch what you eat."

"That won't take long," Lucy mumbled reminding herself that this is what she signed up for, and it was time to see it through.

Apollyona nodded toward Serena. "Make a hair appointment for her. Ask for Carlos. He'll know what to do with her." She looked then at Lucy, who was wondering what was so perplexing about her hair. "Hair cuts for Vanity Fair models are free. Tip the woman who washes your hair five dollars and Carlos, fifteen."

Lucy left with an address, a three o'clock appointment, and a vaguely familiar feeling of being seen yet not seen. She walked back toward the models' apartment at the Blackstone. In the lobby, she saw one of the finest-looking young men she had ever seen. He was running his hand through his long blond hair and laughing with the concierge. Lucy thought he looked like a European orchestra conductor. As she admired him, another handsome male stepped out of the elevator and said hello. He was Italian-American, muscular, tall, and dark, and wearing a white tank top and little blue nylon shorts. Lucy didn't know which way to turn. She decided on the cozy coffee shop off the lobby, poked some coins in the newspaper vending machine, and then ordered black coffee at a little table in front of the square-paned window that looked out onto 58th Street.

The blond approached, smiling warmly, extending his hand to clasp hers. "Are you staying in the models' suite? I'm Ransom. That was my roommate who just left. We're also in a models' suite at the other end of the hall. When did you arrive?"

"Yesterday. I just met with the agency this morning."

"Did they treat you well?"

He seemed to think they probably had not, so Lucy dared to open. "They want me to have my hair cut this afternoon. And they are going to set me up for a weekly weigh-in. Do they do that to everyone?"

Ransom waved a hand in the air. "They say that to all the girls all the time just to keep them on their toes. I have to run now. Stop by and see me some time."

His words comforted Lucy and she was grateful.

*

The hair salon, on 52nd Street, was a long, narrow, modern space on the second floor with a wall of windows to the street. Carlos, a thin, short man with darting brown eyes, stared at her as if she were a blank canvas. A moment later he waved his fine-toothed comb in the air as if it were a magic wand, then used it as a pointer for her to follow him. After a warm relaxing wash, condition, and head massage by a beautiful Mexican woman, Lucy was served a bottle of water from Finland on a silver platter. She thought of grass clippers as she watched Carlos with his crafty scissors, and she quietly bemoaned the loss of her long hair, now falling in sheaths to the floor. She sat staring at her pert bob in the mirror, noticing Carlos behind her, proud of his latest work of art. She thought the cut more appropriate for someone she didn't want to be: someone cute. Lucy wanted to be stylish. She sighed. She'd try it their way. She defaulted again to her doubt-filled question: What did she know about what worked or didn't in the New York modeling world?

*

When she arrived at the agency, Apollyona and Serena looked up and stared at her. Then Apollyona moved around her again, as if studying a statue, and Lucy stopped herself from cracking up at the absurdity of the situation. Apollyona lifted her chin in approval. "I'm going to set up some tests for you on Thursday. But you have to get some different clothes. Even just jeans and a t-shirt, that's what most the girls wear. Or leggings and brightly colored tees. You can find them cheap at Alexander's." Wonderful, Lucy thought, cheap clothes to look like all the other girls. That would fit with the haircut. She liked her khaki pants and pink-striped Dior top. She moved toward the windows. The street below looked like a board game with moving characters. She watched a tiny man in a navy suit buying a miniature hot dog from a jelly bean-shaped vendor on the corner. Then she heard Apollyona say to a woman in the office who had not been there before, "I feel a lot better about her now."

Lucy turned. Serena's eyes warned, Don't pay any attention to her.

Apollyona stretched out her gaunt arm to give Lucy the address. "Keep working on your diet."

Lucy took the slip of paper, holding the bitter taste on her tongue so that she could spit it out before swallowing it.

*

Lucy thought Alexander's an architecturally uninteresting, overwhelming, nightmare of a place. It seemed a monument to inconsequential choice, with racks and racks of clothing and accessories. She took three steps inside, one look, and walked out. She felt like Apollyona was trying to turn her into a clone. It seemed like the same old story in a different place, people trying to make her different from who she was. She was beginning to think that was the way the world worked, one just had to become someone else's vision of themselves to succeed.

As it started to drizzle, Lucy opened her umbrella and walked on, wondering how long she could do what they told her to do, how much that would cost, and especially how she would stand out dressed like everyone else with a cute haircut.

Pausing at Park Avenue and 58th Street, she stared south at the gilded Grand Central station. It represented everything she was dreaming about, this golden white hub that connected to so many others. She imagined all the trains coming and going, she saw all the ground that was covered in between—the smooth tracks, the bends in them, the travelers' goodbyes and hellos. She loved the way it was both home and destination, arrival and departure.

*

When she arrived at the suite, a large, tired woman and a young, voluptuous girl were sitting on the couch. The girl was playing with a box of Anaïs Anaïs perfume. "Some man gave me this on the plane from Milan, Mama, wasn't that nice of him?" As she stretched out and opened a pint of ice cream, the curls of her long, black hair nestled onto her impressive bosom. Her eyes were big and brown and her lips were plump. A stack of European magazines was piled on the carpet next to her.

Her mother saw Lucy glance at the covers, and said, "Those are for her brothers. She likes to show them the work she has done."

Lucy felt a pang, wondering if she would be able to impress her brothers.

The girl smiled. "I'm only 15. That is why my mama goes with me everywhere."

The mother looked at least sixty pounds overweight. Lucy noticed her greasy hair and gray roots. She had large, dark circles under her eyes, and was wearing stretch polyester and a smock top. Lucy wondered if she had once looked like her buxom, fashionable daughter and what that might be like for her now.

"I'm Dolores. How is work going for you, honey?"

Dolores seemed sincere so Lucy was open. "I just arrived. Today the agency told me they want me to lose more weight before they send me to meet clients."

Dolores shook her head. "Those damn girls are crazy. They said the same thing to the girl who is on the cover of *Seventeen* this month. Well, she marched right out of there and went over to American and has been working well ever since."

Lucy sighed.

Dolores picked up her white vinyl purse, pulled a yellow piece of legal pad paper folded in quarters out of it, opened and glanced over it. "This here's a diet that is guaranteed to help you lose seven pounds in one week. You have to follow it to a T though, honey."

As Lucy stood up from the couch to reach for it, Dolores looked her body over, and then looked at her daughter. "I don't see where this girl needs to lose more weight."

The girl had ice cream in her mouth. She pondered Lucy's body and slid the spoon from her tongue. "She's just a bit wide around the hips," she said before burrowing into the container for another scoop.

Lucy read the diet. One plain yogurt and one cup of black coffee in the morning, a can of stewed tomatoes for lunch, another for dinner. For seven days.

*

The first few days on the diet, Lucy walked and slept as much as she could to not think about how she was starving herself. She was often dizzy and getting a kind of hollow, hungry look about the eyes. She and Ransom ran five miles a night in the park. Later in the evenings, bored with the girls in her suite, she walked down the hall to the male models' suite and hung out with Ransom and his roommates. She liked to watch the newest lodger, a mischievous college boy from Duke. She liked the long shock of tawny hair across his forehead, his golden tan, and the sparkle in his green eyes. Listening to him and Ransom complain and dramatize about regularly posing eight hours a day in a variety of groom's gear for bridal magazines provided Lucy with much-needed laughter.

*

"Beauty shots," Apollyona announced on Wednesday. Lucy wrote down the address and realized it was Hyde's, the man whose slides she'd melted, doused with toilet water, and trashed. How on earth will he capture my beauty, she wondered, as she went.

He didn't recognize her and she didn't remind him. As she showed him the clothes she brought, holding their colors near her face, it dawned on him. "Hey. Wow. You look great, you lost a lot of weight."

Lucy half-smiled, wondering why people couldn't just tell people they looked great and leave it at that.

The hairdresser styled her bob all curly and wild. She slipped on a turquoise top, and Hyde wrapped a white fish net around her neck. "For effect."

He and Apollyona liked the shots made that day. They thought Lucy looked sexy and sophisticated. Lucy thought she looked mean and over-made-up. For Lucy, every picture told a story, and this one told of her dislike for the photographer. She thought it odd that her expression of disdain and indifference was associated with sexiness and sophistication.

*

The day after the last of her stewed tomato diet, Ransom invited her to a little pasta kitchen on Broom Street. They sat at a lovely table for two with fresh daisies in a vase. It was fun for her to be out in the city with a man. Lucy allowed herself a plate of tagliatelle with clams and a couple of glasses of white wine. She asked Ransom about his travels. After talking about his work in Paris, Milan, and Munich, he lifted his glass. "You have to see Europe, Lu. We'll travel together."

Lucy clinked her glass with his, searching his eyes for some clue as to why he had never touched her in more than a friendly way. They had been running, laughing, watching movies, and enjoying interesting conversations daily. Sometimes she wondered if only gay men were refined, which was a very sad thought. She suspected Ransom was gay. She didn't ask because when she'd pointed to a woman in a photo-booth photo he had stuck to his bedroom mirror, a vague expression came over his face as he uttered, "That was my girlfriend."

*

On weigh-in day, Apollyona shuffled the weights and Lucy watched them balance out at 131. Apollyona looked at the clipboard in her hand and Lucy's chart. "You have lost six pounds. But you have to go further. In the meantime, we will keep shooting and I have some go-sees for you." While Apollyona wrote the addresses, Lucy wondered if she could face another can of stewed tomatoes. Apollyona handed Lucy the address without looking up from her desk. "This is a good photographer up on 83rd Street. Go and see him this afternoon."

This photographer's studio was a third-floor walk-up. Lucy stepped back when he opened the door. Chris looked like a gentle giant as he ducked to fit into the frame. His bright welcoming smile and handsome Seminole features put Lucy at ease. He looked carefully at the few pictures she had, then asked, "Could I make some Polaroids of you?" She nodded. He aimed the lens at her. "Just look off into the sky in thought."

"That's my specialty," Lucy said, then did.

He shot. "Great," he said as he set the camera back on the table.

"That's it?" Lucy asked, amazed at how brief appointments could be. She mistakenly thought that quicker meant a lack of interest.

She was pleasantly surprised when she answered the ringing phone upon arriving at the suite. "It's Serena, dear. Chris wants to shoot with you tomorrow morning. Be there at nine."

*

He was making coffee when she arrived, then offered her a cup while her hair was being styled. When she stood in front of him and a fan in a white linen dress on white backdrop paper, he cut the fan as if he'd just been struck by a brilliant idea. "Wait a minute." He dashed out the door.

A few minutes later he returned with a large bouquet of daisies. "Here, hold these." They shot several rolls as she held the flowers behind her back like a waiting surprise. Chris cut the fan. "Let's try something. Lie down on your belly."

Lucy rested her belly on the floor, her chin on her crossed arms. Chris lay down on his belly, too. "Just look at me, and give me different expressions."

Lucy looked into the lens as if into the eyes of a lover. Chris clicked until the camera no longer would, then looked at it and sighed. "No more film."

Lucy didn't move; she watched him like prey watches a predator. He shook his head as if he could not believe something, as if he were in the presence of magic. "How old are you?"

"Nineteen."

"Really watch it in this business," he said, the care in his voice sounding as if he'd seen ruin. "I think you are going to make it very big."

Lucy let that in, she walked out of the studio with the wonderful feeling that the beauty in her had been seen.

*

When she weighed in the next week, she had lost another five pounds. 126. Apollyona quickly took the phone and made an appointment for her to test with a famous French photographer. She lifted a black bodysuit out of her satchel and handed it to Lucy. "Wear this."

*

The studio—a huge loft with windows all along the walls—was on lower Fifth Avenue. Lucy's hair was pulled back and clipped up, and her eyes were strongly lined. Barely clothed, she stayed back when introduced to the fully dressed photographer. She watched him bouncing around the studio, wearing a headset while giving her directions via microphone from behind a camera at least two-hundred feet away. The distance between them made her feel safer at the same time it made her feel more like a mannequin. She wondered what it was like to make a living as he did and if he found any meaning in it. To feel less intimidated she imagined him in a bodysuit, too, which made her smile as she took her place in front of the pink backdrop. He came closer then, looked at her face, and ordered heavier makeup. The makeup artist rushed in to fulfill his wishes, adding more powder, and lipstick, and lining Lucy's eyes more thickly, then scurried away. He looked at her, and returned to the camera, talking through the microphone. "Just stand profile, lift your arms straight into the air, and then look at me."

Lucy stretched like a cat and looked across the room toward the lens with both curiosity and warning.

As soon as they finished, she rushed off in her new little black summer dress, one she had been pleased to find at Alexander's the day before. It had a boat neck with a big circle cut out of the back. She thought of it as exposing her wing cleavage. Lucy, both wanting to fly and afraid of it, too.

*

The Water Club was an old steamer converted into a restaurant on the East River. Lucy walked through the plush lobby and up the iron stairs toward the offices. The owner of the restaurant, a tall, slim, proud man with short, gray hair and a finely cut beard the same color as his tailored suit, came to a sharp halt when he saw her. He raised an eyebrow. "Do you work here?"

"Apollyona from Vanity Fair sent me, she told me this restaurant is looking for hostesses."

"Being a hostess is a boring job. Would you like to work as a cocktail waitress on the Upper Deck? You can make more money. See Carol, the manager, ask for her downstairs. Tell her Maximillian sent you."

"Thank you," Lucy said, then scurried down the stairs as gracefully as she could, all the time aware that his eyes were on her tail feathers. Other restaurant workers below stopped what they were doing to watch her descent. Even as she marveled at this attention, she wanted to throw up her arms and declare, "It was not me. I did not do it."

*

That next week, Lucy picked up the gorgeous slides from the shoot with Chris. She accepted the cocktail waitress job and she went to a casting for Clairol. She felt like she was on her way.

Waiting in a reception area overlooking Manhattan, leafing through Esquire magazine, she stopped at an advertisement for a men's cologne. *Life's an Adventure, Live It*, the caption under the image read. Lucy looked at the photo of a dark-haired man with penetrating blue eyes, a French engineer, the small print said, and "I want to meet that man" tumbled out of her mouth. The young woman sitting next to her looked as surprised to be spoken to as Lucy was to have spoken. Lucy's name was called. She closed the magazine. It would be years before she saw that photo again.

*

Just as Lucy thought everything was going in the right direction, Apollyona called to say she would like her to come in for a weigh-in and a talk. When Lucy arrived, she noticed the slide projector on Apollyona's desk, the way Apollyona dodged in and out of the office, and how Bill peeked in and told Apollyona that he heard she was looking for him. Something was disturbing in the way Apollyona was slinking out and in, until finally, she illumed the machine, and projected the slides of Lucy's test with the French photographer onto the wall. Lucy's eyes widened at the beautiful larger-than-life images of her. Apollyona plucked a wooden pointer from behind her desk, then pointed and rested the tip of it over the image of Lucy's belly. She sounded like an economic advisor talking about excess spending as she said, "This is still too much. I am afraid we are going to have to let you go."

Lucy peered. She could make out a slight bump there, perhaps a millimeter. She turned and looked into Apollyona's gray eyes as Apollyona said, "I have talked with Bill and we both agree. He was really positive about you in the beginning, but it looks like you are just not the type. You are a very nice girl. I have even received phone calls about how pleasurable it is to work with you. I just don't think you have the body to be a model." She replaced the stick in the corner and then crossed her arms in front of her as if waiting for Lucy to speak, yet, warning against it.

Lucy, her gut aching, stared at the millimeter bump and then at this woman who never warmed to her from the start. She was thinking about how she was asked to wait an hour for this disappointment.

Apollyona seemed to read her face. "Lucy, when I was your age, I wanted to be a model more than anything else in the world, but finally I had to accept the fact that I wasn't built like a model and get on with my life."

Apollyona wasn't pretty enough to be a model, either. Lucy noticed she left out mention of that.

"You are a bright, charming, pretty girl—you have your whole life ahead of you, it is just silly to waste your time this way."

Though Lucy could see her point there, she knew there was something more going on than a barely visible millimeter swell on her belly. What was clear to Lucy was that Apollyona was projecting herself onto that wall.

Lucy's mind was strategizing how to change this situation. Whether modeling was a waste of her time, Lucy would de-cide. It seemed fruitless to attempt to persuade Apollyona anymore. The best thing to do was quickly accept this sad end to things at Vanity Fair.

Life ahead of her or not, one thing she knew was she was unready to head back to Iowa. She stared out the window, wondering if the cocktail job would cover her expenses. "I'd like to stay in New York, at least for the rest of the summer. Could I work here in the agency as a booker or something?"

Apollyona shook her head. "It's not my policy to hire models just after they have stopped modeling. I think it is better if you go and work at another job for a while and then decide if you want to stay in this business but on the other side. For now, you can stay in the models' suite through the weekend."

Apollyona handed Lucy all of the slides from all of the shoots and Lucy added them to those she was carrying from Chris, which she had been excited to show, but now saw no point. It was a dreary walk down the hall, past the Swedish receptionist and the framed cover girls.

Back on the street on a sunny afternoon in early June, she walked toward the Blackstone, and then, embarrassed to face anyone, she detoured toward the park. She sat on a bench in front of The Plaza, watching people milling and rushing about in expensive cars and clothes, and wondered if a luxury jet-set life were as comfortable as it looked and if it were joyful. Luxury alone wasn't enough, for sure, yet Lucy still wanted to go places in style. Perhaps that was silly, she thought, but she was determined not to turn back. She calculated her savings and how she had not had to pay for anything except food expenses, which made her laugh out loud. She had piles of new slides to use for her book. She would use all this to her advantage and carry on.

*

That night as they ran through the park, Ransom proposed a solution. "Why don't you move in with us? We could share my room. You would have your bed. Depending on whether there are three or four of us, rent would only be four or three hundred a month."

Lucy moved on Sunday evening. On Monday morning, she dressed and made the rounds of all the top agencies. "One said, 'come back when you have more pictures', another said, 'go to Europe', two others said I am not exotic enough, another said I am 'too commercial', whatever that means." Lucy tossed these words in the air that afternoon as she and Ransom ran.

Ransom looked at her. "It means you can make money is what it means. Most of the so-called editorial models, the ones in the fashion pages but not in the advertisements, are making about a hundred dollars a day. They want the kind of money you can make in commercials and ads."

Lucy believed she could do it, but she'd had her fill of rejection, diets, and "looks" for a while. She asked for more hours at The Water Club and began working five nights a week, spending the rest of her time discovering neighborhoods, museums, libraries, and clubs and meeting new people. She never told her parents the agency let her go. She did tell them she had a different room number, and wasn't usually there, so not to bother calling.

One evening, a woman who looked like her first modeling agent in Iowa sat at one of her tables. As Lucy served her a margarita, the woman touched her arm and looked at her in earnest. "I think you should come to Giorgio's model farm in South Carolina."

"Farm?" Lucy imagined a yard full of pecking models being crated and loaded into the back of a pick-up.

"It's a beautiful farm. Girls come and stay, get in perfect shape, learn the ropes of the business. You leave with a great look and a book full of pictures, ready for any agency in Europe. It's only eight hundred dollars."

"No, thanks."

The woman sighed. "Here's my card, think about it, you certainly have what it takes."

Lucy liked hearing that. She was not giving up her dream of seeing the world, only putting it aside. She thought she might find another way. In any case, she was more inclined to believe her dad when he reminded her over the phone. "Getting your degree might not make a big difference to you now, but it will twenty years down the road."

*

"Luce, I want to make love to you," Ransom said the night before she left. They were paused on the gangway of The Water Club after her going-away party.

Lucy rested her head against his shoulder and let him put his arms around her. "It's because you are high."

Ransom lifted her chin with his forefinger and kissed her softly on the lips. "Listen, if I am going to make love with a

57

woman, it has to be you." In the taxi, he kissed her neck, and then his tongue was in her ear, and then he was fiddling with the buttons down the front of her black cigarette pants. He undid them one by one then slid his hand beneath her silk underwear. All of this felt good, strange, and sweet to Lucy.

"Now what do I do?" Ransom asked.

Lucy lifted her chin toward the driver. "Why don't you ask him?"

"Luce, please."

She whispered. He fumbled. The taxi pulled over to the curb at Park and 58th. Lucy was staring at Grand Central Station in the rearview mirror. Ransom's head was resting against her chest and she was playing with his hair. "We're here."

They stood, hand in hand, looking up and down Park Avenue. The avenue, sidewalks, and façades were slick and quiet after a light rain shower. Ransom pointed to the Waldorf-Astoria. "Someday we will live there in a wonderful suite."

Lucy rolled her eyes, she knew they wouldn't. "It's pretty, kind of, to think so," she said.

They walked toward Madison and The Blackstone and then began kissing in the elevator.

They were now living alone in the suite. In the bedroom, Lucy started searching through her drawers. "Random sat on the bed, undressing. "What are you looking for?"

She looked at him in the mirror above the dresser. "Some protection."

"C'mon Luce, I want to feel you. You are not going to make me wear a condom on my first experience with a woman are you?"

"It is not a condom I am looking for if you must know. It's a diaphragm."

"Yes, I must know. I want to know everything. What is a diaphragm? Show it to me, will you? Show me how it works."

Lucy figured she could either offer herself up as an experiment or forget it. It fit well into her sexual research approach, and she was honored Ransom wanted it to be her. He watched her squeeze the gel around the edges of the diaphragm and curled his upper lip. "God, straight sex is messier than gay sex."

"That's hard to believe," Lucy looked at him and said. His long back was propped up against pillows, he tossed off the sheet and Lucy stared at his body. Wide shoulders, tapered torso, long lean legs. An inviting penis, curled in its nest. Smooth, lightly tanned skin. When she sat down on the bed, he pulled her toward him. They kissed and caressed each other lovingly, tenderly, playfully. Lucy felt love and experimentation, little passion. There was the pleasure of two different skins getting to know each other.

Ransom pulled back, stared at the ceiling, and dropped his forearm across his forehead. "It's no use."

Lucy smoothed his hair. "I imagine even a straight man would have difficulty after that many martinis."

As if struck by a brilliant idea, Ransom sat up. "I know. Let's go upstairs and get Randy. That way he can get me excited, and then I can make love to you."

Randy was a handsome Scottish model Lucy barely knew and she had no interest in using another as a jump-start for anyone's lovemaking to her. "You go upstairs if you like, Ransom. I am not up for making love to you through another."

Ransom slipped off the bed and into the bathroom for a long time. When he returned and sat next to her, he whispered, "Luce, are you still awake?"

She pretended not to hear him, it was hard for her to talk about the hurt she was feeling. She listened as he gently closed the bedroom door behind him, and turned on the television.

When she woke the next morning, and he was gone, she felt somewhat abandoned but imagined he, too, was doing whatever it was he needed to do. Her diary was lying open on the dresser. Ransom had pasted a small photo of himself in the upper right-hand corner of a fresh manila page and written, *As you venture back to Iowa, Do Not get detoured by complacency*. Complacency, she thought, how could I?

*

She was surprised at how moved she was to see her parents when she stepped off the plane and how good, yet sad, it felt to be home. She felt something elusive in her had died as she sat with her grandfather in his backyard, eating salted slices of his homegrown tomatoes at the picnic table under the maple tree. The smell of curling leaves was in the air. The red-winged blackbirds were calling to each other, the horses grazed in the sloped pasture beyond the barbed wire fence.

*

Love came and went as Lucy finished her degree. She took many women and gender studies courses as electives and went through an anti-beauty phase where she refused to do the usual things young women do to make themselves more attractive. Her hankering for travel and excitement remained intact, well fed by Ransom's letters and postcards from European capitals. Proving Apollyona wrong popped into her mind now and then.

What marked her most, during those years, was the sight of her mother's knees buckling, her heels spiking into the wet ground as she strove for balance on the gray, sad October day Grandma Bighart's body was buried.

[4]

Unable to let go, Lucy put her modeling shoes back on. At 23. In Chicago. Her agent, Angelina, picked up a loupe and scrutinized the new photos. Without looking up, she blurted, "You need to get to Europe. Now."

Lucy braced herself on the desk. Once again, she was ready to go, and also hesitant.

Angelina looked at her hand. "That's a beautiful ring."

Lucy saw Vic, the man she had decided it logical to marry, placing the little black box on their dining room table three nights before. "I just got engaged."

Angelina shrugged. "It's up to you. Just let me know. I would like to introduce you to foreign agencies when they come to scout."

*

Lucy walked along Michigan Avenue, thinking about Vic. They had similar backgrounds and similar interests, they wanted similar lives. He was a dancer from the Michigan countryside who, like her, wanted a freelance big-city sort of life. It was the first time Lucy was in a serious relationship with someone her age and that seemed a good thing. Her father's words, "Are you sure, honey? You're young. There's no need to rush," repeated in her mind as the cold wind stung her cheeks.

Once home, as Vic chopped garlic and she stirred oregano into the tomato sauce, she reeled out the news. "I always wanted to travel on my own. I can't explain why, but I feel like I can't get married until I have done that."

Steam rose to Vic's face as he strained the water off the spaghetti. "I don't understand why you can't be married and travel alone. I don't mind." He glanced her way, flirting with his eyes. "As long as you come back."

How could Lucy admit that she wanted to be engaged more than she wanted to be married? That she was happy just being a fiancée because it made her feel normal after years of feeling wild and alien? She shooed away his fears and felt hers lingering behind. "Of course, I would come back," she said as she carried plates to the table.

*

"However, in the meantime, dearie, if you want to work here in Chicago, you are going to have to start wearing makeup and dressing like a model," Angelina warned the next time Lucy stopped in. "You have to get flashier. Clients have no imagination. You have to show them exactly what they are looking for. Dress and look the part."

*

When she did, Lucy looked into the mirror and did not recognize herself. She walked into the bedroom and sat on the edge of the bed watching the morning sun, softened through the steamed windows, patching rectangles of light on the cream walls. Vic opened his eyes and blinked a few times. "What's wrong, baby?"

"I look at myself in the mirror, after I don't know how much time of putting all this crap on my face, and what I see is not who I am."

He lifted himself to rest on his elbows and look at her. "You know I think you are most beautiful au naturel. If you want to work as a model, maybe you have to get used to it. Anyway, what you are wearing outside doesn't change who you are inside."

Lucy was unconvinced. She worried the focus on the exterior could pollute the interior. She flopped backward across the mattress. Why can I not shelve this career? she asked herself without an answer other than the urge she carried to go and see. "I am giving this until the end of the year. If nothing interesting happens by then, I'll forget it."

*

"You need some lingerie pictures in your book so you can do catalog work," Angelina said as she sent her off to a shoot.

Lucy flinched, asking herself if it would be unprofessional to tell the graying photographer to stop when he scooped his hand inside the cup of the bra and lifted her breast as if to fit it more perfectly. "Don't worry." He smiled. "It is only for the pictures."

This had never happened to her before. Maybe this was the way lingerie shots went, she thought, then even went so far as to think she could detach herself from her body and watch this stranger moving her breast around like furniture, as if it were a breast on a body she happened to be inside of but not connected to. A contortion somewhat like those one-armed hugs she'd come up with for her grandfather.

When the photographer approached her again, however, she lifted a hand. "I can arrange them. You just tell me what you want."

The rest of the shoot was awkward, cold, and quick.

She would not tell Vic about this for fear of his judgment. Instead, she walked to her friend, Faith's, penthouse apartment on Ohio Street. She and Faith had been friends since college and Lucy admired her for many reasons—among them her cleverness, practicality, beauty, and elegance. While standing on her balcony and looking at Chicago glittering in the night, Lucy talked about the shoot, then sighed, trying to figure out once more why it was so difficult for her to assess what was right and wrong in a man's behavior. She looked at Faith and gently asked, "Am I an idiot?"

"No, no," Faith said, handing her a glass of wine. "That would be him."

*

On a rainy Saturday afternoon not long after, another photographer wanted to put her in lingerie. This was a free test; meaning he offered her shots for her book in exchange for posing for him. She had to do her makeup and hair and bring different outfits. When handed lingerie, she said, "I don't feel comfortable that way."

"What are you wearing under your jeans?"

"Underwear."

"Will you let me shoot you in a t-shirt and those?"

"I guess."

"Bring your jean jacket, too, and your jeans. No shirt under the jacket." He offered her a cup of tea before he went back to finish preparing the set, then pointed out the makeup room on his way. "Put more black around your eyes."

Lucy sipped her tea in the makeup room and darkened her eyeliner, added more mascara. She liked the way she looked like a raccoon. He peeped in and then pointed. "Curl your hair more, there is a curling iron." When her hair and eyes met with a nod of approval he directed her to the set, which was the entire back half of the first floor, overlooking an alley. He was standing just inside the door of the deep, white room, and motioned for her to stand in front of the opposite wall, between the two shaded windows. He pointed to the little microphone below his chin. "To communicate with you better."

Lucy listened to the rhythm of the rain as his voice echoed in the room. "Hold your tummy in, and just look at me. Now play with your t-shirt, lift it a bit." Lucy curled it in her hands. "Now take it off."

"No." Lucy braced herself. So much went through her mind at these moments—questions of how someone could tell someone else to do that, whether that is what she had to do to succeed in this business, and that always took her back to her mother's concerns.

The photographer looked out from behind the camera, "You can still cover your breasts with it, but show your shoulders. You have great shoulders. And keep looking at me that way."

Lucy wondered what way that was as she turned her back, took off her shirt, held it in front of her, and then turned around.

She looked like prey. Little did she know that every man who saw those shots would love them. In the future, whenever Lucy would look at them she would try to figure out why. Was it the vulnerability and fear, or was it the willingness to remain open and receptive in the face of that? What was it that men found attractive? What did they see? How could she know? When she asked, they usually shrugged.

*

The morning of the wedding she sat on the golden spread of her bed, rubbing her forehead with both hands and rocking back and forth as Grandma Pilgrim used to, chanting, "I can't do this. I cannot get up in front of all these people and do this."

A friend scolded. "Get a grip. Of course, you are going to do this. Everyone feels like this before they get married."

Little did she know that a year later this same friend would look at her coldly and say, "I knew it would never last."

So, though Lucy's body was begging her not to, she married Vic.

She felt both like wild filly and master, breaking herself in.

The ceremony and reception took place in the ballroom of a riverboat on the Mississippi in the full color of autumn. They each wrote their vows, and each kept theirs a secret to surprise the other. Lucy looked at her tall and handsome groom and declared, "I will love you and believe in you." She left out fidelity because she was unsure she could live up to it. It baffled her, later, that she had not been more alarmed by this.

When Vic vowed, "I promise to challenge you," Lucy, with one hundred and fifty sets of eyes on her, wanted to bolt.

A year later her mother would say, "I knew as soon as I saw you turn around and almost run down that aisle out of there that something was wrong."

*

"I have a two-month ten-thousand-dollar contract for you to go to Japan on my desk." Angelina's message was the first on the machine the day Lucy and Vic returned from their honeymoon. Vic looked up from the wedding gift he was opening. Lucy stared back at him, her ivory satin dress hanging over her arm, her eyes saying I have to go. He pecked her on the lips and left the room.

Lucy stared out at the last leaves on the catalpa, trying to understand why this was all happening now when she'd all but given up on it. She called Angelina. "Are you sure?"

"Well, I think I know how to read, and I think you are Lucy Pilgrim."

Lucy chuckled. "Wow. I'll stop by tomorrow and sign." She hung up the phone and leaned back in the swivel chair. It was late afternoon, quiet. The light was dappled by trembling leaf shadows on the wall.

Lucy, who had felt in a cage since the wedding, hoped it was just her imagination and wondered if marriage was, perhaps, an acquired taste.

She thought about how when she had talked to Vic about the caged feeling in the cabin and on the beach during their honeymoon, his reply was "You'll get used to it" and that frightened her more.

She wondered if the problem was society's rules about marriage because the mere notion of being a traditional wife petrified her so much that she feared making a meal for her husband might render her subservient. She thought, too, of her father's mention that maintaining her Pilgrim name was ridiculous. "Why did you get married if you didn't want to change your name?"

And Lucy thought about how all family names came from men, so it was her father's name or her husband's name, not hers.

She wished she could just be Lucy and leave it at that.

II. Her Dangerous Journey

[5]

When Lucy walked into Osaka International Airport and saw a Japanese man in a navy blue suit holding a sign with only *LUCY* on it, she was delighted. He bowed as she approached, which she also loved. It made her feel like a queen. She appreciated the respectful distance and the non-touching.

The driver escorted her to a van outside, opening what seemed like the wrong door, and then he drove on what seemed like the wrong side of the road. That, too, made Lucy happy. She was ready for everything to be different.

The last light was fading from the sky. She rolled down her window. It was misty, cool, and smelled like seaweed. Billboards, looped highways, and scattered high rises looked like Lego constructions on the flat, open land. Lucy looked at the blue directional signs written in Japanese and English and it struck her that she was lucky to understand one of those languages. She wondered how a non-Japanese, non-English speaker could get around in this country.

As they entered the city, the modernness of the architecture surprised her, as did the apartment complex the driver stopped in front of. It looked like a two-story American motel, with its interior courtyard, and exterior entrances. She wanted to live in a temple or a bamboo cabin. She followed the silent man upstairs to one of the doors. After he opened it and set her suitcase inside, he handed her an envelope and keys, saying, "Everything you need."

If you only knew, Lucy thought, smiling as he bowed. She did, too, again and again, until she remembered reading the etiquette about allowing the host to have the last bow, so she stopped, and then he disappeared into the night.

Lucy walked through the narrow apartment with the anxious feeling she knew would pass, the familiar one that usually accompanied her on her first nights in a new space. She passed a windowless bedroom across from a bathroom, on her way to a bedroom at the back, in which she saw clothes strewn about. With a pang for home, she lifted the receiver off the pink rotary-dial telephone the size of a peanut machine sitting on a small table in the kitchen. She dialed but could not understand the Japanese recording.

After setting herself up in the empty bedroom, she showered, then lit the vanilla-scented candle she'd brought, and lay back on her single bed listening to music, breathing into the aloneness. After a while, she shuffled through the papers in the envelope—there was a map to the agency, the time she was expected in the morning, and several copies of a composite they had printed.

She looked at the different pictures they had chosen and remembered each shoot. She noticed all of her measurements were smaller and shorter. She wondered what might happen for her professionally in Japan. She watched the candle's flame and thought again about the surprising fright she had felt when leaving Vic, how she had felt like it might be forever and this concerned her. She brushed it off as her tendency to exaggerate, yet the upset stuck in her gut as if some sort of reckoning were due and she was going to have to come clean.

*

The next morning, Lucy was once again led off to be weighed and measured. She had hoped that was over. This time it was by Akiko, the female booker, who looked more like a lab scientist with her bob haircut, long white jacket, and horn-rimmed glasses, with clipboard and pencil in hand. As Lucy followed her, they passed a man sitting on a folding chair. He turned toward them as one does sometimes when there is movement nearby, looked away as quickly, then back again as if he had seen someone he recognized. Lucy smiled, noticing his agility, and lifted her hand in salute. Her body revved and set her back. Akiko watched. "He's Julien. He is from Paris."

Lucy thought him handsome in a real way, different from other male models she had known who looked like human replicas of mannequins. He also seemed older than them, and her. He looked like a cowboy, a movie star, a professor, an artist. She admired the definition of his face and the crystal blue of his eyes. She recognized an uncanny familiarity in them.

She crossed the room and stepped on a platform surrounded by a canvas curtain. While Akiko measured her behind it, Lucy, head, and neck above it observed Julien. He was smoking and watching "The Terminator" on the television in the corner. She noticed his fine wrists and lovely fingers. His jeans, boots, and expensive white shirt. She wondered what it would be like to travel with him, then reminded herself she had a husband, then braced herself to hear Akiko say something about the difference between her real measurements and the ones she had read on her composite the night before. Akiko was silent.

So Lucy asked, "Why are my measurements smaller on the composite?"

"In Japan, women are smaller, so we have to make it different on your card so clients don't think you are too big." Lucy laughed at the absurdity of this, and though relieved not to be told to lose inches or weight, she once again felt over-sized. She was head and shoulders above Akiko. Head and shoulders above all of the people she'd passed on the way to the agency that morning. Akiko gestured for her to follow again, then walked her to the accounting office, where a kind smiling woman at a desk handed Lucy what she was told would be her weekly allowance of ten-thousand yen. It looked like play money.

*

The folding chair was empty when she returned. Five beautiful young American, Australian, and Northern European women were waiting on the two black leather couches in front of the desk that separated the reception area from the bookers' tables. All were scheduled to be driven to a casting together. Lucy sat down to wait. Two more women arrived. "Hi, I'm Caprice, from Texas," one drawled and Lucy noticed the smiling mischievous mouth and lips, the wide brown eyes. She had perfect pale skin and long ringlets of auburn curls fell over her shoulders.

"And I'm Joy, from Perth," said the petite elf-like woman next to her. She had translucent skin, twinkling blue eyes, and was wearing fire-engine red lipstick. The blond of her short bangs was barely visible under the hood of her black cape.

Akiko raised her clipboard in the air. "Time to go!" As Lucy stood she quickly discovered she was the tallest of the group, by at least three inches. She stayed to the rear to feel less giant-like as they all followed Akiko out the glass door, down the escalator, and through the commercial complex to the van waiting outside. Lucy sat in the back thinking about the seven or more years between her and these young women while listening to them chat about the clubs and boyfriends. Looking out the window as they were driven through Osaka, she reminded herself that this is what she was there for: to see Japan. Except for a line of budding cherry trees, however, all she saw was one tall building after another in a grid-patterned city.

The models filed into the lobby of one of those high rises, then crowded into an elevator, then flowed into a reception area on the 23rd floor, entering a board room where ten Japanese men, in what appeared to be the same navy blue suit, were seated at a long, narrow glass table. They each had a clipboard, a glass of water, and a pen in front of them. One at a time, Akiko presented each model's book of pictures and spoke emphatically in Japanese while nodding toward the model. The men nodded, too, accompanying each nod with a short guttural closed-mouth sound. They never lifted their pencils from the table.

This scene reminded Lucy of the panels of Miss America judges she had seen on television. She thought she would be unable to present herself like this in front of a table of American men. She liked the exotic touch of being in Japan and being exotic to them, it made her feel exotic, as she never had.

The fact that she was physically bigger than any of them added to her comfort in this situation. Enjoying the windy sound and upbeat cadence of the language, Lucy looked out the windows behind them, at other high rises and gray sky, then at a tall, purple orchid in the corner of the room. Not understanding the language, and therefore how each model was being sold, put her further at ease. She considered the body language of each model next to Akiko and watched how their posture and poise did or did not change as they were talked about. When it was her turn, she looked each man in the eyes, smiled, nodded, then didn't know what else to do as Akiko went about singing her praise and smiling at her, and them. She watched the men's faces for clues as they looked at her pictures, and looked back up at her, their eyes following her height in astonishment. They nodded among themselves. She nodded back.

She stayed quiet in the van, staring out the window on the way back to the agency, observing the backs of the other women's heads, overhearing tidbits of those who missed their boyfriends, couldn't wait to get home, had worked so long the day before, were working tomorrow, and were going out tonight, were wondering who else would. She felt too old to be there but was happy about the opportunity. She learned no one could dial or receive overseas calls from their apartments except with agency intervention during agency hours, which cleared the confusion about the fascinating and bewildering pink phone. She had yet to meet her roommate Patience, who was expected back from a work trip that evening.

*

"Come with us to the clubs," Caprice said, as everyone was leaving the agency. Joy nodded. "Jubilation is where everybody eats. Then they usually move on to Bamboo for drinks and desserts." They seemed young but fun to Lucy so she followed them, through the sleek and shiny underground metro system with escalators four hundred meters deep, to the red line. At the Shinsaibashi stop, she was relieved to walk up into the fresh air, even amid the thick after-work crowd on the pedestrian street. They strolled past Pachinko parlors with bright colors, flashing lights, and clinking sounds of metal balls and tokens dropping. There were exclusive gadget boutiques and American fast-food franchises next to noodle stands and sushi bars. Lucy enjoyed the viewpoint of being heads above the crowd. Caprice and Joy stopped in front of a red brick building and pointed to the neon signs jutting out from the windows above. *Jubilation* was written on one of them in green, the letters dancing among clef notes.

Upstairs, and inside, it was dark. A young Japanese man in a tuxedo welcomed them from behind a black lacquer reception desk, surrounded by burgundy velour walls. While Caprice signed her name on a clipboard, Joy looked at Lucy. "Give him one of your composites." Lucy did and he filed it in a drawer with others, then handed each of the women a pile of lime green play money, Jubilation Dollars. Joy held them in the air. "These are for food and drink. We get twenty a night. Just because we're beautiful." Lucy felt guilty being granted privilege without earning it.

They rode the elevator further upstairs, then sat on a plush velvet banquette in the VIP room, at a table for four. The opposite wall was glass and looked to the dance floor and bar below. The ceiling was mirrored. The smell of freshly waxed floors lingered in the air. The pounding music reverberated through the glass. Lucy held her hands over her ears. "People eat to this music?"

Caprice sighed. "Oh man, you sound like Julien. Wait, don't sit down. Let's move these two tables together because he said he and Felix were coming, and I want him to sit next to me."

"There he is." Joy pointed with one of her delicate fingers. Caprice looked toward the elevator, then smiled like a child at a treasured toy. Lucy turned. Julien nodded and smiled at her. There was a younger and taller man behind him, with long, fine, chestnut hair, a blue bandana around his neck, wearing a black leather bomber jacket. He sat next to Lucy.

"I am Felix, from Paris," he said. He had a ferret-like, searching look in his kind hazel eyes, along with a set of lips that seemed perpetually posed for a kiss.

Julien sat across from Lucy. His smile moved her and she buried evidence of that as far out of sight as she could. His tie was loosened, his shirt open enough to see the arches of his clavicles. They reminded Lucy of her own. She trained her eyes away and looked at the menu. "So what is good?"

Julien looked at her. "I eat the Macedonian every day."

"The same thing every day?"

Felix nodded in agreement with Julien. "It's good, why not?"

Lucy shrugged. "It's worth a try."

Both Frenchmen looked at Lucy as if decoding what the word *worth* meant.

The Macedonian consisted of spiced cubes of beef, fruit cocktail, and rice. It was good, and it was free, but such free-loading, or exchanging beauty for food and drink, approved as it was, would take some getting used to for Lucy. Yet insisting on paying didn't feel right, either.

She spoke French, much to Caprice's dismay and Felix and Julien's pleasure. Felix raised his eyebrows. "You are the first American I hear speak French. I no think they know." Lucy smiled, liking his *no* for *don't* and pleased to surprise him. Lucy kept her eyes averted from Julien as much as possible.

As they ate, Joy told them she had been a dancer in Perth. Caprice complained that she wanted to model in Europe, but was too short. Felix wanted to make enough money to spend months in Thailand riding a motorcycle and getting stoned.

Lucy looked at Julien. "How did you get here?"

"Excuse me?"

"I don't mean by plane or train. I mean how is it that you are here in Japan as a model?"

He smiled. "It's a long story. A woman I worked with left our office and then became a casting director. She called me one day to come for a casting. I won the job and that led to others. I received calls from New York and Germany to come and work and then Captain came to my agency in Paris. This is my second time in Japan. I worked so much the first time I felt like I missed something. I wanted to come back so I sent a fax to ask, Captain said yes, come again, and here I am."

His life sounded to Lucy like the one she wanted. That must be the attraction, she told herself, knowing how prone she was to fall for men she somehow wanted to be. Except for

Vic, this thought struck her then, she had never wanted to be him, and this had made such good sense to her, this only wanting to be herself with a man, that she'd married him.

Lucy sensed a certain escapism binding all these foreigners together in spirit. They all seemed happy to be away from wherever they called home. It was strangest for Lucy to admit this, and she wouldn't because she was married.

She noticed that Caprice was ready to undress and arrange herself as dessert on the table for Julien if he so much as hinted he might like that. She also saw that he didn't brush her off, but didn't return much. Lucy suspected a certain carelessness with women's hearts and then wondered if she did with every man. By the time they finished their meal, she had decided he could be an amusing friend and was a pleasant sight, but no more, no matter what her body was calling for, and regardless of her inquiring gut.

After the waiter cleared their plates, Felix reached into his pockets and spread a collection of lighters out on the table—one in the shape of a camera, another a hand, another a lipstick. "For you." He gestured to the women at the table. Lucy chose the camera, Joy liked the hand, and Caprice grabbed the lipstick.

*

Bamboo was four doors away and upstairs in another four-story building. They entered another dark reception area and signed in. This one required a Polaroid to be taken for the membership card. Lucy was given another ration of play money. These bills were bigger and a creamy color. As she followed the others up the red carpet stairs to the VIP room, Lucy felt guilty again as she glanced at the crowd below, unwelcome above simply because they were not foreign models, or rich Japanese. People paying a lot of money to be in a room with foreign models seemed sad and ridiculous to her, but it was their life, their choice, she reminded herself as she entered the plush interior.

Ornate chandeliers hung from the ceiling, and one end of the narrow passageway led to a square room with a bar and a buffet table filled with an assortment of sweet cakes and fresh fruit, next to a selection of board games on shelves. The other end of the passage led to the dance floor below, on a stage lit by strobes. The wallpaper was covered in green velvet bamboo and golden mosaics, Lucy ran her hand along it and then slid into one of the leather booths big enough for six, each with a glass wall to watch the dancers. She fingered the base of the small red lamp in front of her and saw there was a call button for the waiter. Felix sat next to her with a black lacquer box and chessboard in one hand, a turquoise cocktail in the other, delight in his eyes. "You like play?"

Lucy looked at his drink and then Julien's. "What is that?"

"A Skydiver. Try it."

And that was how Lucy's life in Japan began. She was escorted to castings and work by day, and then indulged in free dinners, fancy drinks, and society games with handsome foreigners by night.

*

In between castings the next afternoon, the van stopped. Akiko turned and shouted between the driver and passenger seat, "You have twenty minutes break." From her back window, Lucy saw more concrete and tall buildings, but this time something new—little market stalls lining the street, separated by curtains of green tarp. Some had flowers, some vegetables, some fish. Lucy sniffed the air as she ducked through the door. It was a gray day again and mist hung heavy in the air.

Julien was standing on the sidewalk. He wrinkled his nose. "Fish. It smells like fish."

Lucy shook her head. "Seaweed."

He shook his. "Fish."

Lucy smiled and shook her head again.

"May I join you on this break?" Julien asked.

Lucy nodded.

As they passed different stalls, Lucy pointed to the flowers, turtles, fish, and food that interested her. She noticed a certain quiet came over her while in his presence alone, and a feeling of wanting to be very precise and sparing with words. She stopped in front of what looked like a miniature race track filled with water and watched the tiny plates of different pieces of sushi floating around an oval bar. "Do you think we just pick up what we want and—" she turned to look at Julien.

He wrinkled his nose again and slid a French cigarette from its fancy pack, then a silver lighter from his pocket. She noticed his manicured fingernails, the agility of his hand. His black leather belt was closed with a silver oval buckle, and his black cowboy boots were polished and shined. He was wearing a tailor-cut blue shirt with black pinstripes under an open, fitted jacket. Lucy wanted to muss his hair. She was both attracted to and repelled by his cool attitude. He looked at her suede jodhpurs, asked, "Do you ride?" and then lifted his cigarette to his lips.

Lucy noticed the time on the black face of his thin gold watch. "We have to go. Now."

Akiko was standing halfway out of the front passenger door, shaking her finger. Everyone else, five other models and the driver, were waiting inside the van. Lucy quickly climbed into the back. "It was my fault, I was slow deciding what I wanted to eat and lost track of time. I'm sorry."

Akiko shook her head, stern-faced. "He always late."

Lucy turned to Julien to apologize. He gently dismissed her concern with a wave of a hand. When that hand grazed her thigh, she was relieved to see her leg remained steady. She inched toward the window, away from him.

"You working tomorrow, Lucy," Akiko said and saw the surprised look on Lucy's face through the rearview mirror. It was only the second day. Lucy couldn't believe it was happening so fast. "They choose you from composite. For magazine. You will go to Tottori. You must be very early at station. I will give you map and directions after casting today. You must not be late. Client will meet you and drive you."

*

Throughout most of the three-hour ride to Tottori the next morning, Lucy slept. When she woke, they were parked. It smelled like the sea, which was not far but hidden by the fog. All that was visible were massive dunes of white sand. Like a puppy, Lucy followed the young woman who had met her at the station. The rest of the crew emptied the van of equipment, and the makeup and hair artists carried their supplies into a thatched cottage where Lucy sat on a pillow in front of the fireplace. The makeup artist wrapped a towel around her neck, then pleasantly surprised Lucy by massaging her face. In between applications of creams and powders, Lucy opened her eyes and glimpsed the stylist unpacking, pressing, then hanging the clothes for the shoot. She hoped they would fit.

They didn't. She had to crawl back inside of them to make it look like the sleeves were long enough. With the tight shorts hitting her above her thighs, and the cotton cap sitting on top of her crown, she looked like she was wearing a younger sister's clothes, and though she did her best to appear comfortable and happy, each time she saw the perplexed look on the stylist's face, she wished she could explain in Japanese. She pushed a bicycle through the dunes smiling at the camera, then ran, twirling and flying a Hermès scarf through the air behind and around her. As she thought about what she was doing, she began to wonder why the Japanese wanted an American model in their magazine. Why were they using pictures of the descendants of the people who firebombed and destroyed their country only forty-four years before as examples of beauty and charm? Lucy tried to imagine what they looked like from above, there in the dunes: an American female model, a Japanese photographer, and his Japanese assistant holding a reflector; a Japanese stylist darting in and out trying to make the clothes look like they fit, a Japanese makeup and hair artist dashing back and forth to powder her nose or touch a hair back into place, and the Japanese representative from the magazine, overseeing it all. The trail of their voices echoing through the quiet, "More *genki!* More *genki!*"

Lucy cupped her hands around her mouth and shouted, "What is *genki?*"

"Big, big smile, happy smile! More *genki!*" The stylist opened her arms as wide as Lucy imagined they wanted her to smile. She tried, but it seemed so forced, so fake, time and again, as if her mouth wasn't big enough for it. Or as if the smile they were looking for was not in her. Maybe they wanted her to jump, dance, fly? She was happy when it was over. During lunch they all sat on cushions in front of the fireplace, steaming bowls of miso soup in their hands. Lucy felt like a privileged visitor from another planet as she listened to the language, and exchanged smiles and nods. She wished they would photograph her doing that instead.

*

Upon her return to Osaka, the metro stopped at Umeda, where the agency was located, and when the doors slid open, Julien and Caprice walked in. "Lucy!" Caprice drawled in her Texan accent, "I wondered where you were today!"

"In some amazing dunes."

"We are on our way to watch some movies we rented." Caprice held them in the air.

Julien looked like a squirrel eyeing a nut as he invited Lucy. "Would you like to join us?"

Caprice lived in the apartment above Lucy. Why not, Lucy thought and went.

As they settled in to watch the film, Julien sat down in the middle of the three-seat couch, opened and stretched both arms along the back of it, and looked at the young women as if suggesting a harmless cuddle. Lucy, who had never experienced a harmless cuddle with any man except her father, nor wanted part of any threesome, laughed. "You're dreaming." Caprice plopped next to him and nuzzled her forehead into his shoulder. Julien shrugged a *what would you do?* at Lucy. She shook her head, then sat on the floor, and leaned her back against the couch.

At the part in the movie when the female protagonist, played by Meryl Streep, rushes out of her house to begin an affair she's been fantasizing about, Lucy shook her head. "Just watch, her mother will die while she is in bed with her lover."

Julien slid his toes under Lucy's thigh as if in a gesture of compassion. Lucy wrapped her palm around his heel, caressed the arch of his foot, then wondered what the hell she was doing and stopped. The film was ending, and as Lucy predicted, the woman's mother died while her daughter was in illicit ecstasy. Lucy stood up and said good night. Caprice's mouth was hanging open. "How did you know that was going to happen? You must have seen this movie."

"Nope. Never saw it. Just an educated guess. Women usually are skewered for affairs. Men usually are forgiven."

*

The next morning Julien came knocking. Standing there with morning in his hair and empty, open palms, he asked, "Do you have any eggs?"

Lucy, in wet hair and a white terry robe, waved him in, then held out a carton of six. After he insisted he only wanted two, she put the carton back in the mini-fridge. When she turned, he was standing there with an egg in each palm, looking at her lingerie hanging above the sink. "Aren't these the strangest things?" She meant the chandelier-shaped pink-and-white plastic contraption with clothespins dangling from it. She blushed when she realized she could be mistaken for talking about her panties and bras. Julien pursed his lips. Lucy moved to show him the way back out. "Excuse me, now, please. I have to get ready for a casting."

Julien shrugged. "We could walk together."

"I need to be at the agency by 10."

"Me, too. I will come back and knock."

She wondered about Caprice, the night, she preferred not to know.

She enjoyed walking with him through the streets of Osaka. Quietly.

*

Tomy, the men's booker, who Lucy thought looked like a Japanese movie star, with his long hair, dimples, and sparkling brown eyes, escorted a group of models on their castings that day. While they waited on a long, cold platform for a train to an outlying location, the smell of exhaust in the air, he looked at Lucy like he knew a secret about her, then showed her the chart on his clipboard, "You have a trip next week. You will go to Okinawa for Panasonic. One hundred thousand yen per day. That's because it is an internal video, not a commercial video, which pays more. Means they want to use it for the company only, not for advertising. You will go with Patience. Happy?" Lucy was thrilled to be booked for a trip and less thrilled to be going with Patience. She nodded. "You will like." Tomy's dimples deepened with his smile. "It is tropical."

*

Okinawa was warm and blooming. The smell of the sea lingered with honeysuckle. Lucy and Patience were escorted to their hotel, situated along a strip of apartments, shops, and restaurants at the edge of the island. Lucy was relieved to be given a key to her room since living with Patience was wearing on her. After the driver gave them instructions to meet in the lobby at six a.m., Lucy dropped her overnight bag on the double bed, then opened the window to low, green hills. Patience knocked at her door. She looked like a lost raccoon as she peered in. "Lucy, what are you going to do?"

"I'm going for a walk."

"Aren't you afraid?"

Lucy shook her head, then she reluctantly offered, feeling sorry for Patience, and responsible like an older sister, "Do you want to come with me?"

"Just let me get my purse." Patience scurried.

They walked along the strip that looked like many other beach fronts in many other tourist towns. There was an off-season ghost town feel to this one. Many places were boarded up, and the night coming on carried a chill. Lucy looked around. "I wonder where the military base is."

"What military base?"

"The U.S. has a base here."

A drunk couple swaggered out of a bar, toward Lucy and Patience. The man's scruffy face was a blend of Caucasian and Oriental traits, and the bulge of the blue t-shirt that contained his belly fell over his jeans. His girlfriend looked like him, with longer hair. He slung his arm around her shoulder as they approached Lucy and Patience, then reached out, opened his palm, and curled his fingers as if preparing to grasp. It appeared he was aiming for Lucy's breast, but she gave him the benefit of the doubt until he lurched forward and squeezed it like an air horn. Lucy grabbed his hairy wrist and threw his arm back at him. His girlfriend let out a peal of laughter. Patience, who had been looking the other way, turned at the sound. "What happened?"

Lucy kept walking. "That guy just grabbed my breast."

Patience lifted her hands into shaking fists. "What? Let's go get him."

Lucy waved a hand. "I don't want him."

"Aren't you angry?"

"What good would it do? It's already done."

"Get revenge!"

"Living well is the best revenge," Lucy said, raising a finger to emphasize her point.

"I don't get it."

Annoyed and bored by the simple revenge fantasies of most people, Lucy hated explaining things that seemed obvious to her. So she was often curt in these instances. "Think about it, and you will," she said as she pushed open the door of a convenience store, shaking her head, not interested in expending energy promoting endurance to Patience. "A 7-Eleven in the middle of the Pacific," Lucy said, at the same time she thought that sign of market globalization a pity and would have preferred a Japanese family-run grocery. Yet, she browsed the aisles for some American comfort food, then settled on a package of Nutter Butters, which she had not eaten since she was a girl. She'd only have a few, she decided, thinking about fat. Then she remembered how she used to think more fat would stop men from touching her, but that had not worked either.

Back in her room alone, she stretched out on the bed and held the cookies on her tongue until they melted, watching Japanese television she didn't understand.

Her breast felt sad. She cradled it in her hand, caressing it lovingly, soothing her nipple. The problem with ignoring what had been done to it was first in the pronoun; she thought of it as it, rather than as her, and thus what had been done to her, not just her breast. She forgot, for the most part, while her breast remembered, storing up all these assaults to be triggered by unsuspecting, loving fingers in the future. Lucy rarely fully enjoyed other hands than her own on her breasts, loving as they may be. It always put her a bit on edge. What was curious to her was how much it turned her on to have them suckled.

*

At dawn, the driver escorted them to the botanical gardens, where the crew was setting up. During breaks from being filmed while biking through the gardens, Lucy lay on the grass and watched the Japanese women tending flowerbeds under their wide-brimmed straw hats. She leafed through the pocket Japanese language book she had brought along and wrote to friends and family. Patience plopped down next to her and looked at the postcard she was writing. "How can you stand to be away from your husband for so long? Aren't you worried he'll have an affair?"

Lucy thought it interesting nobody ever asked if she would. They always asked about her husband instead. "One, no, it's not easy to be away for so long, and two, he could have an affair even if I were there. Are you suggesting that I don't do what I want to do in case my husband might have an affair while I do?"

"Come on, you know what I mean. Men have needs."

Lucy slid a few blades of grass through her fingers. "Don't we all have needs?"

"I was always taught that men can't control theirs."

"Why do you think women are taught that? Who is being controlled by whom there?"

Patience looked confused, then as quickly, disinterested, in the way people do when they want to dismiss something as too complex that might challenge their ways of living and thinking. Lucy noticed attention at these points often shifted to basics. Patience confirmed this when she said, "I'm hungry. I wonder when we will break for lunch and what it will be. I can't bear another bento box. How long do we have to stay out here and how many more takes? I hate not knowing. I hate not being able to ask and understand the answer. I hate waiting. I hate the way they keep nodding and smiling at us. This is so boring."

Lucy stretched her arms to encompass the hills, the gardens, and the South Pacific surrounding them. "Look where we are, biking through these gardens and getting paid a thousand dollars a day for it. All that smiling and nodding, by the way, is a respectful and wonderful change compared to what I am used to in this business."

They ate a lunch of rice and fish in a small roadside cafeteria then drove to a wooded valley where the crew pitched a tent, set up lights, and built a fire. Patience and Lucy waited. Lucy walked in the woods, occasionally shooting pictures of the location through the trees, noticing the crew were all wearing the same white fishing caps.

Twigs broke under her feet as she approached the van where Patience was pouting. She looked in. "They have to wait for it to be dark to shoot this scene, so we can sit in front of the fire under a starry night."

Patience curled into a ball on the seat. "And then what? A dinner of fish balls and rice? It's freezing. This is awful and boring and stupid."

Lucy smiled. "I think your name was given to you with great hope."

"What are you talking about?"

"Patience, dear Patience, patience."

*

When they returned to Osaka, Lucy asked Captain if she could move. "I'd like to live alone."

"There are no one-bedroom apartments available."

"An apartment near mine is empty." Lucy turned. She had not seen Julien come in. He was standing behind her.

"It's farther away," Captain said.

"It's not that far. I'll take her there. I have time."

"That is a three-bedroom apartment." Captain looked at Lucy. "You can only move into it if someone else moves in with you." He raised an eyebrow at Julien, then took the keys from a drawer and handed them to Lucy. "You both need to be back here by three."

As the doors to the subway car closed, Julien placed his hand on Lucy's thigh. She saw that he kept talking, she watched his eyes, lips, face, and free hand move, but she heard only her desire and her fear of it.

The walk down the hill from the station was also hypnotic, their warmth and color contrasted with the gray and white cool mist around them. Lucy nodded when Julien pointed out the passage to his place, a metallic pedestrian overpass at the bottom of the slope. He then aimed his finger at a cluster of tall white high rises in front of it. "It is in that building."

Every car that passed on the shrub-lined street was white.

Lucy spoke. "Have you noticed most of the vehicles here are white, with white interiors?"

Julien shrugged. "They like it."

She smiled. "I hope so."

At the 7-Eleven at the bottom of the hill, Lucy stopped in front of a basket of onigiri to the side of the entrance. She liked these seaweed-wrapped triangles of rice with mayonnaise and crab in the center. She was going to buy the one in her hand until Julien wrinkled his nose at it and said he didn't like the smell of them on the breath. She dropped it back on the pile, not wanting to risk the possibility that the whole time she was talking to him he might be recoiling from her. It bothered her to please him, though; she noticed that, too. She brushed her fingers along the thick hedge as they turned off the street and followed a curved sidewalk. She looked up, counting twelve floors to the top. There were small balconies with plants and many windows.

The elevator doors opened to a smoky, mirrored interior with a musty smell. Lucy slid her hands behind her bottom and pressed up against the wall a good foot away from Julien. They were facing in the same direction. She sensed his comfort with this sensual tension between them, imagined his expertise and experience in that field to be vast and she was very uneasy, doing her best to remain calm. She felt more in control as the seductress than seduced, and now that she was married, being seduced seemed more guilt-free than seducing. Lucy wondered, too, if this was a game for Julien or if he wanted to know who she was and could be her friend. Her body felt like a divining rod close to a treasure, so she focused on the red neon lights as each flashed until ten and was relieved when the doors opened to the hallway. It, too, was confining—long, narrow, and empty with doors on each side, like a dorm. Keeping her hands to herself required concentration. They faltered as she unlocked the door of the apartment, then she held them behind her back as she let him pass.

She flipped the light switch, again, and once more. "It doesn't work."

"This was my room," Julien pointed to the right as he strode through.

Lucy paused, looking in, deciding to choose it would be too close for comfort, yet she liked knowing he had lived here, it gave a familiar feeling to this foreign place, and she liked, too, that he was pushing her to live where he had. It made her feel special to him.

She turned and saw him opening a fuse box on the kitchen wall. He flipped a switch and the lights came on. She walked into the bathroom and flushed the toilet, then turned on the water. Satisfied with the pressure, she walked into the kitchen. Julien was checking the water and gas. The two other bedrooms were next to each other at the back, each with its balcony. Tatamis. Double-sized futons on frames. She passed through each one, enjoying this feeling of shared domesticity while wondering whom she thought she was fooling pretending this was just a routine apartment check.

She liked, too, the charge of electricity between them in this closed space, the vitality in the air, yet she had left the doorway to the hall open for that very reason, so some of that, and she, could escape. Her next strategy would involve asking Caprice to remain an obstacle by offering her the other room. She looked at Julien. He stood in the kitchen, leaning up against the table, watching her. She paused in the doorway of the room she had chosen. "I want this room."

He jingled the keys in the air. "It's yours. Now, come, I will show you my place. It is right across the street."

Lucy sighed. "Can I have a rain check?"

"A what?"

She smiled. "It's an expression, it means I would like that but not right now, will the possibility still be available at another time in the future?"

"But what has that to do with rain?"

"We'll see. Come on, we need to get back to the agency. We are professionals aren't we?"

"*Oui, oui, oui, oui, oui.*"

She shook her head. "It's never a simple yes or no with you is it?"

He looked at her like she may be smarter than he thought, then followed her out the door saying, "*Non, non, non, non, non.*"

*

After the afternoon's catalog shoot, Lucy met Caprice on the Midosuji bridge. Gigantic neon signs loomed above them from every direction, advertising Johnnie Walker, Coke, and Camel cigarettes. Lucy leaned over the balustrade to watch reflections off the river as Caprice pleaded with her to come to dinner. "If you'll come, he'll come."

Lucy looked up. A distant plane passed through a slice of dusky blue sky between two silver high-rises. "It's not always easy to watch you touching each other. It makes me miss Vic." She left out the part about how she also was reticent to enable Julien's messing around with an eighteen-year-old girl, half his age, and less than keen to watch the eighteen-year-old girl throwing herself at him.

"Ask Felix to come," Caprice said, nudging her shoulder. "He likes you."

As Lucy wrinkled her face in confusion and said to the river, "Are you suggesting I replace my husband with Felix?" she turned to hear Julien say, "Will you come, Lucy?" as he hugged Caprice.

*

The Indian restaurant, Moti, was on the fourth floor of a twenty-story building. Elevator doors opened to a large softly lit room overlooking the river. It smelled like curry. There were tables surrounded by banquettes. The three of them followed the maitre d' through the center of the red-carpeted room. Julien paused in front of a large clay oven. "That is where they make the bread." Lucy looked inside and her face flushed with the heat of the glowing hollow and the excitement to be doing something new. They were then seated in a banquette next to the window, Caprice next to Julien, and Lucy opposite him. As they looked at the menus, Caprice suggested, "What if we order different things and share?"

Julien shook his head. "I will have my own plate. I don't like to share."

Lucy looked up. Perhaps it was a language shortcut, she thought, instead of an overall statement about who he was. Yet, she, too, preferred to have what she liked rather than share what she didn't. She admired that he was taking care of himself, and saying what he wanted. "I have never eaten Indian food before so I'll share if you like, Caprice, if you would like to share this spinach dish with me." After the waiter left with their orders, Caprice excused herself to use the restroom.

Julien leaned forward. "Lucy, what is on your hand?"

Lucy looked at the circle of sunburn on the back of her hand. "It's from the bicycle gloves I wore in Okinawa." She lifted and turned it to face him, then chuckled as she said, "Branded with the Japanese flag."

Julien looked into her eyes, and said, "I'd really like to kiss you some time."

Lucy's head dropped like a shot bird's. She stared at the rings on her finger. She couldn't blame him for stating his desire, and she found his timing vicious. Even though she thought Caprice was dimwitted, she felt compassion for her ignorance there in the bathroom as the man she was pursuing was now pursuing the woman she was using as bait. Had Lucy been uninterested in kissing Julien—it was their desire he had given voice to after all—she would have rolled her eyes and changed the subject, or laughed it off. Alas, she still thought she could find a way to maneuver through this attraction looking good, which was difficult while both feeling guilty for wanting the kiss and admiring his boldness. She was also angry with him for putting her in this position.

Caprice returned. She was refreshed, powdered, and playful. "You were all talking about me, I hope."

Lucy sat up straight, collecting herself and averting her eyes from Julien once again. "We were just getting to that."

Lucy thought of the apartment she wanted, how much she wanted to get away from Patience, and how she needed a roommate to do it. She took a deep breath, and then said, "Caprice, would you like to be my roommate in Tennoji?"

Caprice's eyes widened. "That is where the Penthouse is."

Lucy looked confused. "Penthouse?"

"That is what they call the building the guys live in. Where Julien lives. I'd love to be your roommate."

While Caprice simpered at Julien, Lucy glanced out the window at the high rises across the Midosuji. Julien reached for his cigarettes, and Caprice reached over the table and lifted his portfolio from the chair next to Lucy. She stood it on the table, then opened it and turned the pages. Each was a different image of Julien. He was dancing in a tuxedo, offering a woman a glass of cognac, smiling behind the wheel of a Ferrari, playing golf, sitting in the desert. There, at the desert shot, Lucy's eyes widened. *Life's an adventure, live it*, she read, then looked at him, then at the picture again, then at him again. It was the advertisement she saw in the magazine in New York when she first traveled to model.

It was the kind of occurrence people scarcely believed when it happened in real life, yet were willing to think plausible in novels and films. She smiled to herself. She could feel Julien staring at her. She liked his impatience, the way he looked like he might say, Out with it already, if he knew how.

Caprice stared at her, too. "What?"

"I saw that ad years ago, and when I did, I said, 'I want to meet that man'."

Julien raised a finger. "That is a very good sign."

Caprice pointed to a different photo, one in which Julien looked so mean Lucy backed away. "I like this one," Caprice said then looked at Lucy to see what she thought. Lucy shook her head.

After Caprice closed Julien's portfolio, she leaned into Lucy and said, "Your husband is very handsome. I saw his picture in your apartment this morning. You must trust each other very much. I think a good relationship must be all about trust."

Lucy looked at the river, while Julien squared his shoulders, and said, "It's not about trust, it's about feeling."

Caprice knitted her eyebrows at him, then looked at Lucy, who was for the first time hearing someone else say something she often struggled to articulate. It was about why the word *commitment* bothered her so much. It smacked of something willed, rather than felt, more about promise than passion, more about deals being made than life and love being lived. So Lucy changed the subject, thinking of the ad, where she had read Julien's name and profession in the caption. "So, Julien, what kind of engineer are you?"

"I work with electricity."

"That sounds more interesting than modeling."

"It is at a desk in Paris every day. Drawing. What I like about this business is the *fantaisie*." He pronounced the s like a z, saying fantasy in French, raising one hand as if doing a trick. "It is fantastic to receive a call one day to go to Japan, or the Algerian desert, or New York on a moment's notice."

Caprice shook her head and shook her index finger in the air. "But this is not reality."

Lucy pinched her forearm and then rapped the table with her knuckles to highlight the density of things. "Then what is it?"

Caprice shrugged.

Julien smiled. "That is a very good question, Lucy."

Lucy said goodbye to them on the bridge.

From then on, Lucy's reality in Japan shifted to early morning running—zooming up and down steel stairs, across bridges, past noodle stands and family-owned shops opening for the day on people-less streets in the gray, cool, pre-spring mist while listening to the Pretenders and Zucchero sing—then working. Her jobs included many hairstyle and lipstick changes and flinching as young Japanese female stylists slipped at least fifty different shirts and jackets on and off her daily, pushed her hands away as she tried to button them, held skirts and pants in front of her, and gestured for her to step into them, and then zipped them for her.

"Look, you can just hang the clothes right here." Lucy pointed to the rolling clothes rack. "I'll put them on, I'll be careful, I promise."

She was unsure if they understood her or not when they shook their heads, giggling. They slipped high heels on her feet and stood back to take a longer look. The sleeves were always too short, so yanking them to cover her wrists was also part of the routine. As soon as she moved on the set, the sleeves shot back up and stylists rushed at her to tug them down again. When she pulled at them herself to save time, they all raised their index fingers and shook them, shouting "No, no, no!" as they ran to do it.

Lucy often felt like one of the mannequins in Henri Bendel she used to stare at while sitting in front of The Plaza. She wished her personality mattered, that what she had to say could be used. Moving or jumping in front of the camera was not getting easier for her, but she was learning to relax into a pose, to be a sort of stand-there model. Years later, in Madrid, when she would lament her lack of movement on set, another model would say, "But I think you are a stand-there sort of model, I mean, that's all you have to do, is just stand there. You're beautiful just like that." There, in Japan, she doubted that was enough as she took in the atmosphere of the warehouse studios. Inside them, it was gray all day except for the bright colors of the elegant suits she was wearing, the pastel backdrops rolled down for each change, and the bright red space heaters near the makeup chairs.

At the same time Lucy's world was opening, it began narrowing into her obsession with wanting to touch Julien while being kind to Caprice. One morning Caprice unwittingly gave Lucy permission as she sat on Lucy's bed lamenting. "I have never met a man like him. I'm trying everything to get this guy and he keeps saying, 'I don't think I am for you, or you are for me,' what the hell is he talking about?"

Lucy rolled to her side. "That is a question for him, not me."

"His answers don't make any sense to me. He talks about being real, being present, about deep communication. Who cares? I'll just go over there and sleep with Boris, who wants me, who's dying for me."

Lucy winced. Boris was a mammoth Australian who looked like he'd gulp a woman down and then belch. "Is that the way you want to make love?"

Caprice humphed. "Julien wants me to do strange things."

106

Lucy fluffed her pillow and repositioned it. "Are they things you think would hurt you?"

Caprice whispered, "He wants me to get on top."

Lucy lifted her head, then her fingers to her lips. As she caressed them, she speculated, Climb on up there and ride seemed too enthusiastic a response, all things considered, so she tempered it. "That's not so strange. It can be quite enjoyable."

Caprice looked away, as if she didn't care, which troubled Lucy. "The other night I dreamed Julien was telling me he couldn't get what he needed from me but he could get it from you if you weren't so faithful to your husband."

Lucy rolled onto her back. She would agree with Caprice's dream if pressed, but she suspected Caprice had conjured this to say what she thought, or, perhaps it was simply to test Lucy. As Lucy watched Caprice stare out the window, she saw another concern flit across her Kewpie face.

"And sometimes I think about women." Shame filled Caprice's eyes. "That's strange, too, isn't it?"

"No, Caprice, it's not strange at all. It can be very lovely."

Caprice turned to face Lucy, "You mean you have?"

As Lucy nodded, Caprice studied her as if she were some rare phenomenon. Lucy, feeling she might direct her next experiment on her, answered with a gentle look of I have enough on my plate then offered another possible reason for Julien's reticence, "Have you ever thought that Julien may have a wife in Paris?"

"He has two daughters and lots of girlfriends in Paris. Maybe he just hasn't found the right woman. Maybe it's me."

Lucy didn't have the heart to suggest it wasn't and Caprice walked out of the room looking like a sulking toddler, with her blanket trailing behind her.

*

The next evening in Bamboo, while Lucy and Julien were alone, Julien reached inside his jacket and lifted a fountain pen and leather date book from his inner pocket then tore out a blank page and drew a map. After marking his and her place with a star, he slid it across the table. "I don't want to make any trouble for you, Lucy."

This made Lucy laugh. "Sure you don't."

"I just want you to know my door is always open. My room is at the top of the stairs."

Lucy studied the map. "Are you married?"

Julien shook his head. "Never. I don't believe in marriage."

"Do you live with a woman?"

"No."

"Caprice told me you have children. They must miss you very much."

Julien nodded. "I miss them, too. But I have to live my life."

That she could understand. "Are they able to spend time with their grandparents while you are away?"

A pained look crossed Julien's face. "My parents are not together and unfortunately, I do not have a very good relationship with them."

Lucy sensed she had touched a wound. "I didn't mean to pry. I only asked because I spent a lot of time with my grandparents when I was a child. It was important to me."

Julien leaned back into the booth. "I lived with my grandparents."

"Why?"

"My parents were students in Paris not long after the war, apartments were difficult to find. The woman who owned the apartment they lived in said they could only have one child in it. So my older sister stayed with them and they took me to live with my father's parents in the mountains."

Lucy thought it rude to ask why they hadn't moved. "So you grew up in the mountains?"

"I spent my first seven years in the Alps. Then my parents moved and I went back to live with them. Then my father disappeared."

"Disappeared?" Lucy was flabbergasted by all of this, especially by the way he talked about it so matter-of-factly. She searched for signs of damage but only found a solid wall. "How old were you?"

"Eight or nine."

Lucy winced.

Julien waved that off. "He came back sometimes but we never knew when, and when we asked why he left us he stayed away longer so we learned not to ask. Then he asked my mother for a divorce. I saw very early that my parents' life was not mine."

"What do you mean by not yours?"

Julien leaned back and crossed one leg over the other. "My grandparents lived just inside the village, and one summer night when I was about 13, I was coming back from a walk in the mountains and I watched my father kiss another woman on the street then walk into my grandparents' house and kiss my mother. I understood, then, that his life was separate from mine."

Lucy searched for something to say to ease the pain she imagined but found no words. He waited. She sat up straight to breathe easier. "I feel so strange inside."

Julien shot a look of warning at her. "Don't take what isn't yours."

It was the strangest context Lucy had ever heard the phrase used in, and yet she understood it because she had taken his story inside and it was making her sick. She had never thought of such a feeling as theft, however. It was odd to her, too, the way he seemed angry at her for feeling for him. Was he even selfish about his pain? Or had he mistaken her compassion as a pity he was too proud to bear? She was too afraid to ask. Julien looked like a tiger patrolling his cage, ready to gnash any hand that reached in. She backed away.

An American man walked up to the table and smiled the kind of smile that could sell anybody anything, at least once. Julien introduced him as his old roommate, Joe. Then Dani, an Israeli, with close-cropped, dark curly hair, and a tender smile sat down. Felix slid into the booth after him. A Scot Lucy recognized from an international perfume ad joined them. They were each, and as a group, an attractive distraction to Lucy, who was now in the corner, surrounded by handsome, lively men. Dani slipped a deck of cards from his pocket. "Does any-body want to play?" They all looked at her.

Lucy thought, why not. "Deal me in."

*

The next morning, map in hand, Lucy realized she ran by the penthouse every day. She jogged in place in front of a narrow three-story clapboard townhouse wedged in between two high rises, then stopped and calmed her breathing.

Her steps creaked on the wooden stairs as she slowly walked them to the top. She wiped the sweat from her fore-head, smoothed her hair, and then knocked.

Julien opened the door wearing a gold towel around his waist. Lucy's glance caught on his chest and then darted to his face. The scent of monoi oil and smoke surrounded him. Light and air flowed through the open window above the neatly made double bed. Genesis's "I'm Counting Out Time" played from a cassette recorder. Lucy looked around the room, at the purple velvet loveseat on the far wall and the low wooden ta-ble in front of it. "This is a great little place you have."

"I am happy to see you in it." Julien smiled, then gestured her in. He walked toward the makeshift kitchen along the same wall as the door. Whatever had bothered him the night before was gone, it seemed to Lucy. "I was just starting my breakfast, would you like to join me for some eggs?"

Lucy shook her head. "I can't stay long. I have to work."

She felt that interesting combination of foreignness and familiarity that arose in her in his company. Eggs for breakfast, just like in Iowa, yet executed methodically. She noticed yolks waiting in their shells on the small countertop as he poured a cup of whites into a pan of warm oil. "You separate them?"

"I like the white cooked and the yolk liquid, so, once the whites become white, I center the yellows, then cook them until they are secure."

Lucy smiled at the delightful language. Secure yolks. Julien added a strong dose of salt and pepper, then slid them onto a plate. The toast popped from the toaster and he lifted it onto the plate, too, then held it out to her. "Are you sure you would not like them?"

Now she smiled thinking of Dr. Seuss and Sam, I Am as she shook her head.

"Or maybe some tea?"

Lucy shook her head again, and then followed him across the room and sat at the edge of the love seat, watching as he punctured the yolks, spread them evenly over the white, sliced through it precisely, then rolled each bite neatly around the tines of the fork. When he cut the thick white toast into small pieces, then stabbed them one by one onto the end of his fork to sweep up the remaining yolk, Lucy said, "They have Texas toast in Japan?"

Julien looked confused.

She nodded toward it. "That is what we call that kind of bread in Iowa."

He finished his bite. "You must tell me about your Iowa."

"I'm not sure where to begin," she paused, then came to the point of her visit. "Would you meet me around 6 at the agency and then we can go for a drink?"

Julien looked at her as if nothing would delight him more. *"Avec plaisir,* Lucy."

*

When they stepped outside the building in Umeda that evening, Lucy stood for a moment enjoying the cool raindrops on the hot skin of her face and chest, then looked around to see if she knew anyone nearby. She was ready to risk what she knew to find out about whatever was rising in her and wanted to do so privately. She asked Julien, "Do you know somewhere near here where we will not see anyone we know?"

He nodded, touched her elbow, and looked into her eyes. "Are you okay?"

"Mmhmm," was all she could say. She opened her mouth like a fish, without words. She felt like she was shedding skin.

They stopped in front of a circular high rise and Julien held the door. She passed through and then matched the pace of his boots as they walked down a long, dimly lit hallway. Julien flashed his membership card at the Maharaja reception desk, and Lucy slipped a composite from her bag, then posed for a quick Polaroid. They passed in front of a bar covered in a mosaic of mirror shards and sat in one of the many tall, curved booths set up in a labyrinthine pattern. Lucy liked how everywhere she turned something was reflecting something else. She could feel Julien's eyes on her but could not meet them. She smiled at the waiter's spiked hair. "Wodka on the wocks, please," she said because it was fun though it felt unkind to mimic his accent.

Anyway, the waiter nodded happily, in perfect agreement.

Julien nodded, too. "The same," he said, then looked at Lucy. "I will join you in your drinking."

Lucy drank quickly, and steadily, then played with the silver cocktail napkin. She saw that Julien looked like a relaxed cheetah with a twitching tail. Out with it, she said to herself. "The problem is this: whenever I am near you all I want to do is touch you."

Julien nodded. "I feel it."

She closed her eyes in embarrassment, wondering what the hell he meant by that. Her body warmed as he neared. When she opened her eyes, and he tenderly then deeply kissed her, she figured he enjoyed this problem of hers.

Julien nicked the end of her nose with his. "I like your kiss."

She could only nod, then dive in again. When sated, Lucy sipped her drink.

The way Julien looked at her made her think he was going to say something sweet. Instead, he said, "You have to help me with Caprice."

Lucy had forgotten all about Caprice. She raised her eyebrows. "You got into that one all by yourself, man, you're going to have to get yourself out the same way."

Julien lifted his hands in exasperation. "But you know her. She never stops, this girl. Pushing herself into taxis with me, following me."

Lucy stared, unflinching, she would have none of this.

Julien insisted on blaming Caprice. "You saw her."

All Lucy saw was an opportunity to ask what she most wanted to know. "Why did you even get involved with her?"

Julien backed away, incredulous. "Lucy, I am a man. She is a beautiful young girl."

The way he said it as if that were reason enough both enraged Lucy and made her laugh, in stutters, as she turned it around and looked at it from different angles. Her grandfather, along with a various number of other men, flashed through her mind. Anyway, it was only a kiss, she told herself, as the young man who had taken her Polaroid walked toward their table.

With both hands and a bow he presented Lucy her club membership on a small silver platter–*MAHARAJA MARU BIRU, Members Card of Foreign Models, Dress Fashionable, come and experience it for yourself* was written across the bottom of the lavender card. Lucy chuckled again as she read, until she saw the date, and remembered it was Vic's birthday.

The time difference, the expense, and the difficulty in calling from the apartment had made communication with Vic rare and difficult in Osaka. She could sense a fleck of revenge toward him in this kissing on his birthday.

She could feel a sort of general go f—- yourself against all men mounting, and it was one she kept to herself. She thought that showing a man how angry he made her gave him too much of a feeling of power over her. So she did what she usually did, and went away. "Excuse me. I need to use the bathroom."

Lucy slid all the yen coins she had into the pay phone on the wall near the bathrooms. Her phone number seemed like somebody else's as she dialed. She thought about the nerve she had to be doing this, then quickly reverted to justice, thinking about Vic's questionable relationships with other women. The answering machine picked up. It was his voice now, and it was the telephone number he spoke, not their names, which made Lucy wonder why he had changed it, and if he wanted people to think he was a man living alone. After the beep, she sang "Happy Birthday," and then returned to the table. Her confusion distracted her anger.

Julien stood, and then held out a hand. "Come with me. I want to show you something."

They walked back through the corridor and underground to the subway system. The walls were filled with aquariums. Their shoulders brushed together as they strolled. Lucy, relaxed somewhat by the anonymity, and by Julien's desire to share something with her, thought this was it, this was as good as it could get with a man, a feeling of gentle companionship and shared adventure. She hooked her arm in and out of his, pulling him closer to the colorful fish she noticed. The passage opened into the entrance of the subway. It looked like an empty space station with its chrome ticket machines, turnstiles, and sparkling white tile and glass. And it seemed, to Lucy, that with a push of the right button, they could go anywhere from there.

They stepped onto the red line and their intimacy dissipated as Lucy searched for familiar faces, especially at the Shinsaibashi station. None appeared.

*

When Lucy arrived home, Caprice questioned where she had been and Lucy lied by omission, saying where, omitting with

116

whom, and remaining silent when Caprice complained about not having seen Julien anywhere. Lucy lay in bed feeling awful about her deception and unable to get rid of the feeling she had something important to learn through connection with Julien. It seemed to her that touching him was a land she had to travel through to find a treasure.

*

For the next week, Lucy kept to herself as much as possible, working, running, and dodging Caprice and Julien. She was relieved when he was booked away for a commercial shoot on a cruise ship and Caprice for a catalog shoot in the mountains.

"You better get on a plane and get home now," Faith suggested when she called and Lucy told her what was going on. Lucy wondered if the kind of marriage she wanted—two people first taking care of themselves and then having fun with each other—was possible.

She certainly didn't want to run away from Japan and what she'd set in motion with Julien. She felt stimulated in every way like when she was younger, when she was doing whatever she wanted, without fear of loss.

That evening she strolled along the river to the Osaka Castle as she often did. The grass was tender green and colorful lights were strung through the cherry trees lining the eastern bank. Boys rowed while family and friends picnicked. Assorted stands offered corn-on-the-cob, octopus balls, apples, candies, and goldfish. Palm readers waited at their tables. On the other bank was a Zen garden: pruned shrubs and trees among rocks, flowerbeds. Lucy liked to sit and watch, imagining her questions would be answered eventually.

*

Ten days later, she stood above Akiko's desk, shaking her head in wonder. Both her and Julien's charts were blocked out for three days in Nagoya. Julien walked into the agency, tanned from the booking, and dressed entirely in white. He raised his arms to welcome her. "Hey Lucy, would you like to go to a party at the White House with me tonight?"

Captain approached from the opposite direction wearing a navy suit. He looked like some kind of game show host with two large white envelopes in his hand, smiling slyly behind his smoky aviator glasses. It was as if were all part of some grand plan, this inviting them both to Japan, and they had reached the climax. "You two must leave for Nagoya Sunday morning for a two-day booking. Good money. Beautiful hotel. You will do the brochure. I have all the information and tickets for Nagoya here. And here are the directions to the party tonight." Captain smiled slyly as Julien reached out to shake Lucy's hand in congratulations.

They stepped into a taxi, then sped along a two-lane street under aqua-colored steel train tracks, until the driver stopped at an intersection underneath a film poster with a larger-than-life image of a French actress in a white bodice and flowing blue skirt, paused on a flowering hill. "You would love that story. I would like to show you that film." Lucy looked up, liking that he seemed to be noticing something about who she was to at least venture at what she loved. She imagined a life in Paris with him, then shook the notion out of her head.

The White House was written in pink neon and flashed from the window on the second floor of a four-story white brick building. Lucy smiled. They climbed white cement stairs into a deep, white room filled with models, bookers, clients, accountants, and other business associates of Captain. One of the pale British models Lucy disliked rushed up to them. "Oh, Julien, it's too bad that Caprice is off in the mountains on some boring shoot missing the party isn't it?" then glared at Lucy, who smiled at her in pity as she often did at mean people.

Lucy touched Julien's arm and walked toward the bar to meet Joy.

As the party wore on, and Julien stayed near, Lucy let herself lean into him when she laughed, touch him whenever she passed. She sang "Bridge Over Troubled Waters" in a karaoke duet with Akiko, chatted with American and Australian models she normally wouldn't have given the time of day to, and shook her head, laughing, as she listened to Joy say, "I'd like to pop these cherries in Hamish's bottom, then eat them out of him." Lucy even sat on Julien's knee for a picture, one she would later stare at, back in Chicago, thinking she hadn't looked more happily beautiful since she was a girl.

She enchanted Captain's clients with her stories of the covered wagons built in her hometown along the Mississippi. "You tell very good story," one said, his index finger in the air.

In the taxi, on their way to Tennoji, Julien rested his head on the back of the seat and then turned toward her. "Lucy, you can have any kind of relationship you want with me, even if you only want to sleep in my arms."

It was such a sweet invitation, and she believed him, but she knew being in his arms would do little for her sleep. She went to his room with him anyway, and after hours of kissing, lay pressed against him, naked, as if imprinting his flesh on hers.

Later, when he was almost asleep, she lay there, amazed he hadn't pressured or overtaken her. It was yet another first as no man had ever not, especially in that position.

She was tired of wondering where, exactly, the line not to be crossed was. It felt like some weird kind of hopscotch, she could kiss, but not snuggle, snuggle but no intercourse. All of this laid out through experiences she and Vic had already survived in their brief time together. It was a twisted approach to loyalty, looking for keeping something sacred between her and Vic as if she could say I did this, but not that, and it would be okay. How was she blind to the fact that she was already on the other side of the line? Lucy nudged Julien to his back, rolled on top of him, and put him inside of her.

"What are you doing?" he whispered.

"Breaking through. Please don't move." It seemed so ridiculous and virginal to her, but that was all she wanted then —to cross the line so she could stop thinking about it. It was done. Onward.

*

As they walked hand in hand through Shinsaibashi the next night, and two midwestern women from the agency waved through the crowd, Lucy felt shame and pretended not to see them. Julien waved back, so she had to look, then, and smiled shyly. Julien leaned into her. "Are you embarrassed to be with me?"

"I'm embarrassed because of me."

"But nobody here even knows your husband."

They knew she was married, and Julien knew they knew, too, which made Lucy think his reasoning odd. What did it matter who Vic was to them? This was more about her feeling of shame at being blatantly unfaithful. She thought Vic should be the first to know, as ridiculous as that sounded because he'd be the third. Calling him up to clue him in sounded even more absurd. "I don't care if nobody here knows my husband. I still don't like it."

Julien pulled his head back in like a turtle. "You think too much."

"I can't think less. I've tried. Maybe you should think a little more."

"You should just live and do what feels good."

"I do what feels right, it doesn't always feel good."

"*Oui, oui, oui, oui.*"

"And this little piggy cried all the way home."

Julien's eyes looked puzzled by her chant and she liked this. She was saved from explaining her joke by pointing at Felix waving from the entrance of Jubilation.

She loved watching him and Julien speak French, their pursing lips and fluent hands. They both turned toward her at the same time, as if looking for an accomplice. Julien touched her arm. "Would you like to go to the baths?" Felix nodded to encourage her, but she needed no encouragement. Julien reached for her hand, as if, he, too, thought she might be hesitant.

What is it with these French guys? Why do they think American women are so ignorant? Lucy thought but did not say.

"We'll have dinner after. Come, it's just down the street. The men are separated from the women, though." Julien lifted his arm around her, and she enjoyed that. "So unfortunately we can't be together."

They all walked into a narrow brick building. The baths were upstairs in a white-tiled space. Julien, Lucy, and Felix were offered thick, white towels that smelled like hot lemons at the white semi-circle reception desk. Opposite white hallways led to more white rooms. I'm in heaven, Lucy thought, or a cloud.

As their paths diverged, she followed the female signage, hung her clothes in a white locker then entered another large open white-tiled space where ten naked Japanese women of varying ages and sizes were washing on wooden stools under a line of low nozzles that ran through the center of the room. The women turned, then looked up as Lucy entered, smiled, then sat on a stool to rinse herself looking at the others for direction. The woman next to her held out a bar of soap and nodded. Lucy smiled, then scrubbed, studying the large baths that lined the edges of the room.

She tested each one before getting in, jerking her hand away from the ice-cold one. The electric one made her nervous with its zapping, erratic currents. She climbed into the hot bath and sat between two older women with pink, steamy faces and short, wet, black hair. Lucy nodded as they did as if meeting on the street.

Felix shouted, "Hey Lucy, do you like?" and Lucy glanced around quickly until she saw him, perched over the partition between the baths. The women in the showers ran for cover. Lucy covered her smile with her hand as she watched her bath partners' shoulders jiggle in silent laughter.

*

In the bullet train, speeding toward Nagoya at dawn, Lucy sat near the window, sipping steaming green tea. She liked watching the cities and towns flash by in seconds, smearing white, gray, steel, and streaks of neon across the otherwise sparse, open landscape. She turned to Julien. "Do you believe in destiny?"

He looked at her. "Yours or mine?"

She lifted her chin toward the man across from them, his head back and mouth closed in sleep. "His."

Julien almost laughed. She was noticing it did not come easily to him. "Destiny is not fatality. There are many crossroads. We decide which direction we will take."

"I agree; we always can choose. Or, at least, we can choose what we want to do with what appears."

In the taxi, on the way to the castle, Julien rested his hand on Lucy's thigh. "Put on lipstick."

Lucy glared, not liking being told what to do, still, she rummaged through her satchel, looking for the tube, uncomfortable. "I usually show up for shoots with a clean face."

Julien nodded toward her portfolio. "And get your card out to present to the client when we meet. It's always better, more professional." Lucy shifted her body away from him, wondering why he thought he knew more than she did about everything, and why he was always telling her what to do. Gray sky and the stone walls of the castle filled her window view. The taxi turned, then slowed along a circular drive. *The Nagoya Castle Hotel* was written in gold on a panel of windows at the lobby entrance. It looked to Lucy like a lush life was about to begin. They were greeted by name, then led inside to one of the restaurants and a plush job.

*

A group of eight seated at a round table looked around the dining room in anticipation, then smiled knowingly when they saw Lucy and Julien. A man with a round belly, glasses, and a happy face stood, smiled, and bowed. "I am Toshiro, the photographer." He lifted their composites and held them in front

124

of him like a matchmaker, glancing at them, then Lucy and Julien, then back at the images, until he nodded his approval. The other members of the team left their seats and huddled around to look, first at the composites, then—as if they couldn't believe they were real—at Lucy and Julien. Toshiro gestured to a nearby table for two. "*Dozo*, breakfast?"

As Lucy finished her coffee, a thin man in a navy cotton fishing hat, carrying a silver tackle box, walked up to their table like a soldier reporting for duty. "I am Yohji, makeup artist, please come with me." His eyes followed Lucy's height as she stood, and she tried the shrinking thing again which still didn't work.

In the lobby, Yohji introduced her and Julien to the Japanese couple they would be working with. Miyoki had kind eyes, and a porcelain face, and was wearing bright red lipstick, her long thick hair clipped into a tail with a mother-of-pearl barrette. Naoko had a noble look about him, wavy, dark hair, parted on the side, an oval European face with Japanese bone structure, and broad, strong shoulders. He was a head taller than Lucy so she moved next to him. In the elevator, Yohji pointed to Julien and Naoko. "You two share room." Then he nodded toward Miyoki and said to Lucy, "She live in Nagoya. So you have own room."

Julien traced an imaginary line between Lucy and himself. "We are married."

Yohji shook his finger at Julien. "No."

Julien nodded.

Yohji turned toward Lucy. She was bracing herself with the wall behind her. They were all looking at her, waiting for her to speak. She hated this manipulative part of Julien, but at the same time, she loved his audacity. As she thought why not, she once again felt sick with the lie, not toward them, but toward Vic, who was beginning to seem like her imaginary husband. She always imagined him watching these scenes.

When she nodded with a rusty feel in her gut, Yohji turned back toward Julien. "Sorry I did not know."

Julien looked at him like a pastor forgiving a sin.

Yohji pivoted back as if it had dawned on him that it had taken Lucy an inordinate time to answer and if he moved fast enough he might catch a false look on her face.

Lucy met his glance.

He threw his hands in the air. "Guess nobody knows."

*

They stepped into make-believe land as they were photographed as if on a couple's vacation, which they occasionally shared with Naoko and Miyoki. In between takes of them stepping out of a taxi, registering alongside each other, enjoying cocktails in their suite, dining in the rooftop restaurant, the Chinese restaurant, the French restaurant, at the sushi bar, working out at the gym, relaxing by the pool, sipping aperitifs in the cocktail lounge, perusing porcelain and pearls in the gift shop, or lounging in the splendid lobby, Lucy darted glances at Miyoki, who was doing her own makeup while Yohji retouched hers. Miyoki nodded slightly to Lucy each time in some sort of deference Lucy could not understand. She didn't speak English, and Lucy only knew some words in Japanese. Lucy also saw how Yohji catered to her while he ignored Miyoki. When she was alone with him, Lucy asked, "Why does Miyoki do her own makeup?"

He looked away. "She, local girl. You make much more money."

This bothered Lucy. Later, on the set, she talked to Julien about it. "That's not right."

"It's normal. We come from farther away."

"It still doesn't seem right." Even if she could understand the economics of it, it bothered Lucy to consider herself more valuable than another. Julien seemed much more comfortable in that role, which somewhat impressed her. She admired the way he seemed to consider himself special because she wanted to feel that way about herself, but not at another's expense.

That evening, everyone was looking for Julien to begin the shoot, while she was waiting on set. He emerged from the sauna and steam rooms in a bathrobe, holding a towel around his neck. Even though he saw the entire team waiting for him he did not apologize or hurry, as Lucy knew she would have. She studied the way he didn't act subserviently. She wanted to be more like that, yet, again, something was off about it. He was not approaching them as equals, with respect.

Eventually, Julien, dapper in a black evening suit, strolled across the thick cream rug covering the gleaming oak wood floor in the luxurious lobby and took his place next to Lucy on the tawny velvet sofa. Toshiro cupped his hands around his mouth and shouted from behind the camera, fixed on a tripod fifty feet away, "Talk and smile, please."

Lucy fake smiled at Julien. "Nice steam?"

He looked so suave and de-boner, Lucy heard her brother say it in her mind, and she smiled as she thought about explaining the pun. Julien stretched one of his arms behind her, loosened his shoulders, looked her in the eye, and said, "I would like to make your clitoris as big as a nut."

The shutter clicked on Lucy's frozen smile and Toshiro shouted, "Again!" Lucy cracked up. The shutter clicked and clicked. She took a deep breath as she pondered the possible pain, or not, of a swell that size.

Julien kept his cool composure, never taking his eyes off her.

She did her best to restrain her laughter, as she said, "I used to love to gather acorns in the pasture."

Yohji flitted across the set. "Now they would like to shoot some pictures of you having dinner, then will leave you to enjoy it."

The chuckling and punning relaxed Lucy enough to enjoy the rest of the evening, especially dinner in the rooftop restaurant, and especially after the crew was gone and she and Julien were alone next to the window with the castle's pagodas filling the view.

Without cameras pointed at her, Lucy drank wine, ate lobster, and slipped into the mood and place that would let her go even farther.

*

Lucy was a visionary when making love.

With her first lover, she had often seen children running on a country path in spring. With Vic she saw a recurring image of being in a Victorian room, unable to see anyone above the waist, surrounded by burgundy velvet walls, black taffeta, velvet purple skirts, and men's tuxedo pants–a sense of her being an unnoticed child at a sophisticated late nineteenth-century cocktail party.

That night, in the darkness of the Nagoya hotel room, as Julien lifted his hips, and Lucy arched backward from her agitated perch and grasped his ankles, an image of camels moving across a golden desert at sunset filled her mind. When she gasped at the beauty and vividness of it, Julien paused. "Am I hurting you?"

Lucy curled forward, glided into his arms then nuzzled her head into his shoulder. She loved the feel of his heart beating under her cheek.

"What was it?"

"I saw camels. And gold. Everything was gold."

There was a pause.

"I want you to give me yourself totally," Julien whispered.

She lifted her head, kissed him deeply, and then entered another dream world. Gigantic morning glories opened, one after another, as she moved on top of him, feeling herself slinking through the jungle like a leopardess. Tall grasses brushed across her face, and then she saw a clearing. There they rolled on sun-drenched earth beside a glistening turquoise lake.

The thought of entering Julien excited her. Voices crept into her mind: You are not an animal. You are not a man. You are a woman, and this is not your husband. Her kiss and movements changed, she became tentative.

Julien stopped kissing her, pulled back, rolled away, and stared at the ceiling. "I am feeling someone else's energy. Not just yours and mine."

"I understand. I feel it, too. I don't know what to do about it."

"You need to get clear," he said, then rolled away, and dove into the other bed.

Lucy's nerves scattered in every direction, searching for the lost contact. She felt abandoned but unable to articulate it. She stared at Julien's profile. His eyes were closed. She was afraid to ask him anything. She tried to sleep, but her body was electric, and the image of the journeying camels repeated in her mind. Julien's *I want you to give me yourself totally* began its haunt. Yet his jumping away told her he only wanted part—her light, not her dark.

*

The next morning, disconcerted that on top of dealing with Julien being miffed at her for not making love right, she also had to contend with Yohji pummeling her face and threshing her hair in what felt to her like some kind of twisted hatred for women. Lucy lifted his hand from her face, then moved it more gently to instruct him.

He carried on as if her head were stone.

She excused herself and dashed for the bathroom where she turned on the water so he would not hear her, then hung her head directly over the toilet so the tears fell straight down and did not run the mascara he had just swathed on.

When she walked into the rooftop restaurant Julien was playing "Misty" on the piano. Lucy saw he had everything she appreciated: good looks, music, intellect, daring, refinement, and handyman capabilities. If only he could drop the selfish, arrogant, and manipulative parts, she mused. But then would the daring boldness she admired go with them? The arrogance bothered her the least. What she liked about his was that it was upfront, he said things as he saw them. He was honest about believing he was superior. He was different from many people she met, or knew, who walked around being arrogant while acting falsely humble, hiding behind a veneer of altruism, using what they considered others' misfortune as a building block for their esteem. All Julien seemed to be hiding was pain, and Lucy could relate to that.

She loved hearing him play, she knew how but didn't let on, and when he lifted his head and looked at her, she saw the tiger-who-had-not-succeeded-in-dominating-the-tigress-of-his-choice look had gone from his eyes, which dissolved the tension enough to carry on and enjoy the rest of pretending and picture-taking. Yohji shouted from a table set for breakfast for four, "Foreign couple on this side, Japanese couple here."

When Miyoki smiled at Lucy so freshly, Lucy thought there is who I was.

*

At the team dinner on the last night, she looked up now and then to watch Julien across the round table. He was drawing a map of Paris on a white paper napkin for Toshiro. He sketched the Seine, and the Eiffel Tower, and then after marking his neighborhood with a star, with the butt of his pen he showed Toshiro his way home. Lucy imagined riding with him. But, she was on her adventure, she kept reminding herself, not theirs. He was disturbing her itinerary. Whether it was possible to share adventure and an enduring love story she had yet to find out. There was perhaps more to trust and commitment than either of them thought.

"Hey, Lucy." The female stylist smiled. "Is true that everybody in Chicago carry a gun?"

Lucy lifted her hands. "Not everyone!"

Cars whistled in the distance as Julien and Lucy slid into the back seat of another white taxi. The driver's white-gloved hand reached for the address of the agency apartment. "So much whiteness," Lucy murmured as they swished through the streets, passing *The Hotel More*, written in flashing green neon. Lucy glanced back and thought, there it is, available in a hotel, the more everybody—or is it just me?—is looking for. Julien kissed her neck. The taxi slowed, and yen was passed over the seat. Cool air floated in as the driver pushed a button and the door opened. Lucy loved the feel of Julien's palm on the small of her back as they entered a narrow, dark stairway.

It was another modern studio apartment, with a bed in the far corner next to a window, the room dimly lit by a distant streetlight. Once again as Lucy reveled in lovemaking, a vision appeared in her mind. This time, she saw the entire congregation at her wedding, gifts in hand, looking at her as if they had been duped. She considered the timing inopportune.

"What am I going to tell—" her voice broke. She curled into herself and covered her head with her hands.

She was afraid Julien was going to ditch her again; at least there was only one bed in this room.

Instead, Julien whispered, "Don't," and then wrapped his arms around her.

She nestled the crown of her head under his chin, and felt safe, then, there, for that moment.

*

Back in Osaka, Lucy was drinking a cup of green tea after a long day of catalog shooting when Caprice walked in with her hands behind her back. She set a package of Lucy's favorite Japanese chocolates on the table in front of her. "Everybody thinks I should hate you, but I just can't."

Lucy sorted through the subtleties on Caprice's face. She figured those from the party talked, or maybe Boris told her he had seen Lucy leaving Julien's room the morning they left for Nagoya.

Caprice lifted her chin and looked across the table. "I saw it coming from the first time y'all looked at each other. I feel sorry for you. You have a lot to deal with ahead of you. Are you going to break up with your husband for Julien?"

Chocolates and pity and none-of-your-business questions, Lucy thought, as Caprice moved to the couch and looked at her with half-cast eyes, like a cat preparing to brush up against her body.

Lucy went for the sweetness in front of her first, opened the box of chocolates, carefully removed the gold foil from one, then popped it into her mouth. She let it melt on her tongue until she could feel the contours of the whole almond at the center. Caprice watched as if waiting for something more. Lucy slowly chewed the almond, looking into Caprice's eyes, then gently said, "Thank you for the chocolates. I'm relieved to hear you can't hate me. Please don't worry. I can take care of myself. And, if I choose to break up with my husband for anybody, it will be for me."

Caprice looked like an actress who had been given the wrong lead line in a play and now was lost at what to say or do next.

*

"Overseas call, Lucy!" Akiko peeked around the column, held out the receiver, and offered Lucy her chair.

When Lucy heard Vic's voice, she rolled as far under the desk as she could. "Hi, listen, this is not the best time. Can I call you back later?"

"You sound strange. What is going on?"

They had talked about these things before—she had told him how it scared her when she was attracted to others, and his response had always been to say it was normal. So she didn't hesitate now, though she did look around to assure no

134

one was listening. "I am finding myself attracted to someone and it disturbs me a bit."

"Well, that happens, but I think the problem is that we're not together. I want you to come home."

"I will come home before I go anywhere else."

"Go anywhere else? Oh, Lucy, you haven't. Have you?" Lucy opened her mouth but no words came out. She started to say she was sorry but Vic stopped her. "I'm standing alone in our apartment surrounded by your stuff. It's pouring down rain outside. You've just told me that you are fucking another man thousands of miles away. I'm in agony, and you're sorry?"

"I never vowed fidelity." Lucy was shocked at her utterance.

Then shocked again by Vic's reply. "I'm going to pack up all your shit and send it to your parents. I want an annulment."

Lucy saw her parents at their front door, receiving large boxes full of her stuff. "Please leave my parents out of this."

Vic hung up.

Lucy sat with the dial tone in her ear. Akiko walked by and dropped a box of tissues on the desk.

Lucy wiped her hands, and face, then took a deep breath and threw her shoulders back, and stood. Like a person walking away from an accident with an invisible injury, she moved toward the exit.

Tomy was waiting. He looked at his watch. "The casting is not far, we can walk. Julien is coming, too. This afternoon it's just the two of you."

Lucy excused herself to go to the bathroom, shied away from her glance in the mirror as she splashed cold water on her face, and then had to look. She looked better than she felt, she saw. She slapped herself lightly on both cheeks and added a few strokes of mascara and some lipstick from the new tube that had just arrived in the mail from her mother. Her mother sending her lipstick was a new thing, and oddly comforting for her.

*

Julien arrived and began searching her eyes like a detective who has seen something out of place. She was silent as they walked, then waited in a posh reception area. He reached over and lifted the shoulder of her jacket. "Take this off before you go in there. Show them your shoulders and waist. And take your hair away from your face."

Too tired to argue with him, she thought, who knows, maybe he's right. He most likely thought he was doing her a favor, Lucy assumed, as most people who told people what to do thought they were doing them a favor. Yet, she still saw all unsolicited advice as arrogant no matter the pile of good intentions behind it. Anyway, even she would have admitted she looked striking in her snug sleeveless top with her hair clipped back if she had looked at herself. She was more elegant than with the oversized jacket and wild hair, frizzed from the humidity of the day.

As soon as they left the building, Tomy said, "You have the job, Lucy! A big one for a poster. Two-hundred-fifty thousand yen for only half-day!"

The words bounced off her.

Julien grabbed her arm. "Thank you, Tomy is what she meant to say."

She was grateful. As well as fed up with Julien's Svengali attitude, even if his suggestions were useful. Arguing with him seemed useless. She was exhausted, anyway, and still in shock that she had told her husband she was having an affair by default and long-distance telephone. She wanted to get away. She thanked Tomy and rushed off, leaving them both standing there, confused.

*

Julien called that night when she didn't come to the clubs and invited her for a bicycle ride. She rode on the handlebars as he pedaled her through the small streets of Tennoji in the dark. She loved having the warm, wet breeze on her face, watching the spattering of warm lights in the low buildings, and seeing Japan, dark and sleeping. Lucy pointed to the crescent moon rising, and then glanced at the bikes they passed, parked up against trees, or walls, unlocked. "Where did you get this bike?"

"I borrowed it. Now you tell me, what is happening with you?"

"I told my husband today."

Julien swerved. "And?"

"He wants an annulment."

"Let him have it."

Lucy wondered if Julien saw something she didn't.

Julien felt her sigh and turned to look.

Lucy whispered in his ear, "Please take me back to my place."

"I thought we would sleep together."

"Not tonight."

She dismounted as soon as they arrived. He backed away when she leaned forward to kiss him. Now he was mad at her, too, she saw.

*

As she showered, she thought it telling that Vic's first response had been to let it all go, to say their marriage had never happened because she was loving someone else and acting on it. She knew she wouldn't respond like that. She'd be hurt, angry, and scared, but as she didn't think she was throwing her marriage away by sleeping with Julien, she wouldn't throw her marriage away in the reverse situation. She might, though, if Vic slept with someone else in a meaningless way. She never understood how meaningless sex was more forgivable than meaningful sex to most people she'd asked. She thought those folks had it all backward. Why anyone would want to be with someone who had sex with people they did not care about was beyond her.

Lucy went to bed.

Caprice slipped in next to her during the night, and Lucy stirred. "Lucy, you were crying in your sleep." Breezes floated through the open window. Lucy rolled toward Caprice, as if she were her baby sister, spooned her from behind, and fell back asleep.

*

At her sayonara party in Bamboo, Caprice threw her arms around Lucy, and kissed her on the lips, then murmured in her ear, "When I came into your bed the other night, I was looking for something more."

The hotel sign in Nagoya, *The Hotel More*, flashed in Lucy's imagination.

Felix waved from the corner of a booth. "Hey Lucy, are you coming to my Sayonara tomorrow night?"

Lucy put her hand on her heart. "You're leaving us, too?"

Caprice left, and Felix left. Joy was still there, though.

"He's gone. I'm here alone. I'm going to stay longer to work," Lucy told Vic on the phone. "I will come home at the end of the month."

Vic's voice was full of disdain. "What can I say? You've taken all the power. I'm going to do what I want now."

"Weren't you doing that all along?" Lucy asked. "Also, if it makes you feel better, send the stuff to my parents. Move if you want."

This time she hung up, then left to meet Julien at Maharaja.

He was sitting in the booth where they'd first kissed, with a hard look on his face. She'd stayed out of his bed, except once, since Nagoya and she suspected that to be the reason he was pouting. That one time she was in his bed had been another failed attempt at letting go of her guilt. As he stared at her in that hard way, she imagined this must be his way to express anger, by lancing darts with his eyes. She sat down across from him anyway and relaxed in the booth. "Captain agreed to extend my visa."

He lifted his chin toward her. "How do you feel?"

She dropped her head back on the banquette and took a deep breath. "Free."

Julien spoke evenly. "You are not free. Now you have two."

She sat up in confusion, thinking she had none. "As I told Vic, I am staying here longer for myself," she paused, to let *for myself* enough space and time to sink in. Then she threw a dart of her own. "Not for you."

Julien flicked his ashes into the ashtray. "But you must admit to yourself, at least, that you are staying to be with me."

Lucy backed away looking at him and thinking, don't you know, you aren't even here anymore?

"This is crazy. Vic is angry with me because of sleeping with you, and you are angry with me for not sleeping with you."

Julien shifted position. "You are only letting yourself receive the worst of everything instead of the best."

Lucy stared a what the f— do you know? at him, and asked, "What exactly is the best coming at me right now?"

Julien lifted his chin again in a way she did not like. "You know, Lucy, making love is more than just a pleasure, it is about communicating at one of the deepest levels."

Lucy smoothed her skirt, remembering. "I must admit it has always been more of an experiment in pleasure for me. But I do understand what you are saying, and I feel it."

"Have you ever had an—?"

She was surprised Julien was having trouble saying the word *orgasm* and she laughed realizing he thought she'd never come in her life.

Julien's chin shot further into the air with her laugh.

She took a deep breath. "Of course I have. I love them. I miss them."

"So you know how, but you don't want to give it to me?"

Lucy shook her head in confusion, asking what with her eyebrows.

Julien rephrased his question. "You know how to let yourself go but you just do not want to let that happen with me?"

"I want to. But," she paused again and looked away. She still did not want to tell him how Vic came to mind when she was in that position. His idea that she was holding herself back from her pleasure on purpose seemed absurd to her. She thought of the ways he had pulled back. She looked at him again and used her softest voice. "Why don't you let yourself go with me?"

Julien looked as if he couldn't believe she had the nerve to even ask him such a question. "I am not going to unless you do, why would I? It would be a tremendous loss of energy. It has to be a total share. Why even get in bed with me if you cannot be there completely?"

Lucy's stomach ached. Her head hurt. She had stayed out of his bed for this reason and he was angry about that, too. Again, gently, she spoke. "I want to give you as much as I can."

He looked at her in disbelief, as if he could not care less, then snapped. "What do you give?"

Lucy considered herself a rather generous soul, yet was amazed she had no ready answer. It wasn't her nature to consider herself a gift anyway. Befuddled, she was, thinking why is he sitting here with me if he has no idea about what I have to give? Her anger rose as she wondered, and she pointed at him, doing her best to control her voice. "So let me get this straight, you want to keep the control, but you want me," she thumbed herself, "to lose it?" She paused. "Exactly what kind of share is that?"

Julien drilled his eyes into hers. "I control myself to fulfill your pleasure, our pleasure, and yours is a major part of mine. I know women who climax many times during lovemaking. That is the great advantage you have. Men have one big explosion, losing everything. A woman loses nothing."

Lucy looked for her bag, ready to choose flight over fight once again. She had never seen or heard anything like these control issues, this notion of gender advantages or disadvantages while making love. What she could not believe was that a woman had nothing to lose in the exchange. She calmed herself down, then raised an eyebrow. "Interesting theory."

Julien glared. "It is not a theory. It has been practiced, experimented. I know it is true."

Lucy was unsure if she wanted to continue in a sexual relationship with this man. What was supposed to be a pleasure appeared complicated. She took another sip of her drink and changed the subject. "Captain made an appointment and reservations for me to go to Hong Kong Friday. I'll have to leave the visa papers at the consulate that morning, then stay through the weekend and pick them up on Monday morning."

Julien surprised her by saying, "We could go together."

She shook her head. "I want to go alone. I think it will be good for me."

It was Golden Week, the first one of May, the longest and—for many Japanese workers—the only Japanese vacation of the year. Lucy lifted a map from her bag and spread it over the table in front of them. She pointed to Katsurahama Beach, which she had circled in red pen. "But first, I want to go here. This island is called Shikoku. Would you like to come with me on the night boat?"

Julien slipped a cigarette from his pack and leaned back. "You just said you were going to Hong Kong."

"Not until Friday morning."

"Take an overnight boat to stay one day and night on an island and then come on the overnight boat back?"

Lucy nodded.

She knew by the way he almost smiled that he would come.

[7]

The ship pulled into the dock at dawn. The sun was hidden behind the clouds, and it looked like rain. Lucy and Julien quietly sauntered down the gangway toward the path that led up a hill. Under a small thatch-covered square with vending machines, Lucy slid coins into a slot below a picture of coffee beans dancing with a cow while a packet of sugar was poured over them. Two cans of sweet, hot coffee with milk plunked out. As she and Julien walked up the hill sipping them, Lucy hooked her left index finger in his belt loop, then stared at it as some sort of unconscious accomplishment in reaching out and holding on.

Their feet scrunched along the gravel, and she closed her eyes to listen. Scanning the area, the island of Shikoku did not seem foreign to her. At the top, the vista opened and spread. The gray of the sky highlighted the green of the grass. Man-made structures were scarce and scattered. Chickens pecked in a nearby yard. Locals bicycled by, carrying open umbrellas. It was spitting rain, a misty morning. Lucy pulled the map from her jacket pocket and measured the distance with her finger and thumb to the palm tree she'd circled. "It doesn't look that far."

Julien blew smoke in the air and then shook his head reproachfully. "You must look at the scale to measure correctly."

Before Lucy could suggest that Julien looks at it himself, a passing car slowed, and then backed up. Two young Japanese men in jean jackets smiled from the window. Lucy showed them the map, then pointed to Katsurahama Beach. They pointed to the back seat of the car and opened the door. Cigarette smoke and loud music streamed out as Julien and Lucy ducked in. Lucy rolled down the window. The driver pointed to the cassette player on Julien's lap and then to his ear. Lucy ejected the tape and handed it to his friend. The Beatles sang "All You Need Is Love" as they pulled out on the road.

The driver looked in the rearview mirror at Lucy and Julien. "Where from?"

Lucy pointed to her chest. "Chicago."

Julien nodded. "France."

Both friends smiled at each other as if they had come across a rare alien species. Lucy looked out the window, thrilled to see the horizon and open land for the first time in six weeks. They drove on, listening to the Beatles, smiling at each other, traveling along the Pacific on low land into clearer weather.

Three hours later they arrived at a beach. A white pagoda trimmed in red sat on top of a shale cliff where cedar trees grew. Three boulders formed an ellipse from there into the sea, a bamboo bridge connected them. The driver pulled to the edge of the parking lot, and his friend handed Lucy the cassette. She pointed to them, and then to the beach. They nodded and walked with Lucy and Julien.

"*Kirei*," Lucy practiced what she thought was the Japanese word for beautiful, hoping she stressed the correct syllable. The young men nodded again, bowed, and then turned to go. "*Dove?*" she asked for where? The boys pointed to their watches, the car, the place on the map where the ship docked, then themselves. It dawned on Lucy and Julien then that these

146

young men had driven them there out of generosity, perhaps curiosity, and were headed back. They waved away Lucy and Julien's expressions of disbelief. Lucy offered the cassette as a thank-you, but they wouldn't take it. She made the gesture of drinking, and eating, then pointed to them. "Coffee? Lunch?" They each refused with a shaking of the head.

"Amazing people," Julien said after he and Lucy sat on the sand, looking out over the water. Seagulls swooped and dove into the silver waves. It started to drizzle.

Lucy looked toward the cliff, and then lifted her nose toward the stairs leading up and over it. "Want to see what's over there?"

Julien was leaning back on his elbows, squinting at the hazy sky. "*C'est dommage que le soleil se cache.*"

"I love it when you do that."

"Do what?"

"Speak French to me without realizing it."

"You are right. I did." He seemed softer than usual. "Maybe I am comfortable?"

Lucy raised a finger. "That is a very good sign."

They climbed the stairs, passed under a wooden threshold painted red, and then looked down to another beach and a small village. Walking through it, they passed square one-story homes spaciously placed and furrows in the open ground where planting had begun. Gardeners worked, their wide-brimmed bamboo hats deflecting the rain. The drizzle turned to steady drops.

Under a cliff on the beach, protected from the rain, they sat throwing stones at a can, listening to the ping when they hit, the roar of the wild waves, and their sizzle as they broke the shore. As they watched lightning flash on the horizon, and the rain died down, Julien placed a hand on Lucy's thigh. "Let's walk."

Inland among cedars and pines, a man stood guarding the opening of a huge canvas tent. Cheers grew louder as Lucy and Julien approached. They looked at each other, shrugged why not, then bought a ticket from the man, and went in. In the center was a ring, and in the ring were two dogs in a face-off, growling at each other, each one had bit-up and dangling bloody ears. Drunk and drinking men were shouting bets with beer cans in their hands, and cigarettes hanging from their mouths. It smelled like sweat and blood. "I can't take it," Lucy whispered into Julien's ear, "I'm going outside, back to the beach."

Once there, Lucy breathed easily, and watched families playing in the rain, umbrellas in their hands. She thought about her own family and how they would disapprove of her affair, then kept walking along the boardwalk and timber, letting the scents of pine, cedar, and salt fill her. She felt freer than she ever had, despite Julien's belief that she was not, that now she had two attachments. What made her feel free was pleasing herself, risking the life she knew for one she wanted. She watched raindrops disappearing into the sand, thinking how one life absorbs another, until she heard, "You didn't miss much." She spun in the direction of Julien's voice.

He looked so warm and alive, like a long-lost friend against the gray and green backdrop. She kept to herself how happy she was to see him standing there, and how familiar he looked to her for the first time. Maybe it was his casual clothes. She loved seeing him in sneakers, they made him less intimidating to her. She loved being in nature with him, too. To tell him how happy to see him she was, however, seemed imprudent to her. She thought, then, of a friend's husband who once told her, "I think you are afraid of men, Lucy." She still wondered about that and decided she both was and was not.

What she most hated to admit was her fear to be herself completely with a man, yet was it only men she felt that way with?

She liked being with men her height, as Julien was, meeting eye to eye. Big men repulsed her. The mere possibility she may be physically overpowered kept her back. What also kept her back from Julien, other than the fact she was married to someone else, was the knowledge that saying no to him was difficult. She worried he could persuade her to do things she'd never do alone—yet this also attracted her.

So she was hiding and waiting, wanting him to prove his love first, and then, well, maybe she'd fess up to her tender feelings for him.

Some part of her knew she'd settled for less than she wanted with Vic, and she wondered if that meant she was using him, however graciously. She also wondered if everyone was using everyone else and if it was only a question of how. In any case, using someone made her think less of herself. She'd given up on her adventurous solo life by getting married, tethering herself to a certain security, and she found that, too, a less-than-admirable quality.

There she was on a beach in Japan with a handsome fellow foreigner, one she felt deeply attracted to and had been strad-dling in ecstasy weeks before, and she stood back from kissing him because God forbid what if that made him think she loved him? Then God knows what he might do to her, right?

She pointed to the water, all these thoughts and feelings guarded. "The tide is coming in. I think we should check our bags."

*

They returned to their cliff cove just in time. Julien gestured to a spot farther inland with his chin. "I think that will be a good place to camp."

"I saw some tarp we could use for a tent near a construc-tion site."

"Tarp?"

She liked watching his eyes turn inward as he tried to un-derstand vocabulary without asking. Little did she know how difficult asking anything was for him.

She curled her index finger toward her. "Come, I'll show you." They crossed the beach, then the two-lane blacktopped road to where Lucy proudly displayed her find. "We can use it and bring it back in the morning."

As they removed and folded it, Julien scanned the area. "We need sticks and wood for the fire." He pointed to a dozen bamboo branches leaning against the wall of a shack. "I can use some of those for the tent."

Lucy crammed the tarp into her backpack. "I saw a little grocery store where we can get something to eat."

They entered new territory in their relationship as they co-operated.

*

A tiny woman with silver-streaked ebony hair rushed out from behind the counter in the little market, wiping her smooth hands on her apron. *"Kombon wa,"* Lucy said, and lines crinkled around the shopkeeper's eyes as she smiled and peeled out in Japanese. Lucy raised a hand to halt her, to say I do not understand, *"Wakaranei."* The woman thought Lucy didn't understand the idea, rather than the language, so she kept going, her sharp eyes flashing.

Julien, an aisle away in the three-aisle market, held up a package of cocktail weenies. "What about these?"

"Great, get two. Have you seen any marshmallows?" There was confusion on his face again. The woman smiled at Lucy. Lucy looked at Julien. "You know, white, puffy, we used to put them on sticks when we were little kids and toast them over the bonfire."

"Is it some kind of cheese?"

Lucy laughed. "Forget it. I'll send you one someday. They're light." She was leaning over a display of saké cans piled pyramid-style on the floor. She lifted one, then looked closely at the metal tab with lightning symbols on it. She imagined, when pulled, this tab would start a heating process within the can. She carried four of them to the counter. "Warm saké and weenies by the fire!"

"Weenies?"

Lucy pointed at them. "These are weenies, cocktail weenies. It's also slang, you know, *argot*, for the man's *zizi*."

Julien pulled his head back in horror. "What is?"

Lucy chuckled. "Hasn't anyone ever told you to keep your weenie in your pants?"

Julien furrowed his brow, really trying to remember. "I don't think so."

Lucy kissed his cheek. "Why am I not surprised?"

"How about some chips? Tomatoes? Cheese?" He lifted each suggestion in succession. The shopkeeper and Lucy watched as he placed each item on the counter. Lucy scrutinized the individually wrapped cheeses with the laughing cow on them. She squeezed one. "What is this?"

Julien raised a finger. "Cheese is very good for you, you know. The cow is a very generous animal."

Lucy smiled to herself thinking he may like Iowa, after all, as she watched the shopkeeper add everything with pencil and paper. They counted out the yen and were handed their picnic dinner in a white plastic bag. It struck Lucy then, that they had seen only Japanese people all day. She had the feeling this woman rarely saw foreigners. It gave her pause how at home she felt on this tiny Japanese island with a man that frightened her, yet somehow all of a sudden didn't.

*

It was black dark when they stepped outside. Warm lights from houses shone in an odd pattern from the hidden landscape. The wet road glistened. The rain had stopped. Julien

152

lifted a broken wooden chair at the side of a garbage container and studied it. "I think it's too wet."

Lucy thought there may be more so she opened the steel lid of the bin and peered in. "Jackpot. There are two more in here, and newspapers."

Back at camp, Julien pulled a long white candle from his bag, secured it between rocks, and lit it. Lucy set the cassette player nearby and the Beatles played while Julien broke the chairs over rocks. She balled the newspaper, he positioned pieces of the broken chairs in pyramid form. Then, by the light of the fire, he pounded four holes deep into the ground with a stick and a large stone. Together they inserted the bamboo. Lucy filled sand and pebbles around them. He handed her one end of the royal blue tarp, and they spread it over the tops of the poles, weighing each side down with more sand and rocks. The extra tarp hung over the front edge as a door flap, swinging open toward the large rock and fire.

As Lucy watched Julien spear the weenies on a stick and position them in the fire, she asked, "Were you a Boy Scout?"

He nodded.

She tried to imagine him in the blue outfit and yellow scarf that her brothers had worn. She wasn't afraid of her brothers, it occurred to her then, though it also occurred to her that sometimes she worried if she said what she thought, she might lose their love, too. She wondered if keeping her thoughts to herself was a kind of withholding, a lack of generosity. Hoarding them, was she? *Nah,* she said to herself.

Yet, the questioning went on inside her, sometimes she felt like a question factory. Was it presumptuous to consider her thoughts a gift to others? Was she demeaning herself to think they were not?

She liked to think she was assessing where they might be useful, or at least, recognized and appreciated. Yet another part of her harbored the fear that if recognized in all her pain and imperfection, she'd be unlovable. Even at that moment, she decided to keep to herself that this was her first camping experience, imagining such knowledge would only reinforce her novice status in Julien's mind, giving him yet another opportunity to lecture her.

Oblivious to all this mind chatter, Julien stood, wiped his hands on his jeans, and removed the weenies from the flames. Lucy opened two saké cans. They sat in front of the fire, quietly eating and sipping, watching the night sky unveil. The batteries, dying in the cassette player, distorted the music and the Beatles sounded like strangled warblers. Lucy shut it off. When the seat of the second chair became a bright red ember, she stood, saying, "I want a longer view of this."

Julien also rose, and they walked toward the water side-by-side. Their bare feet sank into the damp sand at the shoreline, and they turned back to look at the first home they made together, a little blue pup tent between rock and fire.

They fell asleep with their heads poking out of the tent, watching the sky until their eyes closed. Lucy removed her shirt as the sun rose, then edged a little further out to soak it in. Julien rose, lit a cigarette, and milled around. Lucy could hear him but kept her eyes closed until he chided her. "Do you like to expose yourself?"

She sat up. "And you think I'm the prude?"

He nodded toward the village. "People are arriving." She shimmied back inside the tent. After she came out dressed, he took off his t-shirt and lay on the warm sand in the same position he had suggested she should not. Lucy stood above him. She looked at her watch. "We need to go. If I miss the boat tonight I'll miss my plane tomorrow."

Without opening his eyes, Julien said, "You can go the day after."

Lucy smelled the fire in her hair as she bent over to gather the saké cans glinting in the sun and sand. She was hurt by his behavior and imagined it was because she had kept her hands to herself throughout the night. She decided she would leave with or without him. "I guess I will be hitchhiking by myself."

Julien sat up. "It's a pity we have to leave now, in the sun."

Lucy, pleased to see movement, smiled. "It will come with us."

The first person to stop and offer a ride was a well-dressed pretty woman wearing lots of gold and driving a sleek black sedan. She spoke English and watched Julien through her rearview mirror as if he were a tasty food she craved. Lucy looked at her watch, then the speedometer. She leaned toward Julien's ear. "Do you think it would be rude if I asked her to speed?"

Julien looked at her as if she were outrageous. "It would be very rude."

Hot, Lucy leaned forward to slip her sweater off. Julien caught her arm before it accidentally smacked the woman in the back of the head. The woman looked back and forth at them through the rear-view mirror. "You know, there is a very important bridge being constructed on this island."

If it's between us, Lucy thought, it better be a sturdy one, that's a long stretch.

Standing on the highway under a scorching sun, Lucy kicked the gravel. "I think she was going farther but just didn't want to take us."

Julien flicked his finished cigarette into the ditch. "She probably didn't want to take *you* any farther."

His meanness took her by surprise and to that hellhole of wondering what she had done to displease. She looked at him hard. "It is three o'clock now. The boat leaves at six. Do you even care if I make it?"

He took another cigarette from his pack. "And if I get stressed and nervous like you, what will it change?"

He had a point, she knew. They walked for an hour or more on the quiet highway, Lucy behind Julien, or at least a foot away when at his side. She was once again in the strange dance of being close to him without being close to him.

A car roared past their outstretched thumbs.

They walked on. As Lucy was thinking of the old film where the woman lifted her skirt to attract a ride, a white Nissan approached and stopped. A kind, older couple nodded energetically, knowingly, when Lucy showed the man behind the wheel the port on the map through his window. She lifted her finger to point at her watch. Julien grabbed her arm. "Just get in the car."

Once in, Lucy sat as far away from him as she could. She was starving, so she unbuckled her backpack and took out a bag of fruit bars. There was only one left. She offered it to the woman, then the man, both refused, then reluctantly to Julien, who shook his head and then glared at the crumbs that dropped on the seat and floor as Lucy ate it. She picked them up and pushed them into her pants pocket, glaring back.

By five forty-five they still weren't there. The boat sailed at six. The driver picked up speed, giving Lucy reassuring glances from behind his gold-rimmed glasses through the rear-view mirror. From the top of the gravel road that led to the dock, they saw the gangway being pulled in. The man lay on his horn, stuck his head out the window, waved, and shouted in Japanese. Gravel spit widely from his wheels as he drove down the hill. The plank reversed its motion and was set back on the cement. Passengers watched and some cheered from the upper decks as Julien and Lucy ran on.

It had raised halfway back up by the time they arrived at the top. They turned to see if their saviors were still there, and the man and woman waved. Lucy blew kisses. As they sailed out of the bay between high slate cliffs, Julien yanked her away from the rail by her belt loop, spinning and facing her in the direction of the sunset, wrapping his arms around her from behind.

"A perfect red ball dropping into the sea," she said.

"No, Lucy. We are moving, not it."

She rested the back of her head on his shoulder. "I like that metaphor."

She could feel his lips moving on her cheek as he said, "It's more than a metaphor. It's true."

She sighed. "It's also a metaphor."

*

The next night in Bamboo, Julien drew a map of Hong Kong and the New Territories and told Lucy about a ferry to Lantau.

In the morning, before she left, she gave him pleasure in a way that she knew would be difficult for him to control, and it was. He let go for the first time. It was the first kiss she'd given him there, and a goodbye, a dare, a steal. Yet, he didn't stop her.

On the way to the airport, she wondered if had he let her hijack his almost defenseless missile, so she could feel the strange emptiness of such a power play. Her focus was too much on him. What if she had asked herself what she was trying to prove, instead?

Was his desire to see and feel her orgasm the same as hers to she could affect him? Was it a common desire to move another to surrender or uncontrollable pleasure?

Whatever the answer or reason, the feeling she carried away with her that morning made Lucy Pilgrim decide never to play that game again.

[8]

On the plane, Lucy looked into the clouds and thought her oddest fear was that of feeling the same comfort with Julien that she did with Vic. Why did it scare her to feel as comfortable with both men? Because she'd married Vic, in part, for that feeling, and now it appeared she could have married herself instead.

Green, smooth mountains appeared in her view. Pastel high rises thrust from the ground, and Lucy smiled thinking how they looked like the houses she and her brothers and sisters had cut out of refrigerator boxes and painted in the driveway. Modern highways split and curved into the ancient landscape. "Welcome to Hong Kong, it is eighty-eight degrees Fahrenheit," the pilot announced as the plane skimmed over the buildings of Central, then North Point.

Lucy took a taxi to Central, left her passport and the necessary papers at the Japanese consulate, then stepped from their air-conditioned offices out into the wet heat. People moved rapidly around her like busy ants. Street workers crawled in and out of trenches in between sidewalks and bamboo scaffolding. Fruit vendors carried their wares in boxes strung around their necks. Red, blue, and green double and single-deck trams clattered down the middle of the street, clanging. Bicycles darted in and out, their bells ringing. Lucy walked, amid the sounds of drills, hammers, and shouting voices, mesmerized by the otherworldliness. She passed wooden barrels filled with fruits and nuts, next to tan rotary telephones sitting on tables, with signs that read FREE FOR PUBLIC USE.

She doubted she could sit down and call Iowa or Chicago or Osaka. She didn't want to anyway. She walked on.

Live chickens hung upside down on strings. A man teased snakes, bit off their heads, spat them into his hand, drained their mouths, and auctioned the liquid as an elixir. People dressed in designer clothes wearing gold sunglasses, gold watches, and gold chains clipped past this spectacle without looking twice. There were greasy cafés next to two-story fancy restaurants. Markets with rows of tables piled with fabrics of every color and texture imaginable.

*

Come early evening, Lucy stretched her legs on a wooden bench at the back of the Star Ferry and rode across the harbor from Hong Kong Island to Kowloon, the Mainland. The sea breeze dried the perspiration covering her body. Junks, with their high sterns and four-cornered sails, floated by. Passenger ferries, tankers, small sailboats, immense yachts, cargo ships, and tiny fishing boats steered by one man sailed about the harbor. Victoria Peak loomed above the congested high rises of the island as the sun dropped behind the haze. Lucy watched an old man, relaxing on his haunches at the back of a small wooden boat anchored in the middle of the harbor. He was smoking a cigarette and looking out over the water in thought. She was struck by his flexibility and wondered what it took to maintain that, because she, too, wanted to remain agile as an old woman.

After the ferry docked, she walked into the nearest hotel. It was posh and too expensive for her budget, but she liked the bar. It was cozy, woody, accented with hanging plants. Foreigners dominated the scene. Lucy watched the people, trying not to stare, as she leaned back in a leather armchair, sipping from a frosty glass of beer. Many different languages were being spoken, by faces and bodies in so many different colors, shapes, and sizes, yet the same feeling of unwinding permeated the room. Lucy wondered what she would do if she saw Vic, or Julien, walk in and was relieved when it occurred to her that she preferred neither would. To her, that seemed like some sort of progress. Content to be with herself, she wanted to continue walking and seeing. She considered not sleeping, but her feet were aching. Her thin-soled sandals were melting, eaten up by the hot pavement. She was sweaty, dirty, tired.

Throughout the day, images of living alone, having many lovers, and limitless options collided with warm memories of the home and life she and Vic had made together. She told herself that if he loved her, he would at least try to understand, then she asked herself the next logical question—how could she be doing this if she loved him? I am doing this for me, she answered, and it has nothing to do with him, and he, we, may benefit from it. She deemed that an outrageous response that felt both right and selfish to her.

*

She checked into The Empress, the closest hotel she considered affordable in Tsim Sha Tsui. "We will need your passport, please," the young woman at the reception desk said after Lucy handed her the American Express card.

She checked into The Empress, the closest hotel she considered affordable in Tsim Sha Tsui. "We will need your passport, please," the young woman at the reception desk said after Lucy handed her the American Express card.

Lucy showed the papers they had given her that afternoon. "It's at the Japanese consulate."

Up in her room, after a long cool bath, Lucy sat on the bed, in front of the oblong ornate mirror, looking at herself as if she were someone else. She looked leaner, sharper, and more mature. Here I am, on the other side of the world, alone, exploring, she mused, maybe I don't need anyone.

She needed food, though, so she called room service and smiled, a bit later, watching a young man in a tuxedo roll a silver tray into her room, bow, then lift a silver dome and serve her a cheeseburger and fries on china.

After her meal, she called Vic again and then hung up when she heard the answering machine. It was seven in the morning in Chicago. She wondered if he was sleeping elsewhere. She picked up the remote and pressed a button at random. A pretty Chinese woman in a red suit gave the stock report in English, with a British accent. Fascinated, Lucy changed channels to watch other Chinese male and female faces speaking with these accents. It jarred her, she wanted to tell them to stop. They looked like puppets in the wrong hands.

The receptionist called the next morning. "I am sorry but your American Express was not approved."

"That's very strange. I will be right down." It was the first time Lucy had used it since she left Chicago. Most of her money was at the agency in Osaka. She called Vic who was still not there. This time she left a message with this news. In the shower, she budgeted the nine thousand yen she was carrying—it was just enough to pay for the room. She had two nights and three days to go before she could pick up her visa and get her plane back to Osaka. As she imagined sneaking out, she was relieved to remember they didn't have her passport, even though she had told them where it was, and that she would go there to pick it up on Monday.

Downstairs, when the receptionist tried the card again, it bleeped as unapproved again. Lucy fidgeted. "Is there an American Express office nearby?"

"Yes, there is, right over on Jordan Road. Here is the address."

Lucy walked out without paying, pretending she would come back, but knowing she would only if she could get the office to approve the card. It would be another first, doing such a thing, but she didn't know what else to do.

At the office on Jordan Road, the agent behind the desk looked up from her computer and said, "This card has been canceled by the primary holder."

"My husband," Lucy had trouble with the pronunciation of the word. The agent nodded. Lucy thought how ironic it was that telling Vic the truth had led him to distrust her. His action also took care of the guilt she had been feeling, in one fell swoop. Tina Turner singing "What's Love Got to Do With It?" came to mind as she walked out onto the street.

It was ten in the morning and already very hot. The strap of her backpack cut into her sunburned shoulder. Other than the yen, she was carrying a pen, a notebook, clean underwear, and a deck of cards. Her feet were pink, swollen, and bleeding in places. She saw a sign with an arrow pointing in the direction of the Kowloon-Canton Railway, and thought why not?

*

At Sha Tin, she stepped off the train and followed another sign, this one pointing toward Ten Thousand Buddhas. She climbed four hundred and sixty stone stairs barefoot, up the side of a mountain, then sat under an ancient eucalyptus tree at a rock table and chair, among singing birds and teeming insects, the faint traffic noise three hundred meters below. Sweat drenched her silk tank top. Her feet pulsed. She wondered where she would sleep. She told herself to just keep going, it would become clear. In an outhouse nearby she relieved herself in a hole in the ground, then cleaned herself with a leaf. As she passed under a stone archway, sheets and cotton shirts, a load of whites, hung from a string between trees on the other side. No one was in sight. Then she spotted the temple entrance, it was made of gray stone, framed in red, with gold Chinese characters etched upon it.

Lucy passed through it to an open courtyard, where the interior walls were the color of lapis lazuli. A color that stopped her in her tracks and deeply soothed her. She looked up, and her eyes, then body, followed a procession of Buddhas traversing the roof of a shrine at the far end. Underneath these

Buddhas was a glass coffin of sorts. She read that what she saw inside of it was the embalmed body of the monk who established the temple. It, he, was covered in gold leaf. She liked to imagine herself that way, alive. She continued to walk around inside the lapis lazuli walls and noted each of the ten thousand Buddhas on the grounds she looked at was unique. Where are the goddesses, she wondered, and then she saw one that looked like a woman and wore gold; she was carrying a wand, sitting atop a royal blue half-dragon half-dog. Lucy liked her and her wand, and in the spirit of gathering her strength, she sat under her for the next three hours, her head and back pressed against the cool cement walls, leaves rustling in the eucalyptus tree above her as parakeets hopped from branch to branch.

Like an opened cage, her mind emptied.

After she descended the mountain, she saw a Caucasian couple waiting at a bus station in front of the railway station. "Will this one take me back to Tsim Sha Tsui?" The man nodded as the woman told her it would. The woman asked, "Are you studying here?"

"I have been working in Japan and came here to renew my visa and travel around for a few days."

"Please tell me you are not staying in that awful place, that Chungking Mansions where my children have stayed for six dollars a night."

"Where is that?"

"I believe it's on Nathan Road, but I've heard simply terrible things about the place. Dark. Tiny. Shared showers and baths."

"Have you stayed there?"

"Most definitely not, dear."

Lucy made a mental note of the address. A red double-decker bus appeared and then stopped at their feet. "This one will take you back to Kowloon on the scenic route." The man nodded, and Lucy climbed up the stairs and offered a handful of coins for the driver to choose from. She sat near a window. After they skirted Golden Hill Country Park, Lucy stepped off, to step on another to ride across Rambler Channel, just because she liked the name.

She was the only one on this bus, sitting in the middle back seat, looking out the window, taking in the sights, sounds, and smells. She saw the bus driver watching her throughout the ride as if wondering if she knew where she was, or what she was doing. She changed buses again at the Container Terminal, staring at the barges lined up, imagining their port destinations around the world, wondering about sailors' lives, and whether they were lonely.

As she rode along the coast of Kowloon, she was once again mesmerized by the harbor, enthralled by the size and mystery of the ships riding at anchor, docking, and unloading, the movement among them, and the distance they had traveled. It was the Grand Central Station of the South China Sea.

She stared, too, at the small villages crammed into the mountainsides and wondered if she could live like that and if she would ever feel at home in anything but open spaces, which also made her wonder how far one can travel from where one starts. She rode the Star Ferry to Central wishing she could ride until morning. It made her want to have both of her grandmas at her side to say, would you look at that? After a tram ride to Victoria Peak, and a stroll along its pine-lined paths at sunset, she reluctantly walked down the hill into thicker and thicker civilization.

*

It seemed everywhere she looked she saw jewelry stores and wedding rings. She stopped in Harry's Bar and ordered a beer, then sat alone at a table for two. She wondered again why she was so afraid of Julien, why did she worry whether she could measure up? Then she decided that she'd done enough wondering and walked again until she found the Chungking Mansions, met Luna the manager, a Filipino woman she immediately trusted, and checked into a cell-like room.

There was a cot against the wall and a small mirror above it. One exposed light bulb, surrounded by cobwebs, hung from the middle of the cement ceiling. Lucy believed the spiders would stay in their web. She reminded herself she was only going to sleep there. A Filipino man was talking to his young son in the room next door. Luna told Lucy the father and son lived there. Lucy's eyes widened. "They are lucky to have a place and to be alive. Many others keep their belongings in locked cages near the port by day, and sleep in the cages at night." Lucy was speechless, wondering how they had imagined their freedom when leaving their country, and if they had known what hardship lay ahead. Or, worse, she thought, had they been fooled? She didn't think it kind to ask. Nor did she ask Luna that night when she went out with her and sat with friends of hers drinking beer in an island pub, watching the crowd, and pretending not to understand the men that sat down next to her and offered her drinks, dinners, trips.

Despite all the challenging evidence, Lucy was determined to believe in an evolved world where men were considered more than predators, and women were considered more than prey.

*

On Sunday, she woke early to ride a ferry to Lantau Island, and from its prow, watched the massive cluster of Hong Kong diminish and disappear. Once docked at Silver Mine Bay, she boarded a rickety bus and sat in the back seat dodging branches that caught in the open window, as they zoomed up and around the mountain to the place Luna told her she must visit. Six hundred meters above sea level, the bus slowed onto a gravel plateau and stopped in front of the gated entrance of Po Lin Monastery.

Lucy followed small wooden signs marking a footpath, past stables where children were riding horses. The air was light there at the top of the world. Lucy imagined herself as a tiny figure on the globe as she arrived at the summit of the fuzzy mountains, and then rested in front of a small stone structure that looked like a shepherd's cove. Sheer clouds wafted in until the path she had trodden disappeared, totally enveloped in white. The clouds passed on, the shrubby knolls reappeared in front of her, and then the veil of white recovered the view of other mountains, sea, and small port villages. It went on like this for hours, Lucy watching. Each time she attempted to rise, the ground held her tailbone like a magnet, so she let it. Warmth gathered and welled there. As the sun set, she walked back down the path, arriving in time to ride the last bus, to catch the last ferry.

*

At the airport, she eyed the security guards, worried she might have the hotel bill and handcuffs thrust before her. She breathed easier once on the plane.

Back in Tennoji, she took a long, lathery shower. Then she smoothed milk-and-honey lotion into her skin, dressed in her khaki adventure pants, and turtleneck black sweater. While lacing her boots, the image of Julien waiting for her in Bamboo moved her in a way she had no words for, and she would ask herself often about the mysterious flush of energy when she remembered it.

She felt desire rising again, which made her realize how her days in Hong Kong had emptied her of it. She felt new, and dashed out the door, breaking herself to a lively gait instead of a sprint. Barely able to sit still through the five stops on the metro, she picked at the wool pilling on her sweater. The only other passenger in the car, an older Japanese man in a business suit, snapped his fingers and then pointed to her mess on the floor. Lucy gathered the lint and shoved it in her pocket.

In the velvet of Bamboo's reception area, she flashed her card and picked up the pen to sign in. A few lines above her signature, *Julien, 007*. She took the stairs two at a time to the

VIP lounge where she saw he was sitting alone. When he turned and saw her, the warm welcome and delight in his eyes told her more than he ever had. She dropped into the booth. He nuzzled his nose into her hair, and whispered, "I am very happy to see you."

*

Hours later, after her stories were told, and they were back in his room, kissing, fully clothed, Lucy eased him back onto the bed. As she lowered herself on top of him, she came. One of her favorite ways to come, in increasing reverberations. She rolled to the side, then whispered, "That has never happened to me before. Like that, I mean. Still in my clothes. Just from my desire."

Julien caressed her cheek and looked into her eyes. "It is very important that you know it is not me that makes you feel like that. It is you. It is what you are giving me. It is yours."

What was she giving him, she wondered, her desire for him, her love of him, her excitement? In any case, what amazed Lucy most was the way Julien gave her pleasure back to her, telling her she was the source, not him.

This was new to her and she thought about it the next morning in the shower. She had always felt like a victim of desire, as if it was something outside of her, more powerful than her that came to rest on her, and was out of her control. As something the other had that she wanted—more about the other, than her. Understanding that it arose within her, and came from her, she could consider it creative and constructive instead of something she had to submit to or conquer.

Perhaps, she considered then, it was the way she loved another, more than was loved by them, that turned her on. It would take her a while to consider it could be both.

*

A week later, while waiting for the train to go to work in Kobe, Lucy called her parents to wish them a happy wedding anniversary. By the gentle, inquisitive way her father said, "How are you, honey?" she could tell he sensed she was in what he would call a pickle. She stood at the payphone, watching three men slurping udon at a nearby noodle stand, wanting to tell her dad what was going on and not knowing where to start or trusting he would understand.

"I'm hangin' in there," was all she could say. She hung up the phone needing to face the life she had left behind, so she could figure out how to go forward.

The next day she talked to Captain, then made a flight reservation, then left Vic a message telling him when she would arrive and not to bother to come to the airport, she'd take a taxi home.

Home felt strange to say, she wondered where that was.

*

"So you've decided." Julien salted the Macedonian dish, then looked into her eyes and raised his brows for confirmation. They were at Bamboo, in what had become their regular spot. This life had become a new home, she thought as she nodded.

His movements slowed. "Well, I hope you'll be a good girl for yourself."

Lucy cocked her head, thinking girl? She was uninterested in an argument. "Please explain to me what is–" she raised her fingers to put quotation marks around it "a good girl?"

"Be strong. Go your own way. Drive your own life, do not let the energies and pressures of those around you steer you."

Lucy listened, liking what she was hearing. She was also trying to picture her life with him no longer in it.

Julien leaned back and looked at her from a different angle, as if he, too, were sizing up what would soon be gone. He spoke. "I had a dream yesterday morning. I was driving my car in Paris and was very happy. I was with someone I stayed very well with, but she didn't have a face in the dream. Her father's presence was there, telling me to take care of his daughter, that she was really loving me."

Lucy closed her eyes to hold back tears. She had no idea what would happen, how she would feel, if she would still want to be with Vic, or him, she knew she had to find out, to move forward, one step at a time. "I can't stay longer. I feel like I'm hanging in limbo."

Julien nodded. She watched his Adam's apple bulge as he swallowed.

After the waiter cleared the plates, Julien slipped a fountain pen out of the inside pocket of her jean jacket, which he was wearing, then spread a white napkin on the table between them. He drew two stick figures, then black arrows from one to the other. "You have this kind of relationship, one giving to the other and then the other giving back, that is, one always

172

waiting to receive before giving to the other." He drew another stick figure farther away from the two, then an arrow from one that traveled on to the third. "Then you have this type. One giving to the other, and the other giving to another." Lifting his pen back to the two in the center, he drew arrows from each of them and joined their ends in the middle space above them. Drawing a spiral around that space he said, "This is the best—each giving one hundred percent and fireworks happening where it all meets."

Lucy was pleased they thought alike on this point while annoyed that he seemed to think he was the one who knew, and she had yet to learn. She pointed to the drawing and said, "Much easier to draw than to put into practice."

Julien wrote *theoretical* in the top left-hand corner of the napkin then slid it her way.

That night before sleep, she kissed him and whispered, "Why don't you beg me to stay?"

He covered his forehead with a hand and looked at the ceiling. "I may as well pee in a violin."

"Why a violin?"

"Exactly," he said, "it's pointless."

He wrapped his body around hers.

The way he held her so closely throughout the night made Lucy feel that perhaps he loved her more than either of them knew.

*

After one last job in Hiroshima, then amassing piles of yen into an envelope at the agency, after Moti, after Bamboo, and after all of the other good-byes had been said, Julien and Lucy and Joy sat in a private room of the elegant bar where Tomy had invited them, drinking whiskey on the rocks and listening to Tomy play the piano. Julien stretched his legs out on the booth and rested the back of his head on Lucy's shoulder. She slipped her hand inside his shirt.

"Someday, someway," she whispered, then looked at him, both believing and not what she'd said.

He seemed okay with it, she noticed, but it was strange for her.

How do any of us know what the words that tumble from our hearts will come to mean?

In the hours before she left, Lucy slept astride him, enclosed in his arms. At dawn, perched above him, she caressed his body and traced the lines of his face. Any movement away from him wrenched her. She was surprised at how painful it was to leave him. She'd been telling herself he'd be a tender memory in her life and she'd go on. Now tears covered her face and chest. He held her hips and softly spoke. "Go now, and don't look back."

Lucy wanted one more look in his eyes. She gently pried the left one open with her thumb and forefinger. The intensity of his regard shot her hand down as if he was saying how dare you to peek into my pain? Yet, it was his pain that told her their relationship was meaningful to him. She curled into him, and then, slipped away. She dressed watching him. He never opened his eyes. After opening the door, she paused, raised her finger above her shoulder, and pointed in the direction she was headed. She didn't look back.

He would write that it was sunny with a warm west wind the day he woke up and she was gone.

Lake Michigan looked like a vast shimmering aquamarine as the plane lowered in the sky. Lucy was surprised to see Vic when she walked off the plane. She noted as she hugged him, the way he held himself stiff in his new clothes. When he looked at the engagement and wedding rings on her finger, laughing and sneering at the same time, she took it as payment for the pain she caused. It made her think he had dressed up to come and torture her. As they walked to the parking lot, "How much money did you make?" was the first question he asked.

Lucy winced. "I have around seven hundred thousand yen in my pocket," she said as he lifted her suitcase into the trunk, then slammed it closed with a nod.

On the highway, as Vic jerked the stick shift and she sensed he imagined it as her neck, she rolled down the window and let spring in.

Chicago had gone from gray and bare to lush and green while she was gone. Lucy felt herself blossoming with it. She was as full of a sense of possibility as Vic was of rage. His anger was understandable to her, but not his behavior. She kept asking herself, Why is he here? Why does he want me if he thinks I am so awful?

The first thing she noticed when she stepped inside their home was that their bedroom was gone. In its place was a new study. That is where Vic put her suitcase. She turned around to where the study used to be and saw the new bedroom. The formerly cream walls were now painted drab steel and covered by ivory sponge marks that looked as if they had been slammed there. The bed was hidden behind the door, shoved into a corner. Vic looked at her proudly. "What do you think?"

Her face fell and nausea filled her stomach, she was heartsick to see how unattractive it was. She couldn't stand to be in it, she felt the sponge marks coming at her.

He nodded toward their former bedroom. "I couldn't sleep in there anymore."

She nodded, too, and then slid around his body to get out. As they walked toward the living room, she stopped and reached to lift Lovey, who scrambled from her and scampered down the hallway with her sister, jumping on and off the walls. "The cats are running away from me."

Vic looked over his shoulder. "Can you blame them?"

Lucy sat on the couch and then leaned back, telling herself to stay calm, and closing her eyes. When she opened them, Vic was standing in front of her with a tray of chilled champagne, two flutes, and a small platter of Lucy's favorite curried grape salad. He sat down next to her, looked into her eyes, and lifted his glass for a toast. "Welcome home."

Lucy touched hers to his.

Vic forced a smile as he asked, "He never left Japan did he?"

With her mouth full of bitter bubbles, Lucy shook her head.

Vic bored his eyes into hers. "You slept with him last night, didn't you?"

Lucy closed her eyes and nodded. The champagne was still in her mouth. She was holding her breath. When she heard his shaming, "And it was your friend's boyfriend," she opened her eyes.

Vic was looking at her as if she had committed a heinous crime. "We have big problems here." He leaped up and away.

Lucy set her glass on the coffee table. "I wondered what we were celebrating."

Vic paced in front of the rocking chair. "To stay you need to realize you've made a mistake."

"A mistake?" Lucy asked, knowing calling it that would be dishonest.

Vic threw his arms in the air, then picked up Lovey, and stroked her fur. He looked at the cat lovingly, then at Lucy as so much less deserving.

Did he want her to be jealous of a cat? She was confused but happy to be seeing what she was seeing. It was revealing more of Vic to her.

He saw the question in her eyes and said, "I don't know how else I can forgive you."

Lucy looked around the room. It was understanding she wanted, not forgiveness, though one led to the other she imagined. In any case, she was not about to let go of all she'd gained inside herself through her illicit relationship. She looked out at the full catalpa trees, their leaves bouncing behind the screens of the open bay windows. She could smell the freshly cut grass. The day looked too beautiful, to her, for this ugliness. She turned back at Vic, who was looking at her as if she were an ogre, took a deep breath, and said, "I am sorry for the pain I caused you. I'd like to see if we can build a new relationship from here."

He lifted his chin as he did on their wedding day when he vowed to challenge her. "You have to admit you were weak."

Lucy looked into his eyes. "It took a lot of strength for me to do what I did, and it was important." She loved hearing herself say this, and was pleasantly surprised by her calmness while doing so.

Vic scoffed at her declaration. "I want you to stay, but no more traveling alone and no more contact with him." He sat in his grandfather's rocker, looking at her as if it were the moment for her to throw herself at his feet and beg for mercy.

Lucy, meanwhile, was trying to imagine never venturing on back roads alone again, never walking through an airport alone again, never talking or writing to Julien again. She couldn't believe Vic thought this attitude would inspire her to stay. She was amazed that Vic thought he owned her.

Had she known then that he told everyone they knew about her affair, it would have been somewhat clearer to her why he felt the need to prove his domination. Lucy sensed that this was all an act, so she put it aside. "Let's get outside, that will help. I'm going to take a quick shower, and then how about if we go down to that Mexican restaurant on Armitage for lunch?"

Vic looked at her like he could not care less and like he was doing her a huge favor to even be talking to her. "If you want."

*

After a margarita, away from their home, he seemed more like the man she knew as he sat across the table from her listening to her talk about Hong Kong. She delicately sidestepped the story of how he'd left her stranded by canceling the credit card. He even smiled and let a compliment slip out. "You look great."

At that moment she could see a glimmer of understanding in his eyes. She thought him more generous when he said, "Whatever happened over there must have been good for you."

The good feeling was dispelled when she paid the bill, with Vic standing next to her, and the owner looked at her and asked, "Are you French?"

*

That night, each time she approached the bedroom, it was as if she walked into a countercurrent that whipped her about-face and marched her back to the living room. She made up an excuse of needing to drop something off at Faith's but instead drove up and down Lake Shore Drive until dawn.

After the expected "where have you been?" and her honest answer, Lucy lay down next to her husband, but touching him felt untruthful to her. She could still smell and feel Julien on her skin despite the showers. When she closed her eyes, she was in his bed in the penthouse. When she opened them, she heard Vic say, "The ball's in your court. It's all up to you."

She thought, aren't there two of us here? but kept quiet. She was confused about what ball, anyway, what game, and why it was all up to her. Especially when Vic was the one declaring the rules. She guessed it was up to her to accept them or not.

Acid burned in her stomach when she thought about staying. It disappeared when she imagined going off on her own, then came back again with images of divorce. When she thought of Julien, she ached, too. Yet she knew, deeply, it wasn't about leaving one man for the other. Instead, they both felt like obstacles to her self-reliance. She knew she had to go further on her way in the world first, that it was still too early to enter into full partnership, and she was as scared as she was desiring of that. She lay stiff, on her back, wanting to move away from Vic, but not wanting to hurt him more. She began to see how she had trapped herself with her longing for security, and now as it was crumbling she could see how false it was. As soon as the light came, she rose to make some coffee.

The phone rang around nine. Lucy answered it in the study. It was her father. She imagined him at home, looking out over the valley, as he asked, "Lucy, what's going on over there?"

The way he always seemed to sense when she was adrift, wherever she was, comforted her. "Well, I'm trying to decide whether I want to stay married or not."

"Already?"

Lucy paced in silence, twirling the cord, seeing his point.

"What is it? Drinking? Drugs? Gambling? Has he hit you?"

Lucy was surprised by her dad's list of justifiable reasons. "No, it's me. I got involved with someone else while I was in Japan."

There was a pause, then her dad asked, "Why'd you tell him?"

Lucy pondered. This was, after all, the man who had taught her to do unto others as she would have them do unto her. "Because if it were me, I would want to know."

"Well, that's a whole different can of worms," her dad said, and Lucy imagined cans of people intertwined with their lovers. Tom went on. "I don't have any experience with that. All I can tell you is this; you made a commitment and you broke it. What you have to remember now is if you stay, you're making another one."

That piece of advice rang bells of clarity in Lucy's mind.

That evening while she ran along the train tracks, it dawned on Lucy that what she had given herself with her honesty was a second chance. Would she marry Vic again? became the pertinent question.

She came home, opened the futon, and set up her bedroom in the office. She slid off her wedding ring but left her engagement ring on, and over the next day's breakfast, she told Vic, as sweetly and as softly as she could. "Let's think of this as a new engagement. Let's decide if we want to marry each other again."

She watched the ripple of shock move through his body. Looking back, she would marvel at her nerve. Yet, she meant it.

Vic stared at his plate, suspicious, his fork poised above it. "You've never made eggs like this before."

"It's true. Try them. You might like them."

Vic threw his fork on the plate. It rattled as he pushed it in her direction. "You think you are going to turn me into him, is that your plan?"

Lucy watched. "I just like the eggs," she said, foreseeing a life of hiding in the pantry if she wanted to eat them.

She was quite sure Vic had had at least one affair, too, but she was not interested in titting for tatting. He was circling the table now. She wished they could read the *Tribune* and chat about current events, or just quietly move around in the same space, touching, or kissing each other as they used to. Those days looked far away. Even though she was sitting nude at the breakfast table as she often did when at home.

Vic stood above her. "What kind of birth control did you use over there?"

"My own."

His eyes went wild. "You used absolutely no protection with this guy?"

"I trusted myself."

"Trusted yourself, Jesus Christ."

"How dare people do that in this world," Lucy said as she stood and walked out of the room.

Vic was soon hot on her tail. "You could have gotten pregnant. Do you realize the risk you took?"

Lucy stopped, and turned, ready for battle. She was so tired of men thinking she did not know what she was doing. She wiped a hand between her legs to show him the blood she felt beginning to flow. "Satisfied?"

He stared at her as if for the first time. Then she saw another thought move across his eyes.

He raised his chin again. "You talk about how you want to give me yourself as you are now," he spat this out as if she were worthless, then pointed to the bedroom. "But you have given me nothing in there."

It is a privilege, she thought, not a right. Lucy gnashed her teeth. She focused on his eyes and enunciated each word. "Until I see some respect out here, you will not be seeing me in there."

*

A few days later, Lucy was resting against a willow tree by the lake in the afternoon sun, after having stood up for herself one more time in a battle with Vic. She could feel, as she relaxed, a sort of gathering heat in her lower belly, and a strengthening pulse between her legs. It resonated upward and outward and made her feel giddy, like a child who has just been told a delicious secret on a ride. It felt to her, in the beginning, as other excitement had, but yet it sprung from no apparent desire. If she desired anything strongly at that moment it was simply to be herself, freely. And to be loved, or at least left alone. She felt a power surge at the crux of her. Maybe it was the approaching summer, she wondered. Or maybe it was because she had laid more claim to herself than ever before since returning from Japan, and her body was responding in celebration, saying yes, yes, yes, keep going, yes like that. She looked around, saw she was alone, lay back, closed her eyes, and came.

The passing cyclists, scampering squirrels, docked sailboats, and everything around her took on a sort of oneiric glow after coming like that, and it was more difficult for her to discern where her skin ended and the earth, grass, water, sun, and other people began. It was as if her walls were dissolving. She took this as a sign she was on the right path.

It was interesting to her, too, how the source felt feminine, how she had the impression there was a goddess inside of her, and the pulsations were like delightful labor pains, a birthing of wave after wave of pleasure, the goddess swimming in them, then, finally, as if it were she, Lucy, the goddess, being birthed in pleasure. Whatever it was, she liked it. She wondered how many women felt it, why she had never heard about it. It seemed such wonderful news.

*

When she walked in the door, Vic handed her a letter from Julien as if it were more evidence for her prosecution, and then followed her into the study. She opened it in front of him to insist she had nothing to hide. He sat on the futon and she could feel his glare from the corner of her eye as he watched her face warm and soften as she read. How sweet it felt to her to know that she was missed, loved, and wished well. What an ache it caused in her to read the details of Julien's life in Japan without her, how he felt she was still there, like a ghost beside him, how he was waiting for the phone to ring and for it to be her.

She came to the end, and read *We both deserve the life we are working on, it is uneasy, tormented, but so exciting*, then read it again and again as if it were code. It occurred to Lucy that Julien might have known and understood her better than she thought. She was surprised he used *we* and *working*, pleased that he had seen she was indeed working on the life she wanted. Noting their way was uneasy, perhaps different yet similar, also intrigued her as he seemed to her to prefer the easy way, and she was given pause when she read his admission of torment. She read on. *Keep going, I have my way to love you, just send me a sign, as you did when you left my room, last sad Wednesday.* She knew then he had seen her raised finger pointed in the direction she was going. She wondered for a split second why she had left, yet couldn't imagine herself still there. She looked up to face Vic's disdain, then dropped the open letter on the desk, said, "You can read it if you want," and went to the kitchen for a glass of water.

When she passed by again, she watched the way Vic's eyes widened and his mouth dropped open as he read. "I want to meet that man," he uttered as he set the letter back on the desk.

At that moment, Lucy knew he understood.

Then she saw the hardness return to his face. He sneered. "Why does he say that his clothes now smell like you?"

"Because I left him the rest of my detergent," Lucy said and left the room, hiding the tears in her eyes.

*

The month of June filled with the matter of who was going to take the blame for the end. They stayed in their separate rooms and lived their separate lives. Lucy started drawing again, something she hadn't done since before she was married. She rode her bicycle for hours along the lakeshore, left news with the agency that she was available for more trips, and saw Faith and other friends, though most were too nervous around her as their young marriages were fragile.

When Vic showed up by her favorite tree at the lake, pretending it was a coincidence, she was unfooled. Already gone, in a way, and bitter without realizing it, she was ready to punish him now for punishing her. He reached out and touched her cheek. "My daughters were supposed to look like you."

She recoiled. "So you married me to breed me?"

Vic looked at her disgusted at her ignorance of his great compliment, then grabbed her hand and pulled on their engagement ring. "I want that back. You are not the woman I asked to marry me."

Saying, "You're right," Lucy pulled her hand back to herself, and slid the ring from her finger. She placed it in his palm, then bicycled home and started packing.

*

As she emptied drawers into suitcases, she came across a green velvet pouch she'd forgotten she owned. She loosened the drawstring, and the tiny gold dromedary charm her Grandma Pilgrim had given her years ago fell into her palm. She remembered her grandmother telling her how she had found it among her own mother's things after she died. Lucy slipped it onto a chain and clasped it around her neck.

That night, passing under elms on a bike ride along the lake, the steady beat of the pendant on her chest brought the memory of the dromedaries she'd seen while making love in

Nagoya. She smiled, thinking camels and gold, what might that mean? then brushed the coincidence off as perhaps trite, all the while marveling at the mystery.

*

The day Vic's brother helped him carry almost everything out of their home, Angelina called. "Both Barcelona and Athens want you, take your pick."

Lucy chose Barcelona and then imagined what life in a city on the Mediterranean might be like as she watched Vic walk through the apartment pointing at things, saying, "Mine," until the place was empty, save for their mattress, some linens, dishes, her clothes, a cassette recorder, and books.

That afternoon, she rented a storage locker on North Avenue, and in between trips of filling it, she rode her bike to the Loop to meet with a lawyer.

Raine, a friend of Angelina's, was tall, broad-shouldered, and handsome with a soothing voice. He asked questions and then said, "We can use the time you were in Japan as a separation. I will draw up the papers, then get a court date."

"How long could all that take?"

"A couple of weeks if there is no resistance."

Lucy knew her speed would be conceived as brutal, but she saw no reason to prolong the agony. She was sure she no longer wanted to be married to this man, come what may.

*

When she arrived home, a huge truck filled with catalpa trees was pulling away from the apartment building. Lucy sat on her bike, staring at the three raw stumps on the corner, thinking about loss, until a car honked her out of her shocked state.

Inside the building, she opened the mailbox, and there was a small cassette case decorated with a map and addressed to her in Julien's handwriting. She was happy to have something to listen to once she entered the empty apartment, now devoid of cats, stereo, telephone and so much else. Upstairs, she walked down the hallway then was struck by the stark view of the red brick apartment building across the street, where she had seen lush spring green leaves that morning. She dragged the mattress Vic left behind to the living room. Eager for company, she put the cassette in her Walkman, lay back, and listened to the tape.

There was a pause, the scratch of a microphone being moved, cars passing in the street outside the penthouse window, and Julien moving on his bed. "It's like I spend all my morning with you reading again your letters. And, I have a lot to say for sure. Let me put some music. Isn't it a good blues? I am quite nude. Totally. And I have a lot to do about your letters." Lucy wondered what that meant. Would he come to Chicago? She had not told him she was going to Barcelona. She listened to the saxophone, piano, and bass play softly in the background and could easily imagine Julien where and how he was. She loved having his voice with her, making love to her across the miles. When the tape ended, silence echoed in the large room, Lucy kept her eyes closed. The faint laughter of children from a carnival at St. Gregory's, two blocks away, drifted through the windows, making her ache for shared joy. She knew, though, that she had to go on for herself, not for, or to, him. She both wanted to be with him and to be on her own.

After a while, to distract her mind, she got up and ate some pasta salad with the one fork she had not yet packed. She began wondering how to get in touch with Vic about the divorce papers. She wondered where he had gone, so she went for a bike ride and from a payphone by the lake, called his parents in Michigan.

Her mother-in-law answered. Once she heard Lucy's voice, hers changed to a lower, colder register, and when Lucy asked about Vic's whereabouts his mother said, "Just to give you an idea how hard Vic is trying to make things work, I think you might like to know that he went to Iowa today to have lunch with your father."

Lucy wondered how Vic and his mother thought talking to her father would impress her. Am I in a nineteenth-century novel here? She also wondered. Her mother-in-law offered solutions to their broken marriage and asked if there were a third party involved.

Lucy thought it best to remain kind yet brief. It was all so embarrassing to her, yet she knew that apologizing profusely and continually would get her nowhere. "The only two people involved in this right now are Vic and me. Thank you for your time and this information. I'm sorry about all of this. I love you."

When her mother-in-law said, "You don't love anybody but yourself," Lucy hung up.

That night, she hopped up on one of the stools at a bar she and Vic liked on Halsted, and when her favorite bartender saw Vic come in, he winked at Lucy, then disappeared. Lucy turned on him slowly. "So, what did you have to say to my dad?" She imagined the two of them sitting across from each other, talking about her affair over lunch.

Vic shrugged. "He had some questions. I answered them. Your family is not very happy with you. You should call them."

Said the man who cut the telephone, Lucy thought. Vic's visit seemed more like revenge than an attempt to fix anything. She smoothed some dollar bills as flat as she could. She placed them next to her half-empty glass, then walked out.

*

Days later, if only her mother, instead of her father, had answered the phone when she called, things might have been different. But it was her dad who did so she gave him the news, from that pay phone that was becoming dear to her near Foster Avenue beach. She liked looking at the lake while she talked. "I didn't tell you more about what was going on because I thought you would appreciate that I handled it on my own. The divorce should be taken care of in the next week or so." She waited.

Her father remained silent. It seemed Vic had done the damage he had perhaps hoped to do. Lucy went on. "I've been offered work in Barcelona, Spain, and I'm going to go." Still no response. "I'd like to come home for the Father's Day picnic. I'd love to see everyone before I leave."

As Lucy watched the moonlight on the lake, she heard her dad say, "I don't think that's a good idea."

Lucy swallowed hard. She wondered, again, what Vic said, why her dad had believed him if he did, and then, what one says after one is disowned, especially if one hopes it is only temporary, and especially if it is because one divorced someone who didn't love them. She was trying to understand, so she asked what she suspected. "Are you embarrassed?"

"Yes, I am. And I don't want to deal with all that right now."

Lucy's ears and heart burned. The lake breeze helped. She smoothed sand under her feet. "I'll let you know when I leave for Europe, then—"

"You take care," he said as Lucy had often heard him say to acquaintances.

"Okay. Bye, then." She gently set the receiver into its cradle. Looking up at the stars, the almost-summer night fresh around her, she guessed it was time she learned to live without her daddy.

*

"Your mom called me and wants you to call her," Faith told her on the beach the next afternoon.

So Lucy called.

"I didn't want you leaving the country without a kiss and a hug from me," Viola said.

Lucy mumbled, "I just feel like nobody understands me."

Viola groaned. "For god's sake, quit acting like you are on a soap opera."

Lucy sighed. "I am going through a divorce. Forgive me if I have a mood or two."

*

She flinched as the uncontested papers were stamped and her marriage proclaimed dissolved. *Dissolved*, Lucy repeated in her mind, thinking that an odd word choice while she imagined their brief wedlock sliding into a puddle on the floor, soon to be swept away.

*

On the first day of summer, Lucy boarded a bus to live Grandma Pilgrim's dream and ride across America. She sat in the back watching it all go by, listening to Four Non-Blondes sing about revolution through headphones. The more she thought about Julien, the more grateful she felt for his presence in her life. By the time she arrived at Penn Station, she'd decided she wanted to thank him in person before she went to Barcelona. So, once off the bus in New York City, she walked to a travel agency and bought a plane ticket to Paris.

View from seat 5B-1, TWA Flight #800

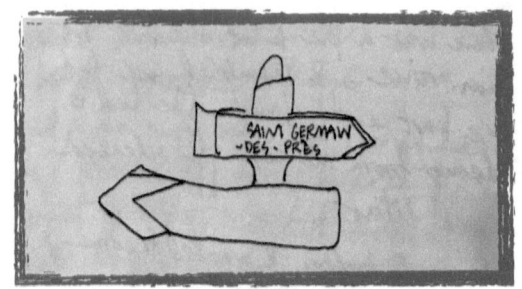

[10]

Lucy climbed the stairs out of the RER station at nine in the morning and walked along Boulevard Montparnasse, an unfurled map in her free hand. The suitcase wheels rattled against the wide sidewalk as she took the Left Bank in, looking everywhere, especially at the sunlight splashing through the leaves of the plane trees. She smelled baking croissants in the air and decided she would first check into the hotel, then buy one.

The weight of the affair, the return, the divorce, the estrangement from family, the moving, it all fell away under that foreign sky. She admired the stones of the Parisian buildings, their shuttered windows and doors and she delighted in the way the street signs looked like empty stages as if each street were an act about to open. In the title position was the street's name, painted in white on blue enamel rectangles framed in green, with fine lines of black and white paint to create shadow effects, making the signs look three-dimensional. There were marquees above them with the number of the arrondissement, as if the 6th, in this case, were the number of a perpetual movement in which everyone who passed through the neighborhood played a part.

The three-story hotel was marked by a painter's palette with the words *Hôtel des Academies et des Arts* jutting out above the lobby window. She had reserved a room at the airport because she liked the name of the place. A bird-like woman in a tight chignon checked Lucy in, and Lucy followed her slim figure up a set of creaky wooden stairs, wondering if this woman's bad mood was simply because she'd tied her hair too close to her scalp. They entered a room with a double bed, a nightstand, a small chair under a wall telephone, and a view of the slate roof. The woman opened what looked like a closet and pointed to the toilet in it. Behind another door, she presented a shower and sink. She held the key in the air toward Lucy and then left without a word.

Lucy splashed cold water on her face, imagined Julien waking to the message she'd left from the airport, and wondered if he would come, then went out for a walk in search of the Seine. After what seemed far too long on Boulevard Raspail, the colors of clothes, people, pâtisseries, boutiques, façades, and even sky, ran together in Lucy's jet-lagged and exhausted mind. Paris became surreal in her vision. When she stepped into the street and was almost hit by a Vespa, she turned back, thinking it wise to rest. In the window of a food shop, she pointed to a cheese sandwich with a 10F sign sticking out of it, then to a pretty blue bottle with an orange peel on it. Back at the hotel she ate, showered, then fell asleep.

*

The knocking woke her, she covered herself with the sheet and rose enough to crack open the door. When she saw his eyes, she fell back on the bed. His hair was long and he had grown a beard. He was shaking his head in happy disbelief. "Lucy-chan, what are you doing here?"

She rolled to her side, patted the space on the bed, and then curled her upper body into his lap. He glided his fingers through her hair and caressed her face and neck as she emitted pertinent details of the weeks since she'd seen him.

When Julien drew her on top of him, their kisses and caresses deepened and traveled, and Lucy, with no need to hold back, no fear, no guilt, no worry, realized that the dam to her full pleasure was gone. She was flowing free, river and source, amazed by how much she contained.

"You are a fountain," Julien whispered.

When she felt empty, her body glided into rest, and peace in his arms.

Until he asked, "What are you going to do?"

The missing *we* pained her. She hoped Julien could not hear her heart skittering in fear of rejection. She reminded herself she had come to see him. That was it. She'd seen him. Her lips moved against his chest. "I'm on my way to Barcelona. But maybe I'll see some agencies here before I go."

"Maybe it is better for you to go there."

He was thinking about what was best for her, she told herself, even though he was suggesting that she go. She'd planned to go anyway, yet here she was again, wondering why he did not ask her to stay. Her insecurity upset the peace and restfulness she was enjoying. She both knew and lamented knowing, that he could not be part of this next step in her journey. Little did she know she may always struggle with the pull toward and away from togetherness, may always fear losing independence in companionship, yet long to be able to depend on someone.

Julien lowered his chin to look into her eyes. "Paris is a difficult market, you know."

She curled into him as if in her cocoon, yet sticking close to his. "Mm-hmm."

"What is wrong?"

She looked out the window at the red geranium on the sill and the slate roof. She was disappointed that he had controlled his excitement and withheld his orgasm throughout all of hers, but she didn't want to talk about that right then. Anyway, she imagined he would say he was doing it for her, but Lucy felt like there was more to it than that. However, she did not know how to articulate that at that tender moment and was in no mood for an argument. She dared to say, "I am frightened by the strength of my feeling for you."

"Lucy, noooo—"

"If you asked me to jump off the Eiffel Tower right now, I'd probably ask you what you would like me to wear on the way down." It was a first for her to admit such a thing to any man and she knew it was not entirely true, yet, she still worried she might sacrifice something essential to be with this man.

Then she wished she hadn't told him that, but it seemed funny, and he was laughing. They both knew she would never kill herself over him. In any case, it seemed courageous, even generous, to her to show him her vulnerability.

Julien reached for a cigarette, kissing her on his way. He looked at his watch. "I must go. It is my niece's birthday. I am invited for a dinner."

Lucy thought about how, in his position, she may have asked him to come along, and wondered why he didn't. She imagined it was too early. She reminded herself she had surprised him, and that she did not know the whole story.

"How are your daughters?" she asked

"They already left on vacation with their mother. I talked to them this morning, all of us sad. But I will go to see them next week."

So, it wasn't about them, Lucy thought.

*

They dressed, walked downstairs, and crossed the street together through slants of early evening sunlight. It was early July, the longest days of the year with light until at least ten. Julien stepped into a TABAC, a tobacco shop, on Boulevard Montparnasse, and, while they waited in line to buy his cigarettes, he showed Lucy the different French coins and bills with images of a beautiful revolutionary woman charging amid an army of men, one breast exposed. *Liberté, égalité, fraternité,* Lucy read, thinking she might enjoy living in a country where they placed a courageous woman and those values on their money, though she wondered about the breast. What is it about the breast? The nourishment, the comfort?

When Julien kissed Lucy goodbye at the top of the stairs leading to the metro, they were framed by mint green wrought iron railings and arches, the name of the metro, Vavin, displayed at the summit. "This looks like an entrance to an amusement park ride or magic land," Lucy said.

Julien pointed across the plaza, hesitating a moment as if it had occurred to him that perhaps it was rude to leave her alone there. "There is a bar called Rosebud over there, you might like it. I will call you."

Lucy placed her finger on his lips. "Don't say it, just do it."

He kissed her once more and she watched him skip down the stairs, and then, before disappearing underground, turn and wave.

She looked around at the Left Bank, which she had read was famous for its artist population, wanting to see small plazas and cozy cafés. The boulevard was too wide to be quaint. At this point, the city was more majestic than she had imagined, and there was a hint of something too perfect about it all.

Alone again after the intense intimacy of the afternoon, Lucy wandered, more floated, for how light and fluid she felt, toward Luxembourg Gardens. There she sat for a long time by the pond, watching people stroll and linger. She was pleasantly surprised to see that all Parisians were not chic. It made the monumental beauty of the city less intimidating. She understood how they could be arrogant; how many other cities were as impressive as their hometown? Yet, that was the outside of it, not the heart of it. She had yet to learn about the people.

A feeling of freedom kept striking her, and at first, she felt a certain panic as one does when one thinks they have lost something, followed by the relief one feels when finding the feared-lost thing still there. She marveled at how she was living her dream, doing exactly as she wanted, on a great adventure, on her own. When her thoughts turned to the unknown, she reminded herself that she had nothing but an appointment in Barcelona on Monday to be concerned about. A train or plane ticket to buy. She'd find a travel agency tomorrow, she told herself. She walked on and found Rosebud, then ordered a martini while watching the reflection of the hanging lights on the bottles lined up behind the bar and observing the few other customers through the long ornate mirror. It was too early for more of a crowd, she imagined, as she looked away from a pair of hungry male eyes.

She sketched the way she imagined she looked as she waited for her cocktail. Then took a sip, feeling like the international adventurer she was, enjoying the jazzy music, the view to rue Delambre, and the simple fact that everywhere she looked she saw something new. She wished to live like that, seeing new things every day. It also flickered through her mind that she easily looked like a lost soul, drinking alone, and she was nagged by the image of coming to her lover's life, and now he was elsewhere, living his. She'd left hers in tatters, she thought. At least she was sure she left something in tatters, yet she was still living her life, right there and then.

That night, when the phone did not ring, she decided it better for her to go to Barcelona right away, then enjoyed the deepest sleep she'd known in months.

The next morning, as she was packing her suitcase, the phone rang. "Bonjour, Mademoiselle, are you ready to go to the agency today?"

She wondered what had changed Julien's mind. "I think I should go straight to Barcelona."

"Wait one more day. I will introduce you to my agency."

All leaving involved was getting on a train to Spain, Lucy reminded herself, and it was only Friday. Why not, she thought, why not go and meet a Parisian agent, especially since Julien was offering, and see. She told herself she could always leave the next day.

As if Julien could feel her coming to this decision, he said, "Meet me at Duroc, you can get there from the station I left yesterday. First, though, breakfast on one of the terraces of Montparnasse, you will love it. I will see you in one hour."

Lucy enjoyed a glass of fresh orange juice, a café au lait, fried eggs floating in olive oil on a tin circular platter that just fit them, and a warm croissant at an outdoor café in Montparnasse. She drew. She took her time.

Then, those metro entrances deceived her. It was a whole different story underground—gray, dark, dingy, damp, not quite a dungeon but more fit for rats and mushrooms than humans. The people seemed pale and unhappy, like automatons. She tried not to stare at the sad, angry faces as she rode.

Julien was sitting on a cement bench when she stepped off the train, his brightness a stark contrast to it all. He folded several pieces of paper he held in his hand. "This is for you. I didn't get a chance to finish it."

Lucy felt the thickness of the letter and was happy to think he had so much to say to her. She slipped it into her backpack.

*

The agency was in a grandiose building on Boulevard Hauss-mann. Lucy stood back, gaping. "Wow, these doors are im-mense."

"They were originally for carriages," Julien explained, hold-ing open a smaller door within one of the larger ones.

Upstairs, Julien spoke in French to a beautiful woman be-hind a semi-circle desk just inside the door. She smiled, nod-ded, and picked up the phone. Lucy glanced around the room at the framed magazine covers of some of the most famous models in the world and didn't even notice that she was not nervous.

A door at the far end of the long room opened and an elf-like man with curly brown hair darted out. He was dressed in a polo shirt, jeans, and loafers without socks. Lucy liked his sprite-like quality, yet, all she found attractive about him were the tanned arches of his feet. He stretched his hand toward Julien and they exchanged conversation in French that Lucy only understood words of, like her name. He turned to her. "I am Léon. Welcome."

Lucy nodded as she had in Japan, and had often unwitting-ly, since, instead of offering her hand.

Léon gestured toward his office. "Please, come."

Julien followed which surprised Lucy and made her wonder why he thought she needed a chaperone, yet she thought telling him to wait outside would be rude as he had introduced her, after all, and perhaps he meant to be an interpreter.

Léon looked like a rascal playing grown-up behind his desk, fidgeting around in his chair as he opened her book, darting glances back at her as he studied the photos as if he'd missed something right away and was now getting it. "Very photogenic," he said to Julien as if congratulating him.

Lucy searched for words to describe how the compliment that belonged to her being given to Julien made her feel. At that point, she was more interested in having a Parisian agent than calling him disrespectful.

Léon snapped her book closed, then, and looked at her. "It is good to work in Japan for the money, but the pictures are worth nothing here. People want to see work from European magazines—especially at your age. Go to Barcelona, work on your book, make some money, enjoy Spain—and come back to see me in September." He opened a drawer of his desk and tossed a t-shirt with the agency's logo on it to her. "And here is a little gift for you."

After the agency door closed behind them, Julien shook his head in disgust. "*Il est con.*"

Lucy turned toward him. "What is *con?*"

"An asshole."

Lucy looked back over her shoulder and grinned. "Are you saying that just because he didn't give you a t-shirt?" then skipped down the stairs. She didn't want to know more about Léon just then, and she was pleased to both have a reason to go to Barcelona and one to return to Paris, and even a time frame. All that was comforting to her mind.

At street level, Lucy struggled with the little door. "How do you open this?"

"It is called *la porte cochère*, Lucy. You open it here." He pressed a nipple-sized button on the wall next to him, and she stumbled onto the sidewalk, laughing.

206

*

After more lovemaking in her room, during which Julien still controlled himself, Lucy declared, *"Je t'adore."* She felt so brave. She had never told anyone she adored them before.

He looked out the window. "Adore is too much of a feeling for me."

She curled into herself, away from him, enjoying the smoothness of the sheet on her skin. She was giving him all of herself now, she thought, as he'd requested in Japan, and here, it seemed it was too much for him. She was not ready yet to ask why. She was not even asking to stay, or for him to come with her, she thought. He lit a cigarette. What is too much, she wondered. Adore certainly wasn't too much of a feeling for her.

"Lucy, I have dinner plans again, tonight, it is another birthday celebration. I must go."

Lucy nodded. She reminded herself she had shown up unexpectedly, and could not expect him to rearrange his life for her.

She toured Paris on foot, through the Tuileries Garden where she rose high above the city in a Ferris wheel. Circling, lifting, once again thrilled, she came there, in the air. She felt freer, each time she came, freer than she ever had. It seemed the excitement mounted at moments when she realized her life was her own to do as she wished.

*

When Julien called the next morning she said, "I gotta go. I can't just hang out in Paris and make love. I need more."

"Just wait one more day. Another agent wants me to make a new picture for their head sheet and today is the last day, but if you meet me this afternoon, afterward, we can walk together, and have dinner." Lucy liked the urgency in his voice, it made her feel valued, and once again she thought, why not, there were worse places to bide one's time, it is what she would be doing in Barcelona until Monday anyway.

On her way to meet him, she walked along the Seine, trying to picture a life for herself in Paris. It seemed fuzzy and difficult. She loved the bridges, but how much time and living could be spent staring at them, she smiled to herself, knowing very well that modeling would be a way, of course, but unsure if that would be enough. It scared her to be on Julien's turf, too. She liked it better when they were both foreigners.

When she reached the Eiffel Tower, she stretched out on a bench and gazed at it, thinking how she preferred it at night, lit. By day, it was too hard, too cold-looking, like the people she saw. She wondered if they, too, were more attractive, lit up, at night. Pigeons scratched in the gravel, it was cool enough to wear a sweater, the sky was gray, and it was July. The letter Julien had given her in the metro was in her hand. He'd begun it on the plane, somewhere between Seoul and Anchorage.

Hi Lucy-chan, you are in trouble, I know it... Something is scaring me, you want, you need, too much to be understood. It means you are not strong enough—if you feel yourself surrounded by misunderstand-

ings, just leave them "on place", not to escape them, but because you still need comfort and security.

She wondered if she was scaring him now, too, if that is what his not wanting her to adore him was about. He underestimated her, she thought, because she was just as strong, if not stronger than him. Not caring whether anyone understood her or not sounded like a lonely way of life.

She walked toward Radio France, where billboards of her would one day hang, and sat outside at the café where she would meet Julien. She sipped mint soda while sketching a nearby pot of nasturtiums on a napkin. She was startled by a warm hand on her shoulder and turned to pounce. Julien smiled, and she noticed his beard was gone. She reached up to touch his face. She loved the way each time she touched him now she no longer felt like she was breaking a rule, and that walking down the avenue hand-in-hand, she felt no urge to look over her shoulder.

As they walked toward the bridge, the Pont de Grenelle, Lucy was surprised to see a Statue of Liberty with her torch held high on the island below. They walked down the stairs, and she and Julien sat at her base, looking out over the river, away from Paris. Lucy looked up. "So, what's this tiny Statue of Liberty you have here?"

"A gift from your country."

"Oops." She covered her face as she leaned back against it.

"It was a Frenchman that designed the original, you know, which was our gift to you. This smaller one here, your gift to us, was erected later, facing the Atlantic, and her big sister."

Lucy looked toward America, which felt light years away from her. The now familiar excitement was gathering, and she closed her eyes. These arousals were so unpredictable to her, she wished she knew where they came from. She imagined creating charts of when, and where, they happened. As the reverberations increased in intensity, why fight it, she thought. When she opened her eyes, Julien was looking at her with wonder, "You don't need me anymore."

Lucy kissed him again. "It's not about needing you. It's about wanting you."

But what did she know, really, about the difference between the two? She had yet to sift through her wants for needs. Her belief that she did not need anyone kept her from understanding what she might need from someone. Needing someone, and needing something, are two different things.

Julien glanced back at the river then, and appeared agitated, "Would you like to have dinner with me in Montmartre, Mademoiselle? Do you mind having pizza in France? I have been craving a Neapolitan pizza since last night but they did not have it where I went." He opened his mouth and bit the center of his tongue. "I can taste it."

It thrilled Lucy to ride on the back of his Vespa. From her seat there, on the hill above Paris, she could see the portrait artists that lined the Place du Tertre, who made her think that perhaps she could sketch for a living. Then she watched a couple argue outside the window the way she and Julien could have if she wanted to bring up the unspoken things that had bothered her during her stay. Julien followed her gaze, then shrugged. "Everyone in Paris is in a bad mood because of the weather."

Lucy looked around the plaza, the restaurant, and across the table, amazed that she was in Paris, and with Julien. The togetherness was familiar in a way, yet the setting and the man were different. She felt like she was on set. She saw that the Frenchman was more at home in France than Japan, of course, and perhaps it was normal that he did not seem as adventurous and carefree here. She glanced toward the pizza chef wiping sweat from his brow, then sliding pizzas into the open oven, then at the table of six behind theirs where a family was talking and gesturing excitedly. She looked at Julien across from her. It all seemed real enough. So why did it seem like a play?

She was thinking, too, about how she had to leave him again. It would be easier now, she felt, as the future seemed more open with the possibility of togetherness if they wanted it.

She had no idea what a Neapolitan pizza was but when he ordered one, she did, too, to try something new. "Mmm, this is tasty, what is an anchovy, though?"

Julien's eyes widened. "You do not know?"

Lucy shook her head.

"They are a fish. A little fish."

She smiled and shrugged. "There aren't any in the Mississippi."

While she sipped the house wine, she watched Julien dissect a second plate-sized pizza, lifting perfect bite after bite. She was struck, at moments, by how she felt part of a normal couple with him as if they had been together a long time and would go back to their home that night, yet she still felt worlds apart.

After insisting on paying for their dinner, which surprised her, Julien unsnapped and rolled out his French checkbook. Lucy tried to imagine herself with one. It looked as surreal to her as the play money in the Japanese clubs.

Outside, they strolled for a while in the narrow, lovely streets, and then sat on the steep stairs in front of Sacré Coeur looking over Paris and listening to a group of Peruvian musicians. "Such happy people," Julien said, looking as if he wasn't one. Lucy sensed a melancholy mourning in him that had nothing to do with her. She wondered what he was not telling her.

In the taxi, Lucy was quiet, watching the rain hit the window shield and trickle droplets the colors of the neon signs they were passing in Pigalle. She rolled down the window to get some air and saw pale, hurried faces scurrying through the rainy night. As beautiful as Paris was, it seemed to her a sad place, a place where nothing was the way its residents would like it to be. Perhaps it was the weather, she thought, yet the Parisians' dissatisfaction amid such beauty and splendor puzzled her.

*

Her nipple was in the crux of Julien's second and third fingers as they fell asleep like spoons. When she opened her eyes the next morning, the first thing she saw was his watch on her nightstand. It struck her the way that seemed to be its rightful place. He kissed her shoulder, then her back, and she rolled to face him. They began to make love.

"Just visiting," he said, as he entered her.

She looked into his eyes. "Make yourself at home."

Then, she became too bothered by his self-control to enjoy it. She could understand his withholding up to a point, but when total it seemed twisted. She deemed it just as twisted to demand that he come. Why did she care, she wondered, why was that important? She had no answer but it still bothered her, as it had in Japan, that Julien thought his energy, as he called it, was more limited and precious than hers. It seemed he didn't trust her with it. It was difficult to call his retention selfish, as it also prolonged her pleasure, but it felt too much like a performance instead of a share. Lucy wanted to feel that he was making love with her, not to her. Again, she did not want to talk about it. She just wanted to go. They could always come back to it later, she thought.

*

Then she was on the back of his Vespa again on a sunny July afternoon, her arms around his waist, cruising along the wide avenues and cobbled streets of Paris, whirling around Place de la Concorde, and the Eiffel Tower, Les Invalides, Pont de l'Alma, crossing what had become her favorite bridge, Pont Henri IV, and racing along the banks of the Seine.

It was like the movies but she knew she and Julien were not a couple nor possibly ever going to be. He did not adore her, though she adored him, albeit less since she arrived. She may see him in September, but she may not. She was amazed at her bravery and where it was taking her.

"*Encore*," she whispered when Julien stopped in front of her hotel.

They both knew she did and didn't mean it.

Julien carried her suitcase outside and then hailed a taxi. Had someone at that moment told Lucy everything she would go through before she saw Julien again, she might never have moved from that spot.

They kissed goodbye, and this time, from the taxi, she looked back. The vision of Julien in the middle of Boulevard Montparnasse—up on his toes, blowing her a kiss as large as his arm could reach—would replay again and again in her mind.

[11]

Barcelona. Lucy's hot spot. Stepping out of Sants station into sauna-like heat at nine in the morning, she peered into a taxi and smiled. "Hotel Continental?"

The driver eagerly offered her the seat next to him, and she slid in, ignorant enough to entertain the idea that the front seat was perhaps where Spaniards sat in a taxi.

Watching his Basset Hound eyes drool and his mouth twitch as he stared at her bare legs, Lucy found it pitiful and laughable, foolish and heartbreaking what people went through over sex. Yet, she enjoyed watching the man writhe, it made her feel potent.

This, too, was new for Lucy. Had she known that the hotel she had chosen, for its central location and reasonable price, was also known as a brothel, she may have understood more clearly this man's behavior. She could not speak Spanish, and listening, she did her best to decode from French.

Lucy noticed what appeared to be another language written above the Spanish on signs, primarily on doors: *Obert. Abierto. Tancat. Cerrado.* She smiled to herself as her mind played with the words: O, Bert, you are a Tan Cat. She was like many who had never visited Spain or studied much about it, who had no idea what Catalonia or Catalan was, or that such a language even existed. She wondered about it, yet she also knew they spoke English at the agency, and that would do to start. She could ask more there. She had another money to decipher. She was carrying dollars, yen, francs, and pesetas. She'd felt richer the moment she changed ten thousand yen for fifteen thousand pesetas.

In a sparse little room with a balcony overlooking palm trees and a plaza, Lucy set her suitcases in the closet and then stood staring across the wide avenue at the university. It looked like a sort of medieval fortress, she mused, where scholars may still be moving about in robes and hoods. It was quiet on that early Sunday morning. She had an entire day ahead of her and wanted adventure.

The man at the receptionist's desk suggested a beach to the south and told her which bus to take.

Lucy sat near the window and rode out of the city on an almost-empty bus. A half-hour or so later, she stepped off along a dusty highway, at a place called Castelldefels, and walked under the shade of parasol pine trees, looking up. In front of her, she saw a bungalow-style restaurant at the edge of the beach. She sat and ate mussels, sipping Coca-Cola, looking at the sea, pondering the best spot on the sand to rent a chair with an umbrella for seven hundred pesetas. She chose one, then lay back, closed her eyes, and occasionally dipped in and out of the water.

She looked back and was training herself to stop that. Her life in Chicago, her estrangement from her parents, those days with Julien, and all that she had lived in those last two months was a faint nipping at her bare heels. In front of her everything shimmered.

The cadence of the language around her confused her. Sometimes she noticed open vowels at the end of words, with

a lingering *s*, and other times all of the letters seemed clois-
tered as if the speakers savored those words so much they held
them in their mouths like tasting wine.

Lucy was silent. She pointed when she wanted something,
and nodded to confirm.

She smiled that evening when she saw a white camel
branded on her chest where the charm had lain. It looked like
a scar just below the star of a freckle. More triteness, perhaps,
still, a simple pleasure, she thought.

*

The next day the agency directed her to another place to stay—
Hostal Campi on Carrer Canuda. It, too, was sparse. It was
also clean, inexpensive, and soon became home. About a
dozen other foreign models rented rooms like hers and a constant flow of young travelers passed through the lobby's
French doors, a bell ringing each time one did. The hostel oc-
cupied several floors of a five-story building, steps from the
bowered pedestrian walk called Las Ramblas. A ramble toward
the sea, as Lucy thought of it.

She imagined the English word must come from Latin, but
when she flipped through a dictionary in the back of a nearby
bookstore, she saw that the origin was believed to be Middle
Dutch. She read: "*rammelen*: to wander about in a state of sexual desire."

"*Quién? Nombre? Ramblas?*" Who? Name? Ramblas? were the few words she could use to ask about its origins which amused the hostel's friendly, frisky chef named Pépé.

"*Lluvia,*" he gestured with his fingers like rain falling, and then moved his hands like the banks of a flowing river, saying "*Rio.*" A river of rain to the sea. Lucy liked to imagine the rut transforming over time into the vibrant passage of pedestrians, artists, mimes, terraces for eating and drinking, flower stalls, birds, chickens, turtles, and other small furry creatures in cages.

For three weeks, she marched around Barcelona in the heat, up and down and across the city, to five or more castings a day. She quickly discovered that modeling in Spain was not as regal or fun as it was in Japan. It reminded her somewhat of those first experiences in New York, and now she did not even have the language to talk to people. She found it exciting, still, to be in a new place and observe it and meet other people from around the world. In the agency, she wrote lists of other agencies around Europe, ready to visit and work in them, too. This made her hanker for Julien, knowing she would prefer to do it with him. She was realizing that his company was a big part of what had made it fun.

For six days she worked for a German catalog and made six thousand dollars. In heat hovering around one hundred degrees, she did her best to appear as if she were enjoying a leisurely autumn stroll through the gardens in front of the palace while makeup artists rushed in and out to powder the streaming perspiration on her face, and workmen hid in bushes to watch her, and the other models, change in the back of the van. During the two-hour lunch breaks, she relaxed in one of the city's shady plazas, eating a light lunch, sketching, and watching people. She loved the way everyone seemed to take time to enjoy a meal and life in general. At dusk, which fell around ten, she ran under the Arc de Triomf, her arms in the air as she imagined herself as a heroine returning from battle, and then through the Ciutadella Park, past old ladies chatting on benches, old men playing cards and pétanque. She often paused to catch cool sprays of water from the immense sculpted fountain, or to listen to laughter or the song of a flute, and then carry on past young adults displaying their affection, and children romping. Those were the moments she missed being close to those she loved the most.

*

Those days when arousal filled and rose in her, Lucy giggled. "What kind of happy drugs are you on?" a British model sitting next to her clipped, as they waited for a casting in the reception area of a magazine.

Lucy grinned. "Pure joy." The woman rolled her eyes. Lucy was taken aback seeing how disparaging people were of her joy. Of joy in general.

She was over the top, perhaps, yet what a way to go, she thought. She was thrilled to be living the life she had long dreamed of.

A few times she did talk about the orgasmic wonder she was experiencing, like once in a neighboring hostel room when four male models invited her in for a chat on her way back from the shower. "When was the last time you had sex?" one asked, and they all looked at Lucy, who paused at this too-personal question yet, felt it was time to start talking.

Everything she had been taught told her she was crazy and shameful to even be in that room with them. She felt her experience was beautiful and important, and imagined everyone must be capable of it. She thought it could revolutionize romance. She asked herself time and again why so much shame was connected to sex. It seemed women were even more ashamed to speak of it than men. Sometimes Lucy wondered if her brazenness was an over-compensation for all women who didn't dare. Sex is intercourse, she guessed, yet, what about these orgasms, she wondered. She took a deep breath and asked, "What do you mean by sex?"

The men all looked confused. Mr. When-Was-The-Last-Time asked, "What are you, some kind of innocent virgin?"

Lucy looked straight at him and evenly said, "Every time."

He laughed, and the others became quiet. She was so tired of the way the word virgin was used. She looked at them all. "Do you know the original sense of the word meant an unexploited, pure, wholesome person? Why should having sex change that?"

They shook their heads. One raised an eyebrow.

"Anyway," Lucy said, now unconsciously running her hand along the curve of the blue bottle of Nivea body lotion she had carried from the shower. "I have had this amazing thing happen to me, where I become aroused all by myself, out of the blue. I can be walking down the street and overcome by orgasm. I know that sounds weird, but it's true."

The man sitting next to her grabbed the bottle out of her hands, saying, "Stop that."

Lucy blushed and laughed as she realized what she had been doing.

Mr. When-Was-The-Last-Time stretched out on his bed at the far side of the room, and ogling her, asked, "How big is your clit?"

"Jesus, man, lay off," the kind man next to her said, staring across the room in disgust, then looked at Lucy as if he was interested in what she had to say.

She took a deep breath and thought to walk out yet froze at the same time that she appreciated the support and interest next to her. She remembered Julien in Osaka talking about nuts. She sighed. "The answer to your question seems irrelevant."

The kind man was looking at her in a protective way that also felt condescending. She was in the middle of a shame attack trying to figure out how to get out of it while still validating what she thought was important. She stood and made her way to the door she had intentionally left open behind her. "Excuse me, this wasn't the place to talk about this."

The kind man reached the door first and held it. "Thank you," he said, then looking over his shoulder, added, "And forget him, he's an asshole."

Lucy nodded and slinked out, trembling as she walked to her room. She was proud of her boldness, yet ashamed of her lack of discernment. She was convinced her experience was not unique and that it was her duty to let others know they contained similar power. Yet, whatever was driving her to speak confused her because it seemed she always wound up feeling ashamed.

She thought men would be relieved and women thrilled to know that they were the main source of their excitement, that no tricks or manuals were needed, and that it was what they did that turned them on.

Yet she could now see how she could too easily be considered some sort of freak show.

The ogling guy climbed to peer over the stall as Lucy showered the next day as if there might be something visible about her inner combustion. It was obvious why no one talked about it, she thought as she shook her head at him in disbelief, and he slid away.

One day she dared to tell two women, two models she was working with that day. The young Canadian woman looked on in a mix of horror and fearful awe as Lucy trembled, needing to talk about it to someone. "I know this sounds weird, excuse me, but I feel like a river. I don't know what is happening to me."

The eighteen-year-old's big brown eyes filled with both kindness and fear. "Maybe you are having a nervous breakdown."

Lucy glanced at the gorgeous blond patrician her age from Texas, who was listening from the balcony of the hotel room where they were taking a break. When their eyes met, the Texan looked away.

Lucy felt on edge. She believed she could handle it, for the most part, and was hard-pressed to imagine a nervous breakdown as orgasmic.

The nerves, she imagined, had more to do with the rejection from her father, her attachment to Julien, and the disconcerting divorce.

What more was there to say about the fact that sometimes she had to go back to the hostel, and lie down and orgasm until she could carry on?

Years later a doctor would tell her that it was a condition women suffered and that a chip could be implanted in a woman's occipital bone that would stop it.

Then, she liked to think it was Julien thinking of her when the arousal hit. The frequency and strength of it, however, compared to his silence, caused Lucy to deem that a long stretch.

*

An annoying model from America who looked more like a battery-operated corpse, a sort of Ken doll gone pale from it all, joined her table, uninvited, at dinner one evening then looked at her cockeyed when she disagreed with him as he blamed the agency for his lack of work and general unhappiness.

Lucy, who was becoming annoying with her changing-the-world-to-a-joyful-place attitude, said, "What if you consider approaching it a different way?"

The young, pasty man pointed his fork at her and gritted his teeth. "You don't know what you are talking about."

Lucy stood, said, "Don't ever tell me what I do, or do not know, again," then dumped the table full of food on him.

Wendy, her Australian neighbor who looked like a sort of hippy Goldilocks, followed her out of the dining room. Lucy's heart pounded, and her hands shook. She turned to Wendy. "Everyone should know how that feels once, though, no matter how stupid it is."

"Ah, Lucy, come on, it's time to follow the crowd."

"I hate following the crowd."

"Just come with me to meet Cosmos."

Lucy chuckled. She couldn't help it. "How is it dating Cosmos? How can you say his name without cracking up every time?"

Wendy had a devilish look in her eye. "We don't talk much. I don't care what his name is. Come have some fun."

Lucy did.

There was a young man that looked part rancher, part-dandy standing on the Ramblas, next to a BMW motorcycle, not far from Cosmos. "I'm Beau," he said, then lifted his shoulder toward Cosmos and Wendy who were kissing deeply. "They're too much. Would you like a ride?"

Lucy shrugged. "Why not?"

"A little more enthusiasm than that, please?"

She smiled. "That would be fantastic."

Lucy loved riding in the July night, past Gaudí's curvy colorful groovy buildings on Passeig de Gràcia–they too were more magical lit at night. And she loved playing pool with Beau in a narrow, cozy bar he frequented in the neighborhood of Gràcia. On that warm summer night, she felt happy to be sitting on a bench in a Catalan plaza, talking and listening to a new old friend.

It seemed to her that the people she came the closest to had always been, somehow, nearby.

Days later, riding in the green mountains above Barcelona, Beau stopped in a village and they sat outside under a fig tree to eat paella while ridiculously arguing about whether life was easy and people made it more difficult, as Beau thought, or whether life was difficult and people made it easier, as Lucy thought.

She lifted her glass. "To your state, the first to declare independence." He was from Rhode Island, which made him even more attractive to her. It was a mythical sort of place in her mind, the smallest state with the biggest ideas, with a capital called Providence.

Beau looked at her differently then. "There are many firsts. It was one of the first to separate church from state, to pass laws prohibiting slavery, two hundred years before it was imposed on the South, and it was the first Union state to send troops when Lincoln asked for help. It also," he lifted his glass, "never ratified prohibition." He smiled, then swigged the last bit of wine. "Now excuse me, I'll be right back."

Lucy smiled at the way he hitched his jeans by the belt buckle every time he stood, looking her in the eyes wondering how much longer she could resist and why. She couldn't believe her luck to be in love with one handsome and interesting man and to have another right in front of her who looked very possibly worthy as well.

Riding along the Mediterranean after lunch, her body pressed against Beau's, she wondered how many men she could love. She asked herself again if it were just a matter of letting go of all the old stories about one soulmate for everyone, and what was stopping her from having many lovers, if she wanted them. It certainly seemed easier to her to deal with just one.

In any case, Lucy felt privileged following him along dusty train tracks to a remote beach he wanted to show her, as she admired his form and the seaside vista. She felt privileged again, and so alive, as they kissed in each other's arms.

It was amazing to feel like a mature and experienced virgin, to consider each time a first. It was the best approach, she thought, and it was a sort of heaven for her to finally feel precious. Why hadn't she felt that way from the start with men? Or when did it go away? She wondered about all that.

When Beau greedily looked at her, as if he wanted to chew her up and swallow her, she backed away. He became angry as if he had a right to all of her since she had granted him the privilege of some.

"Give me the preciousness you've got," he said.

Lucy looked into his pained eyes. "So it's not me you want, it's something I have?"

He looked both confused and as if he had been found out. He rolled away and they were silent in the shady cove.

She, too, lying on the sand and looking at the sea, was wondering what she was talking about.

Though Lucy had thought all the chaos was making her stronger, she doubted it that weekend. For two days she did not go farther than from bed to bathroom, exhausted, sick, empty, and sad.

*

Then she met Hope. In the air, on the plane to Dusseldorf. Her eyes were filled with love as she said hello. It was a comfort to Lucy to meet eyes that seemed related to her own. She felt like they, too, had been friends before they met. They were two of at least ten models traveling from Spain to join fifty-some more to do a fashion show under a circus tent in Essen, Germany. Lucy watched the way Hope walked with a lilt as if her life were a dance. This made Lucy wonder where her lilt had gone and if she'd ever had one. There had been one as a girl, had her grandfather squeezed that out of her, too? This, she did not wonder about, yet.

*

Once back in Barcelona, she wanted to leave but didn't know where to go. What she had loved about the city upon arrival was a prismatic quality in the air. It colored everything, even the sea breezes. It smelled and tasted like openness. But now in August, it stunk. She wanted out.

She thought of her family. She'd sent letters, postcards, gifts, and the agency's number to call for emergencies. She told them not to bother to write because she did not know how long she would stay. More than isolating herself, she felt like she was incubating a new self. She had some direction, yet it was a mostly spontaneous adventure. In ways, too, she was lost, wishing for a guide and knowing no one like her who could point the way.

She had written Julien, too, and was increasingly vexed by the lack of news from him and fighting that vexation in herself. She had yet to learn that one cannot fight oneself and win. Her biggest fear was that her real detector was off, that Julien was not the person she thought he was, and that the love she sensed from him was an illusion.

"I met this man in Japan, and recently surprised him again in Paris before coming here, but I haven't heard anything from him in the last three weeks. Don't you think that's strange?" It was nearly midnight, and Lucy and Wendy were sitting near the gondolas at the bottom of the Ramblas dangling their feet in the water.

Wendy leaned back on her elbows. "Just call him up."

Lucy thought about how easy that sounded and at the same time was struck by how afraid she was to do it. This made her wonder what was wrong.

Wendy looked at her as if she could read her thoughts. "Do it for yourself. Who knows? A million things could have happened between then and now."

Lucy's hands shook as she slid coins into the green pay phone in the lobby. "I don't know what to think not having any news from you. Would you please just give me a call to ease my crazy mind?" was the message she left along with the hostel's telephone number.

Her heart pounded a few days later when she was called to the phone at the hostel.

It was Hope. "What will you do for August, Lucy? Why don't you come to stay with me and my family in Bonica?"

The next morning she went to the agency and collected her money, then left Barcelona that evening, heading north by bus, increasingly relaxed as the noise and heat of the city disappeared. It became greener, and homes were more sparse. They passed castles, horses, bamboo. An ostrich farm. They rode into some small villages of the Costa Brava and Lucy stepped off to Hope's life-giving smile and open arms.

*

"This is for you," Hope said, tilting her head toward the trays she was carrying as they walked together to her car along a dimly lit village side street.

At the dinner table in Hope's home, Lucy could see the Mediterranean across the street, a pool of indigo surrounded by rugged cliffs. It was just before midnight, a platter of cured Serrano ham with freshly sliced melon, and another of salmon were laid before her along with country-style toasted bread rubbed with garlic, olive oil, and tomato, and sprinkled with salt. They drank cava to toast her arrival. Hope interpreted her family to Lucy, and they laughed often.

Lucy wondered if Hope's Catholic parents knew about her divorce and if they would worry about her badly influencing their eighteen-year-old daughter. When Lucy watched Hope argue excitedly with her father during meals, she missed her dad. She mentioned nothing of that, or her divorce, to Hope, though she did speak of Julien.

*

"Who is that?" Lucy pointed to a framed picture of Hope's father shaking a man's hand.

Hope's father's eyes widened, his arms raised, shocked it was not obvious, he said, "Jordi Pujol! President de la Generalitat!"

"What is the Generalitat?" Lucy asked Hope.

"It is the government of Catalunya."

"It's not Spanish?"

"We are not Spanish, we are Catalan," Hope's older brother exclaimed, raising his arms high into the air.

Lucy was too ignorant to have an opinion, but she did find any country that still had a king and queen ludicrous, so her tendency was already toward the Catalan side. It was Hope's father's birthday, and she gave him a card she had drawn for him, with the words *Feliz Cumpleaños, con mucho amor* she had written inside. After he opened it, Lucy saw how he dropped it on the table as if it were infectious, saying, "That's Spanish."

Lucy looked at Hope, not knowing what to do. "How do I say I'm sorry in Catalan?"

Hope shook her head. "Forget it, it doesn't matter. It was from your heart. That is what matters."

"But it obviously does matter," Lucy pleaded.

Hope turned and spoke in Catalan to her father, who smiled at Lucy as if to say it was okay, but she could tell it was not, that there was a mountain of animosity under it all. It calmed her to see it had nothing to do with her. She had a lot yet to learn about Catalonia and its history.

*

It took Lucy ten days of beaches, elaborate and delicious lunches, naps, sunset walks, and nightclubs to get restless. Even more, she felt she was imposing to stay so long with such wonderful hospitality. Her mind was wandering too much to what-ifs: what if her father never wanted to see her again, what if she could not trust her perceptions of people, what if she didn't work enough, what if she ran out of money? Even though she knew she'd survive all that, it didn't sound like much fun. She wanted a change of environment, movement, money-making work, and cool air.

Another reason she had trouble sitting still was that her bottom was bright red from her daring to wear a thong. She had loved being almost naked in the sun and sea, the way it made her feel like Eve in paradise. Now she was lying on her belly in the spare bedroom, airing her burnt bottom. She turned to Hope. "I heard there is a good market in Zurich, and that their agencies are open in August. I think I may go and see if I can get some work there."

Hope looked at her as if she were crazy to want to work during vacation time. "Come on, Lucy. Stay a while longer. You just arrived. Are you just going to go there without knowing anyone?"

"Why not? I've always wanted to see Switzerland, and I can meet all the agencies in person."

"I just need to keep moving right now," she explained the next morning at the train station, as she and Hope hugged.

Hope shook her head, smiling. "You are wonderful and wild. I love you."

*

On the train to Switzerland Lucy read Sartre's *No Exit*. She'd bought it for the title. She was beginning to think that there was no exit from her troubles, as she had hoped, and now she was feeling guilty about all the people she had supposedly hurt in the last months, especially her parents, and Vic. However, she did not know how to fix that.

Where did people get the idea that a painless life was possible, anyway? She wondered. She had hurt people by telling them the truth and then, by doing what she wanted to do. Was there a way to live truthfully without hurting people? And, if not, was a life of truth-telling, then, to be an apology? Would she have to continually say, "I'm sorry for being me"? She wondered.

She did not even think about how worried her mother might be, because she was not a mother herself yet, and as far as her father was concerned, well, he had told her to keep in touch so she did. She sent postcards and an occasional letter, and she wrote to her grandfather, too, but could not bring herself to call anyone.

It had been seven weeks since she had talked to anyone who really knew her. Or had it been, perhaps, her whole life? She wondered about that, too.

*

In Zurich, Lucy sat by the lake dangling her feet in the water near cradling sailboats, timing how long to wait to arrive promptly for check-in at the convent on the hill. She presumed choosing a convent hotel would ensure a beautiful place because all those she knew were in the best spots. She wondered if she could live as the sisters did, in that peace and order she craved.

If it were not for the outfits, she thought, as she followed the nun and the swish of her habit down a long hallway. The room was spacious and welcoming, with purple velvet curtains falling over a wide window that overlooked the city. After showering, Lucy looked over the list of agencies she had carried from Barcelona, circled all five on the map, then walked the cobblestone streets of the center, delighted by the sharpness in the air, the cleanliness, and quietness.

*

Each agency was in an attractive building with a perky well-dressed receptionist who looked surprised after Lucy introduced herself and her intention. "Do you have an appointment?"

"I prefer to introduce myself personally when I can. May I?"

"It's not the usual way. You see, there are not many models who live in Zurich. It is a market more for those who have already established themselves in Paris or Milan. We book them directly from there. But wait a moment, I will ask if someone can see you."

A booker was willing to see her in each agency, to look at her pictures, and to suggest she go elsewhere and contact them again in the future from there.

At the last agency on her list, the owner, a short, fit woman with strict bangs and a page-boy cut, flipped through Lucy's book, listened to her modeling history, then said the same thing as the others. She looked at her again, and added, "I think Paris is the best place for you now."

Lucy fidgeted and looked out the window. She could feel resistance in her bones. She did not want to go to Paris until September when there would be work. What she was resisting was finding out that she had been dumped and duped.

The agent stared at her, waiting. "But Lecon," Lucy heard her slip and smiled. The woman raised an eyebrow. "I mean Léon, at Soinin, told me to come in September. I was told that all the agencies in Paris are closed in August."

The Swiss woman picked up her telephone, dialed, spoke French, and then as quickly hung up. "It's slow, they say, but they are there. What are you waiting for?"

"Nothing I guess. Thank you for your time."

Lucy walked along the lake, back to her room, telling herself it was better to know than to wonder. Once back in the convent, she relaxed in the early evening sunshine streaming through the room. As she lay there on the bed, the sun warming her body, thinking about going to Paris, about how wonderful it was to be able to make decisions like that, the familiar arousal began.

Lucy enjoyed coming, wondering afterward, and yet again, whether it might be life's way, her body's way, of bringing her relief when she needed it. That is how she had always considered the times she had come in her sleep and dreams.

As she looked around the room, and out onto the city's rooftops, she wondered if the sisters knew what she knew. They were hiding it well if they did, she thought. She remembered the story of Saint Teresa and other religious women in ecstasy, yet she'd read it was their communication with God, their devotion to "Him," which was reportedly turning them on.

Lucy could not deny there was an unseen force involved, but it did not feel like a man, or like devotion to anyone but herself.

[12]

Back in Paris, Lucy checked into the Hôtel des Académies et des Arts again and then went directly to Julien's apartment. She was tired of wondering what had happened, she wanted to know. Passing a flower stand as she walked, she stopped to buy a bouquet of miniature red roses. She felt more powerful as lover and wooer than as beloved or wooed.

As she approached Julien's doorstep, she saw a small mailbox overflowing with her letters, postcards, and packages. She fingered through it all, trying to figure out what day he had left. It seemed he must have received some, she thought, but she could no longer remember all of what she had sent or when.

She stared at the tarnished doorknob, imagining his hand there, and then touched it. She shuffled her feet on the steps, imagining his feet there, then sat on the stoop. She snapped all of the rosebuds off their stems and wrapped them into that day's page from her agenda, stapled it with her nifty new pocket stapler, then crammed it all in with the rest of his mail.

She watched the breeze moving through the lace curtains of the slightly open upstairs windows. She wished she could throw her desire to the wind. Was it him she wanted or was it perhaps confirmation of the reliability of her instincts, some proof that she had not been wrong about his sincerity? She did not know. She stood there on the corner of that small side street on the outskirts of Paris, not wanting to go or stay, questions bubbling inside of her. She asked herself if it was him she cared about at that moment or her, and Lucy saw that it was her.

No fountains, no statues, and no beautiful bridges as she walked miles due east. Looking at her map, she saw she would eventually wind up at the hotel. This was not the Paris she had imagined—warehouses, gray and charcoal cement block-like structures. The air was warm and the streets near empty. Having measured the way back with her fingers, instead of the scale, it was much, much farther than she thought, which gave her plenty of time for more questions. She wondered what a life without desire might look like, and imagined death. She questioned how to live with desire, to listen to and honor it, and not go nuts. She asked herself why she wanted to be with this man, what was this compulsion she felt. She wondered, still, how she could have been so wrong to feel that he was responsible. She had no answers, only more questions.

Blisters formed on her feet as she walked along the river toward Montparnasse. When she finally reached the hotel, she decided she deserved a treat and walked across the boulevard to Le Dôme, where she sat in a fancy booth and ordered a seafood platter and a glass of white wine. She enjoyed watching the way people cast surprised and suspicious glances at her as she dined alone with pleasure. The waiter gave her his card at the end of the meal. As did a tall, handsome American doctor she met on the stairs of the hotel when she returned.

She wondered if she had ever had more male attention in her life as in the last few months, or if she had not noticed or allowed it before. In any case, it seemed at every turn, there was yet another man ready to offer her a motorcycle ride, a drink, or a meal.

As much as she wished it untrue, men all seemed to want or expect something in return for their offerings. Lucy wanted to think that human nature was more curious than craving. It would take her decades to understand and accept men's disinterest in being with her unless they felt they could eventually be with her sexually, too.

*

When Lucy walked into Léon's agency late Monday morning, he was on his way out. He looked at her and then at his watch. "Would you like to have lunch with me?"

That was fast, Lucy thought, but why not. "Sure," she said. They walked downstairs and a few doors away to an elegant restaurant. Another Frenchman who didn't speak English, his expensive shirt open to a hairy barrel chest and gold chains, joined them. As Lucy stared out the window at the noon light illuminating the shuttered French doors and balconies on the butter-colored façades across the street, the men's voices registered as if from far away through a wind. Men, she was thinking, what kind of creatures are they? How much can I accept from them and retain my dignity? It seemed she lived in a world of prostitution, in one way or another.

Between bites of grilled lamb, she mentioned she was looking for an apartment. Léon waved one hand in the air as if that gesture alone would make it appear. "I will find you an apartment. I was a real estate agent, but changed." He smiled.

"From selling houses to selling women." He cracked up and Lucy shook her head.

Léon signed the bill, then looked at her. "Come back upstairs to my office." Again, she felt she had nothing to lose by following, yet it all seemed such an odd way of doing business. She was wearing down yet still going and seeing. Léon was a sort of cartoon character for her now, she would watch this show through to the end.

Up there, he scribbled an address on a piece of paper. "I want you to see Christian, a young photographer, good. He lives in the Bastille."

Lucy smirked. "I thought it was empty since the storm."

"What storm?"

"You know, the storming of the Bastille?"

Léon gave Lucy a blank look as he picked up the phone. Lucy waved the joke off as unimportant. Léon hung up. "I'll try again later, he is not there."

Lucy wanted to do something, anything, to move forward, so she asked, "Where can I find an apartment?"

"I told you, I'll do it. Soon, soon. Would you like to have dinner with me tonight?"

Though increasingly suspicious about this not talking much business with her, and then inviting her to restaurants, and then not saying much about work while there, Lucy figured, again, why not.

She met him for dinner at Bellini, an elegant Italian restaurant not far from the agency. Léon was sitting at a long table with flickering candles reflecting in crystal glasses. He was next to a very attractive young man Lucy would one day see on

242

a magazine cover with his princess fiancée. Five teen-aged girls who looked like well-bred daughters of very rich people were also at the table. Lucy sat quietly, observing. As she watched Léon fidget and stutter through the ordering, Lucy wondered if it was a language or a drug problem he had. Then she noticed he hardly touched the food on his plate. She ate asparagus and sole. Mid-meal, his handsome friend leaned across the table to say, "Lucy, tell me about yourself."

As Lucy opened her mouth to speak, Léon slapped his friend's arm and told him to stop, which to Lucy's surprise, he did. Lucy looked at Léon. "Why did you do that?"

He lifted his chin toward the girls and said, "He has enough for himself," then wiped his mouth with the white linen napkin, threw it on the table, and motioned as if something outside was awaiting them. "Let's go."

Lucy was happy to go, even though she had not finished her meal. Trying to understand this man was requiring more effort than she wanted to exert. "I would like to go back to my hotel," she said, as they stepped outside.

Léon insisted on giving her a ride, so she let him. He pulled up in front of a nearby building, and Lucy said, "This is not my hotel."

"I know. It is Régine's. Come in, just for one drink."

Once again, Lucy went to see what she could see. The club was smoky with red booths, chairs, and floors, surrounded by mirrored walls and ceilings, and dotted with more men with lots of gold chains. Lucy kept her distance, looking up in the mirrors to watch Léon kiss a red-haired, curvy woman in a snug, sequined black dress he directed toward Lucy. "This is

Régine," he announced proudly as if Lucy were meeting a very important person. Lucy nodded, the woman smiled, and then signaled to a waiter across the room who glided through the crowd to offer Lucy and Léon a glass of champagne from his tray. Léon darted to a corner to speak to someone else, while Régine smiled at Lucy with a look in her eye as if she was surprised to see someone like her with Léon. As Lucy lifted the flute to her lips, Léon cupped her elbow. "Let's go."

Lucy followed as staying was uninteresting to her, then set the full glass on a small table near the door.

This time, instead of her hotel, he pulled up in front of a courtyard and idled the motor. Lucy was looking at the transmission wondering what kind of man drove an automatic Ferrari. Léon said, "Please come to my apartment. I don't want to be alone right now. Please, just one drink." Lucy's parents, who had taught her to help people, would have been appalled to hear that part of the reason she went was that Léon was lonely and the kind thing to do was to sit with him for a while.

The salon of his apartment was the size of a ballroom, with high ceilings, ornate mirrors, and very modern furniture that he moved toward, touching piece by piece, announcing the tens of thousands of francs he had paid for each item. Lucy nodded politely each time, and then looked out the heavily draped windows as if she could see where Julien might be pulling up to his apartment. She wondered if he already had arrived and just not called, and what he would think about where she was now. She was both embarrassed to be in the lair of such a man and yet, strangely proud to have reached the innermost chambers of the owner of the best agency in Paris.

Léon left the room and Lucy turned toward the fireplace mantle, looking for a picture of his wife, another Midwestern woman, one she had seen on many magazine covers. There was no picture, and Lucy imagined in vain that she would come home and join them for a drink, making all of this look like the friendly chat Lucy wanted it to be.

Léon set a silver platter on the glass table in front of the white leather couch. Lucy's eyes followed a path from the bottle of chilled vodka on ice, to a silver bowl with lemon quarters, to two martini glasses, then to a grapefruit-size mound of cocaine in a blue glass bowl with two little silver spoons sticking out of it. The mystery of Léon's fidgeting cleared. She looked at him and asked, "Don't you have any grass?"

Léon poured thick icy vodka into their glasses. "Grass mellows me out too much."

Lucy stared at the leg he did not stop shaking. "It looks like you could use some mellowing out."

He lifted a heaping spoon of cocaine toward her.

Lucy shooed it away. "I am already nervous enough." She changed the subject to what she wanted in Paris—an agent and work. "Did you reach Christian or find out anything about an apartment this afternoon?"

It was so weird, she thought, to be sitting there wondering if it were rude to ask him if he had done what he said he was going to do.

The more he did not talk about business, the more she believed it was never going to happen, and the more she wanted to make it happen. She did not want to think the only reason he was interested in her was to get her into bed, she wanted to put herself in the company of other world-class models, yet she doubted. And she hated that she doubted. Looking for self-approval was like reaching for a handle inside herself that was not there.

She wondered whether continually giving him the benefit of the doubt was naïve while aware that she was doing her best to respond to him respectfully as an equal. Though this seemed a new experience to her, it was just a change of set design and character in the same old story, and Lucy was still bent on finding a different ending to it, to keep alive her hope that men are more than their sexual appetites.

It was the going and seeing, that dear Lucy was taking too far, one might say.

Léon handed her a glass of vodka. "Do you know how many models have offered me blowjobs to get covers?"

Lucy shook her head. "I always thought it was the other way around."

"And, mothers take off their shoes and play with my legs under the table as we discuss their daughter's modeling future."

"That's sad."

He poured more vodka into his glass and then spooned more cocaine into his nose. "Would you like to watch a movie of some ugly dogs?" He lifted his chin toward an open door. "I can show you in there." She raised both eyebrows. "It's only to watch a movie," he said.

That is how he lured her to his room. On her way, she wondered how many steps away he thought she was from giving him a blowjob. At least for her, it was clear that it was out of the question. She sat on the floor with her back against the bottom of the bed, watching women wearing one-piece bathing suits and high heels, a combination Lucy had always thought ridiculous, parade across the screen. She looked over her shoulder and saw Léon, stretched out with six pillows behind his back, fidgeting his toes and feet. "These are not dogs," she said.

Léon laughed. "They are ugly and fat."

"These women may not be gorgeous, and are too heavily made-up, and are curvy, but they certainly are not ugly, nor fat."

He dismissed her comment with a French *bof*. "Are you comfortable on the hard floor?"

"Not really. Are you ever going to give me a ride home?"

"Why don't you sleep here? You do not have to worry about me, I promise. I am sure my home is more comfortable than your hotel. Why don't you go in my wife's closet and choose a robe or some pajamas?"

Lucy looked at him. She could see his desperation but not hers. They seemed to be desperate for different things, yet, it was the same—connection and comfort. He had a different way to get there or perhaps only one. What moved Lucy was something in his eyes, albeit tiny, which seemed sincere to her. Something else looked sure that he would get what he wanted from her, and she even liked that part, because she was going to prove he would not. Yes, all that wanting to prove was getting the best of her.

Léon smiled and pointed to the walk-in closet behind him. His wide, thick mattress looked comfortable to Lucy and her weary bones. If he tried anything, she told herself, she would go to the couch or leave.

She could not believe she was doing what she was doing as she walked into the closet and then stood looking at his wife's clothes. To make herself feel better, she imagined that his wife, if she were there, would have made the offer of a robe and bed herself, and she would not even have had to deal with him. As she undressed in the bathroom and slipped on the long silk robe, she was even debating whether she might send his wife a letter and tell her what a scoundrel her husband was. Then Lucy stood at the threshold of the closet looking at Léon, thinking, Jesus, I am not getting out, am I? I'm only going further in. He moved to the far side of the bed and offered her a wide space. Her body was happy to lie down. She was dangerously close to separating her body from the rest of herself again.

The phone rang. Lucy listened as Léon told his wife that he loved and missed her, then she sunk into the comfort of the expensive bed and sheets, seeing herself, too, from above, as if watching a clone of herself in a bed in Paris with a stranger. Léon hung up and turned to face her. "That was my wife, Jeanne. Do you know her?" Lucy nodded.

He looked alarmed.

Lucy shook her head. "Not personally."

Léon sighed. "She is in Miami working now. I hate it when she goes. I miss her."

"So be true," Lucy said, unfortunately not even thinking it odd to say such a thing to a man about his wife while lying in their bed next to him.

She had slept in the same bed with her brothers when younger. She would think of him as a brother.

Léon raised his arm, then, to take her in. He appeared genuinely moved by her, and the possibility of tenderness evoked by his gesture moved Lucy to let him hold her. Resting her cheek on his chest, keeping her lips far enough away to make a kiss impossible, she listened to his heart's rapid beating, as her own yowled for comfort.

It took a matter of seconds for the realization to form that she was now in bed with Julien's agent because she wanted to be closer to Julien. God almighty, what nonsense, Lucy heard an ancestor say, and she jerked up and away from this man's chest. Her next thought was of her father. She felt some desire to be held by him in there, too, and it crushed her to see how pathetic she had become. Yet, her desperation for solace seemed valid and believable to her.

She dressed. "This was crazy. I am going."

Léon panicked. "Please wait for the light."

Lucy bit back the pain as blisters burst and oozed when she pulled on the boots. "I'm sorry. I never should have come here."

"Please, don't go. I am frightened when I'm high and alone in the dark."

Lucy shook her head.

He reached for the phone. "Wait. I'll call you a taxi."

"I can't wait anymore." Lucy was asking herself how much time she had already wasted in her life as Léon scurried after her, grasping her arm at the door.

He grabbed a pair of sunglasses off an entryway table with his other hand and crammed them into hers. "Wear these when you leave the building."

She shook her head in disbelief once more, wondering if he kept a stash of shades for such occasions, then walked out laughing to herself that he even thought she would wear sunglasses at three in the morning.

The city was empty. Lucy set the sunglasses on a windowsill then limped until she leaned against a chic boutique, and eased off her boots. She walked barefoot on the narrow sidewalks and the grassy areas along the Champs Élysées until Place de la Concorde, where she sat down to rest. Staring up at the obelisk, she felt like a pawn on a huge chessboard and wished a big gentle hand would break through the pewter-blue sky and lift her to the next best position.

She could not imagine telling—or not telling—Julien about what had just happened. It was hard for her to imagine telling anyone such an embarrassing story, yet she was feeling the need to talk to someone she could trust, though she was unsure who that could be. Everybody seemed to have some agenda behind what they said to her, something they wanted her to do, or some way they wanted her to be, to make them feel better about their own lives.

*

It was half past five when she arrived at the hotel. When the Moroccan night watchman handed her the key with a smile, she wondered if she should distrust him, too. How to trust, when to trust, and whom? These questions appeared to be constant companions now.

Jackhammers in the street woke her at eight. Pillows over her head did not drown them out. She decided to go and see if Léon's work offer was for real.

He was not there. She wondered if he was sleeping as she walked out of Soinin around noon not wanting to see him anyway. When she opened *la porte-cochère* to the blinding sun and the sidewalk, Felix pulled up in front of her on a Harley. Lucy felt like she was seeing the first robin of spring.

"Lulu!" he exclaimed, with open arms, then invited her to lunch on the terrace of a nearby restaurant.

*

"Julien is probably on vacation, you should just wait a few days more." Felix swept his arm along the avenue. "Why do you want to leave Paris, the most beautiful city in the world?"

Lucy was reluctant to tell him what was going on. She deflected his question. "Wouldn't you like to go?"

He nodded, then frowned. "My father wants me to start working at his bank."

Lucy could not imagine Felix suited up in that way and place. She sighed. "I'm thinking about going to New York and seeing if I can work there. I want to feel some familiar ground under my feet. I want to hear American English and speak it."

Felix shook his head. "I think Europe is a better place for you. You are not like the Americans. And, anyway, I am sure Julien will be sad to miss you."

251

Lucy shrugged, wondering both about Julien's feelings for her, and what an American was. There were so many different kinds, after all, and she was most definitely one of them. For now, she was happy to see a familiar face, unexpectedly. The world seemed smaller and friendlier running into an Osaka friend in Paris. She took it as a sign that despite the challenges, life was on her side.

*

Back in her room, feet up and in the open air, she watched puffs of white clouds inch through the blue sky over the slate rooftops, and thought how sad and true it was that she did not want to see Julien now. She felt too insecure to handle it well. Sure, she had money, she could stay in Paris, and see what happened, see other agencies, and even go back and see Léon again, but what if it meant dealing daily with him or characters like him? Going back to Barcelona for work was another alternative, she imagined, but modeling alone did not seem exciting enough. She could do more than that in America. A deep echo resonated when she thought about returning, about going to New York City, and Lucy decided once more that what excited her most was the next right thing to do.

After a nap, she went to the nearest travel agency and bought a one-way ticket. From a pay phone on the boulevard, she called Julien. "I wanted to be all set up by the time you came back but it didn't work out that way. I am leaving for New York tomorrow. I wish you would have called, or written, told me something." Too weak to smash the receiver, she leaned back against the glass wall and then stared out at the empty sidewalk as if waiting for the phone to ring. She even looked back as she walked away, in case a voice might come booming across the wires, telling her precisely where she had gone wrong.

III. Safe Arrival at the Desired Country

[13]

Lucy had a wonderful time in New York without realizing it. She was still too obsessed about all that had happened and not, and all that still might or not, and what she could do about it. Her mind was racing all the while she was living in a simple room in a boarding house near Gramercy Park, meeting friends and friends-of-friends for cocktails and dinners, walking through Central Park, drawing in cafés, visiting the Met, or strolling through the library, scrutinizing the paintings on the ceilings and walls.

What she did realize was she would have to start making money again. When she gathered her nerve to visit a few modeling agencies, they all suggested she go back to Europe, that she would work better there, and that her look was more European. Me and my look, Lucy thought, walking down the avenue. Going back—just those words—bothered her. Forward is where she wanted to go, but where?

One evening in a restaurant in the East Village, as the handsome Swede across from her was attempting to engage her in a game of footsie, and the good-looking Canadian next to her began caressing her thigh, she moved closer to the window. The telephone booth on the opposite corner caught her eye. Why not call him, she thought, and find out. He was the one she wanted to be with, not these guys. She glanced at her dinner companions, then stood up. "Excuse me, I need to make a phone call." They made way for her.

Her breath was shallow and fast as she crossed the street. Julien answered on the second ring. Lucy blurted, "Do I need to come back to Paris or what?"

"Where are you, Lucy?"

She looked up at the narrow green street signs. "The corner of Tenth and Broadway. Anyway, I thought what you felt for me was real."

"Didn't you receive my letter?"

"I received nothing."

"Oh, I wish you had. It explains everything."

"Must be some letter."

"Lucy, what is important is that we both live our present the best we can."

"I know. But I miss you."

"But you can't just keep jumping on airplanes, Lucy. Slow down, look around, it's fall. It's time to lose something."

She looked up again. Crinkled leaves dangled from the branches of the plane tree like deserted cocoons. Lucy closed her eyes. "What more do I have to—?" Her voice broke.

"Oh Lucy, it's good to be empty. That is the way you will find your strength. And you are going to succeed. I am sure of that. And I miss you, too."

"Will I ever see you again?"

"Eventually."

Eventually? she thought. It was clear to her that he was not ready to be with her. To see some movement toward her by him would have comforted her, she thought, but would it move her where she most needed to go? Her insecurity bothered her. She was uncomfortable standing there feeling like a clingy wanderer hoping for rescue. She mumbled, "Sorry to have bothered you," and then hung up.

*

It was cold and windy inside her after that. She felt she was a long, narrow hallway the world was blowing through. Reasons for her to stay in New York became hard to come by. She saw so many struggling to impress, while oppressed, it depressed her. She thought she could go to Chicago, an opener city, where she knew there was work, and she had friends, and eventually, she could venture a bit farther and see if she could patch things up with her family.

*

Were they important, the men that she met, the ones that sparked her? Lucy wondered. She thought it better to think of every human as valuable and worthy.

She spent most of her last week in New York City with Mick. He, at least, seemed not to want something in return for his attention. He was an Australian with keen blue eyes and an extensive map collection, as well as a carefree, optimistic air, and a strong, long-legged body. His spirit and companionship lifted her. It was on her last afternoon when they sat drinking and laughing after dancing at a bar on Third Avenue, the current barged through and from her, and she told him about it. She even took his hand and placed it on her thigh for proof.

It surprised her to see how barbarous this here-to-fore docile giant became. "You b——, you c——, you tease. Why won't you give it to me?" he yelled as they rode upstairs in the elevator of his apartment building. Lucy slapped him hard to snap him out of it, and then stared at her stinging palm. It was the first time she had ever done that to a man.

"I'm sorry, I'm an asshole," he blubbered.

Lucy wondered if apologizing was wrong while she was doing it. "It's partly my fault. I should never have told you what was happening."

She helped him inside where he passed out on the couch while she smoothed his forehead, repeating a care-taking pattern she was not even aware of.

She stood at the window afterward, looking thirty floors down at the colorful constellations of passing umbrellas, wondering why she felt responsible for Mick's behavior. Something seemed off about it that she could not name. It would take her years. She became embarrassed and ashamed yet again, like in the hostel in Barcelona, but still did not feel wrong.

Had she been irreverent? She thought not, yet, perhaps, then again who decides that, and how? Perhaps she had been too playful. Yet that didn't seem right either.

It seemed once again she was supposed to keep this orgasmic mystery to herself unless she was prepared to give it away for someone else's consumption.

She decided she would simply have to accept this as a secret well inside of her that did not matter to anyone else.

Yet, how could it be no big deal? She wondered.

Lucy still felt certain that she was not the only person endowed with this ability and in the years to come she would meet others. At that moment in New York, she thought about all of the different, even violent, ways people tried to get that beautiful orgasmic feeling from another and how different the world might be if they realized they did not need to.

She felt alone, exhausted, and misunderstood.

Little did she know she was returning to the source of her confusion.

*

At first, a change of environment did its usual trick, and the next day as the plane lowered in a perfect blue sky above a glistening Chicago on a warm October afternoon, Lucy felt anything was possible again. Within a week, she'd met and laughed with friends, moved into a residence on Dearborn Street, and accepted part-time work for a Japanese journalist in his office in the Wrigley Building. She called Angelina to say she was back in town. "I don't feel like modeling now. Please just call me when foreign scouts come to town."

And then, finally, she called her mother to say she was coming home the next weekend.

Viola's voice weakened. "But we're not going to be there."

Lucy winced at the lament in her mother's tone, though it was comforting to feel she was missed. She was also grateful she would not yet have to face her dad.

"I'll come again soon. I just need to get some stuff out of the attic," Lucy lied. There was nothing there she needed, she only felt a longing to walk around on the ancestral land, and an inner nudge to see her grandfather.

*

Ernst stood like a stoic sentinel as the bus pulled into the station. Lucy had not seen him since months before the divorce, and he never liked Vic. Hers was the first divorce in the family that she knew of, and she wondered what he thought about it but did not want to ask. She hugged him, jumped in the car, and then rode next to him in silence as she often had.

She was thrilled to see the bend and flow of the river, the cornflower blue sky, and the waves of ocher, russet, and moss in the valleys. She could feel the roots in her soles as she awaited walking on the land. When Ernst pulled into his driveway, Lucy reached for the door handle. He gripped her arm. "Tell me about your life, honey. Did he hurt you?"

Lucy was touched that he did not blame her. She rubbed her bicep where he had squeezed it and said, "No, but you did." She was conscious of the layers to that comment, sensing a chance to tell him that she meant more than her arm, yet that young girl he had hurt's voice was so deeply buried she did not even know how to summon it.

Ernst's face wrinkled in pain, apparently unable to say he was sorry, though she could see he was feeling it. Lucy breathed deeply as she looked out over the pasture, and they walked to the picnic table under the maple. She watched her grandfather's jaw stiffen as he stood there, and she knew it was because he was not sure what to say next to get her to talk. He, like she, hated asking questions. They both figured that people told you what they wanted you to know. He lifted the rake that was leaning against the tree. Lucy watched the narrow yellow leaves jump like fish as he went to work. "Who got the divorce?" he asked.

"I did."

"Was money involved?"

"Not much." Lucy went to the garage for a bushel basket.

"What are you going to do now?" he asked when she came back out.

She lifted the leaves into the basket. "Live," she said, "one day at a time."

When they were standing by the fire pit in the pasture, the leaves flaming and smoking, she confessed. "Grandpa, I was the bad one, in a way. I became involved with another man while I was in Japan. I told Vic about it. He said he wanted to stay married, but all he wanted to do was punish me. So I left."

Ernst poked at the fire for a while then said, "Why'd you tell him?"

Lucy shook her head remembering her father's question, and now it was his father's. "What is it with you people? You're the ones who taught me the Golden Rule. I told him because I would want to know if I were him."

Ernst tilted his head as if moving her words around in his brain, trying to make sense of them. He looked at her. "We all make mistakes."

"I don't see what I did in Japan as a mistake."

Ernst twisted his lower lip as if it were a key in a lock. "There was," he grimaced. "Intercourse," he paused for a better word perhaps, "involved, wasn't there?"

Lucy thought, there's the technical line as she said, "You might call it that."

Ernst stabbed the pitchfork into the ground. "If that man really loved you he would have never put you in that position."

Lucy knew that would come. There was yet another moment she could have used her voice to ask him about the position he had put her in a decade prior. She wasn't thinking about that, though she was thinking defensively, as she often did, as she probably had since that moment. His words of doubt about Julien's love, which certainly were not original, had repeated in her mind often enough. She could not blame Julien for what she had done and she hated that her grandfather thought she had been powerless in that situation. "I put myself in that position," she said, feeling an ache for it.

Ernst stoked the fire. She could tell by the expression in his eyes that he was still trying to figure something out. "Just tell me one more thing. Is this man a Japanese?"

Lucy shook her head. "He is French."

He seemed to understand something then. "A traveler like you?"

Lucy had never heard Ernst say the word travel, nor had he ever called her anything other than her name, or honey. A traveler, she thought, yes, I am, and it made her happy to know her grandfather thought of her this way. She also liked thinking of herself and Julien as two travelers, because, for some odd reason, she never had. She looked out over the pasture to the horizon. "Yeah, a traveler like me."

*

A strong wind blew the rest of the leaves off the apple trees the next morning, and Lucy stared at the bare branches through her parents' kitchen window, thinking of a line from a Cummings poem, *this is the passing of all shining things*. It was lonely in the empty house, and it had been a long, still, night, in which she lay awake listening to the ticking of the clock, thinking about her dad's rejection of her, and the letters from Vic she had seen in her parents' room, filled with details about her behavior and the divorce, alongside his declarations of great love for her. She went to church with Ernst, and then out for a pancake breakfast eaten in predominant silence, except for her "I don't know" to most of his questions, and his "you sure don't know a whole hell of a lot do you?"

The first snow fell, melting wherever it hit the surface. As Lucy hooked her arm in his and they walked toward the bus, he pulled her closer. "I sure do worry about you, honey."

After she hugged him, she pressed her finger on his jacket and chest. "Believe in me." She looked into his eyes to make sure he was listening. "That will help a lot more."

*

It was November when Julien's letter arrived, along with a royalty check from the agency in Barcelona. "Money and love," Lucy said, smiling as she stared at the French postmark, 8-8-88, thinking that's eternity after eternity after a double eternity, and then slid the envelope from Julien in and out of her pocket several times, marveling at her self-control to not rip it open immediately. She saved it for a favorite spot along the lake to read in the sun. *You put yourself too close to me, and it bothers you, as well as me... I would like you to get your distance away from me to grow up by yourself, with no help, and no private attach...*

Lucy gazed at the horizon, wondering how much farther away they could get. She understood him. Familiar to her, he was foreign enough to make her think he was different. She had grown up feeling left alone by her family, after all.

The closeness she felt to him, even attaching the orgasms to him, was what she had been struggling to break away from all summer and still was, and maybe always would.

She could see how this distance from him was building her security in herself.

Yet, why did he want her to be helpless and alone? She wondered.

As she watched sun rays sparkling on the lake, she also wondered whether he missed her, and if so, why he had not moved toward her. Then she reminded herself that he didn't even know where she was. She wished he would somehow find out, and turn up on her doorstep this time. She remembered a college friend from Los Angeles teasing her that she had watched too many romantic American movies in her life and lost touch with reality. "Life is not like the movies, Lucy," she said.

Yet Lucy remained determined to live romantically, not to make a movie of her life, but to live the sort of life she would like to see on screen. She had, after all, turned up on his doorstep. Such things were doable.

*

The day before Thanksgiving, she sat in a rented car, staring at her parents' house. When she saw her father walking across the driveway toward her, she pretended to look for something in her bag. Tom Pilgrim bent down, looked in the window, and then tapped. As their eyes met, a jolt of joy, relief, anger, and sadness tore through Lucy.

When she stepped out of the car, and he opened his arms and said, "How are you, babe?" that glimmer of the intimacy she thought was lost forever drew her, and like a pendulum, she swung toward his chest. He held her there.

When she walked into the house, light and cautious, her mother lifted a hand as she approached and said, "Wait," then climbed onto a kitchen chair to be taller than her, opened her arms, and said, "Now." She took Lucy to her breast and held her.

Along with her parents, her brothers and sisters and their significant others, their kids, and her grandfather she gathered around the Thanksgiving table that afternoon. It was as if nothing had changed and she had not been gone for months. In a way, it was as if she were not even there. No one asked how she was, where she had been, or what she had seen. It was as if she had no life other than this one, to them. It was perhaps too painful for her to think that they were simply un-interested.

Her sister-in-law, Dawn, apologized for everyone while she and Lucy were alone doing the dishes. "We were wrong not to reach out to you, Lucy. It was just that we did not see you or hear anything from you. Vic did not only go to see your dad, he visited everyone in the family. If you would have seen him and how upset he was, and heard what he was saying, you would have understood why everyone was so upset with you."

Lucy scrubbed the frying pan. "What I understand is that wanting to be kind and charitable people, you all supported and believed a guy you knew through me, for two years—instead of me."

"Everyone knew you would be okay."

This, too, confused Lucy. She wiped her hands on a nearby towel and raised them in the air. "How is it that everyone thinks I will always be okay but doesn't trust me? It's okay to hurt Lucy because Lucy can take it, is that it? Does anybody ever ask why Lucy can take it better than anybody else? Maybe she has more practice, could that be it? So let's make her a master at it. Let's just keep shitting on her because she can clean it off and not throw it back. Is that my reward for hard work, more shit?"

"Geez, Lucy, I said we were wrong, okay? Relax."

Lucy could not relax. She saw that her family may never understand her and though she no longer needed them to, she still wished they would at least try. Without knowing how to say it, she yearned to be seen and valued by them as she was.

She still had much to learn about seeing and valuing herself.

A little help would have been a boost.

She was in love with a man who also did not want to help. She was not seeing that connection yet, either.

She both hated and loved being made so differently from the rest of her family. Being there among those she had always known, hugging and carrying on like nothing had happened, had comfort in it, but not enough for Lucy on the edge.

She was glad to return to the city.

*

Christmas neared, Chicago hardened. Lucy, ready to go again, sat in Faith's office looking out at the steely blue sky over the tormented lake. She was watching Faith pace back and forth in front of this backdrop. Finally, Faith blurted, "What would you do if you were attracted to a man that was not your husband?"

Lucy raised her eyebrows. "I think you know."

Faith stopped pacing and looked like she might cry. She flung a hand toward the window. "I don't want to just throw myself into the abyss."

Lucy realized that is where her friend saw her floating, she tried to imagine herself out there over the lake. Lucy in the abyss with diamonds, she thought, then said, "It's where we all are anyway. Even if you think you're not there, it doesn't change that you are."

"I just can't," Faith crumpled.

Lucy craved communion with someone who dared to live freely. She wished she could lie in the embrace of another human being who whispered, "Yes, live."

As she left the building, hungering for touch, she reminded herself it always came when it was right, and lifted her collar before walking north.

*

Angelina clapped and threw her arms in the air when Lucy walked into the Christmas party. "Tokyo called! They want you to come in January!"

"Wow. I've been wishing for a trip. Thank you," Lucy said as she hugged her. She immediately began imagining Hope there, too.

A man with curious, witty eyes was looking her way from across the room. Throughout the next couple of hours, he and Lucy glanced at and approached each other, then told stories and laughed so often that others were drawn toward them to ask what was so amusing. When Lucy commented, "My, my aren't we cocky," and he responded, "We prefer to call it self-assured," she thought she may be able to learn something from him.

They left together and after a drink at Bijan, she accepted his invitation to tea at his home.

*

This is one of those serendipitous moments in life, Lucy thought as she moved around his cozy apartment. She could have done without the poster of Paris on the wall that reminded her of Julien, who she had been trying to forget since she received his letter. When the handsome young man turned on the cassette recorder and it played The Style Council's tape that she had listened to all summer, she felt she was in the right place. She touched his sculptures and lingered over the sketches on torn-out notebook paper scattered around the room. It was like encountering an unexpected oasis on her journey, with a true fellow.

He built a fire, and Lucy relaxed into a beanbag chair in front of it while he made tea. They talked about how they felt attentive when they drew, strong when they sculpted, and playful, too. She was moved by the light in his eyes when he spoke of his dream of living in the mountains. She could see him chopping wood and a woman watching from the window. She noted it was not her. Nonetheless, Lucy was grateful to want to kiss someone she could.

Her body leaped toward his like a long-lost friend there in front of the fire.

As his kisses lowered, she became nervous. She felt resistance in her body, which still seemed attached to Julien. She told herself it was important to let herself be loved by and love another, so she pushed through her body's hesitation, and, unfortunately, farted in the lovely man's face. She immediately covered her own, thinking I will never push again, as she spoke. "I'm so sorry and so embarrassed."

He shook his head as if it was nothing as he rose above her. He wrapped his arms around her and held her for a while, then covered her with a blanket and kissed her on the forehead. "I'm going to bed. You are welcome to join me if you like."

When Lucy woke in the dark, the fire smoldering, she tip-toed into his room. He spooned her, and she fell into a deep sleep in which she dreamed that she was sitting on his toilet looking between her legs, where she saw Band-Aids falling from her, floating like leaves on the water of the basin.

She opened her eyes, and then lay for a while thinking about the strange dream, enjoying the smell of coffee brewing, wondering what had been wounded there and what had healed. She had no answer. Tenderness is what she felt.

*

"Do you think you will ever get a real job and settle down in just one place? With one man?" her mother asked as they lay next to each other on her parents' bed Christmas morning.

"There is one I could imagine doing that with, I think. But he is far away."

"How far?"

"France."

Viola dropped the back of her hand on her forehead. "You are going to live way over there?"

Lucy sighed, it was difficult to imagine at this point, but her mother's question gave her new hope. If Viola thought it was possible, it must be.

Lucy raised her eyebrows at her father on Christmas after-noon hoping to convey that he owed her an apology. To spur him on, she added, "By the way, I've forgiven you."

Tom slapped his palm on the kitchen table as if the apology was a gnat under it, now squashed. "That's one of those things you don't have much choice about, Lulu."

The lights on the tree blurred in her vision as she looked past him into the living room. She could not understand why her father was being so hard on her. Even if he wanted her to face the repercussions and the seriousness of the choice she had made to end a marriage, why he could not say so gently was beyond her. She saw the whole holiday like those lights, the love still there, but blurry.

The next afternoon while she was filling the dishwasher, her dad said, "Your whole problem is that you are too defensive."

Lucy looked up, dirty fork in hand. "That is because I feel like I have to protect the shit out of myself whenever I come to this place."

Tom Pilgrim opened the newspaper and casually said, "Well, then don't come."

Lucy slammed the fork into the flatware slot. "Fine then, I won't."

Her dad dropped the paper on the den floor, then raised his hands in resignation, feeling sorry for what he'd said. "What do you want us to do?"

Lucy glared. "Just forget it," she said and went upstairs.

A sleepless night, fever, and headache left her feeling delirious at dawn and she decided to leave. The snow crunched under her feet as she walked across the yard to say goodbye to her grandfather. Through the window, she could see him shuffling around in the kitchen in his robe. She tapped on the door. He looked at the clock on the wall and then opened it. He could tell she had been crying and asked, "What are you doing up this early?"

"I'm going back to Chicago. Everyone is still asleep over at home but I can't take it anymore. I gotta go."

He gestured for her to come inside for coffee. When she sat in her grandmother's chair, he looked at her the way he puzzled over tomato plants that were not growing correctly. She was tired of being looked at by her family as if something were wrong with her. She missed her grandma. She remembered sitting in that spot as a girl, after having helped prepare supper. Ernst put a cup of coffee in front of her. "You're just a loner in the world now. Just going out in the world totally alone."

Lucy nodded, self-satisfied, thinking it has always been that way, at least someone sees it now.

Ernst shook his head. "And this is no way to be. You will find out. You can't get through this life all by yourself."

"Oh yes, I can," Lucy said, sounding more like a child than she realized.

"You are totally independent—," he said it like it was an affliction.

Lucy interjected another fierce nod to let him know she took it as a compliment. "Thank you."

"—and it can't work. You need people."

There's that again, Lucy thought. The needy network is what she called this kind of talk. Yet she knew people could help, had helped.

She looked at her grandfather. "What kind of people? That's the question."

Ernst straightened up to deliver his blow. "You have no future."

Lucy looked at the World Series ring on his finger. "Is that what you told your son when he wanted to play professional baseball?"

He nodded.

Lucy shook her head in disgust.

"Luckily the grace of God was with him."

Lucy rolled her eyes. "I thought it was supposed to be with us all."

Once again, Lucy left.

[14]

As Lucy scanned the awaiting crowd at Narita airport, memories of Osaka flooded her. Beads of sweat and chills broke out over her body as she ached to see Julien, and ached from that ache. Then, just as in Osaka, a man in a blue suit holding a sign with her name on it bowed. This time she was driven to Roppongi, the center of Tokyo, where the driver pulled up in front of a modern eight-story building between a 7-Eleven store and a flower shop. He walked her inside to the elevator, and the fourth-floor studio the agency had reserved for her, then handed her keys and an envelope, just as a gentleman in Osaka had less than a year prior.

The agency was in a simple office building a fifteen-minute walk away on a four-lane street lined by saplings. It was much smaller than the agency in Osaka and run by a cheerful and kind woman, Tami, who peeked around the philodendron on the counter as Lucy walked in and then introduced her to Oki, a tiny young woman with curious, friendly eyes. She was the first Japanese Lucy had seen with an afro, and she smiled at her colorful clothing. She was wearing an electric blue t-shirt, rainbow-striped wool socks over black leggings, red Adidas volleyball shoes, and a neon orange ski jacket. As they walked out to the street and on their way to the first of many castings, Oki grinned sheepishly and pointed at her head. "I want to be a black person. That is why I did this to my hair."

"Wow." Lucy smiled. "But what will you do about your skin?"

Oki cracked up. "Can you tell me something? What does it mean to 'hang it up'? My boyfriend, he is Australian, he told me that we should hang it up. Is it a good thing?"

"That depends on what you are hanging up," she told Oki. "You know when you take off your coat and put it in the closet?"

Oki nodded.

"That's hanging it up."

Oki looked worried.

"As I said, it depends on what you are putting in the closet."

Oki nodded, working on it in her mind.

*

Lucy's best jobs in Tokyo were as an "older woman" for elegant catalogs. She also did covers and fashion spreads for magazines, often as part of a couple, her favorite was pretending as if she and a handsome young man were on vacation in Chiba. She skied in Hokkaido and played a young mother in luxury homes in Tokyo suburbs. Once again treated like visiting royalty, she loved most those jobs where they played Kitaro's music and gave her massages before makeup to "fully relax and increase her beauty."

All that pretending and posing was getting to her, though. Lucy began sticking out her tongue at the camera or crossing her eyes and screwing up her face for the Polaroid shots made to test the lighting. "Why you do that?" one photographer asked.

Lucy shrugged.

The man straightened the glasses on his nose and then shook his head, confused.

Lucy ventured a guess. "Diversion."

"Diversion?"

Lucy shrugged again not knowing how to tell him how much the job bored her. She didn't think she was being unprofessional because they were only Polaroids taken to test the lighting. She was sure to play the right game with the real film and deemed that enough. The breaking point was the day she was asked, while wearing a one-piece swimsuit, to do some aerobic dance moves in front of a table of fifteen men in business suits. The professional thing to do, it seemed to her, was what was asked. So she did. When they looked at the woman next to her, waiting for her to show them some moves, and she refused, Lucy was ashamed it had not even occurred to her to say no.

"I'm not going to jump around for their perverse pleasure," the model from Texas snapped as they walked out, and Lucy wondered what had become of her to think it was professional to do as she had done. She felt so lost and yet, confident, too, in other ways, it was strange the way she both dared to do as she felt, yet second-guessed herself. Who could she trust, if not herself? How could she peel away that layer of self-doubt?

Still, she was happy to be in Japan again, seeing more and a different part of it. Tokyo was more condensed and tense than Osaka, with even more neon and people so Lucy searched for the open spaces like the graveyards amid high-rises and the wild parks in the center of the city. She loved to run to and around Akasaka Castle every morning and to take long walks at night through Hiro-ho, the neighborhood adjacent to hers. The structures were lower there, and there was a park with an ancient eucalyptus tree, a stream, and across the street, a friendly, woody bathhouse where she often bathed with the neighborhood ladies. In the wee hours, when she couldn't sleep, she went to the clay she'd bought and sculpted miniature fantastic worlds of her own. Sometimes she sketched.

When she was in a social mood, she went to the clubs and danced, or sat and listened to the music and people's stories. The stories were usually about chances missed, love—or what they thought was love lost, intimate abuse or neglect, and strange jobs. Her favorite was listening to an American guy tell her what it was like to be in a male casting and watching him demonstrate how he prepared himself for bathing suit castings by doing push-ups and other pumping exercises.

The nightclubs had names like BingoBangoBongo, Bio, and Lucy's favorite, Java Jive. It was set up to look like Jamaica, with palm trees and chaise lounges around the dance floor, wicker stools at the bamboo bar, and a live reggae band. The clubs were all on top of each other in a high rise, and Lucy often got into the elevator and rode to another one when she was bored. Models drank and ate free in Tokyo, too. Lucy wondered how long it would last as she watched some Australians and Americans, a group the youngest Australian girls dubbed The Wankers, order the bartenders and waitresses around like indentured servants.

She danced a lot in Tokyo, and by herself. It was then she felt freest. Sometimes she had the entire dance floor to herself, she closed her eyes and spun and flew, letting her body move as it liked to the songs she loved most. She often imagined Julien walking her way; she wanted so much to have a chance to be in his presence again, just to see what it felt like. She could neither deny nor fulfill her longing. Then, as if to make her Japanese experience round, another Frenchman appeared.

She and Marcel met in a restaurant, both alone, eating separately until he asked if he might join her. He had warm brown eyes with golden flecks framed by thick, arched brows, full lips she imagined would be pleasant to touch and a long neck that she admired as he adjusted the bandana he wore around it. She noticed the way he checked himself in the mirror, too, before joining her, and this combination of vanity and insecurity made him more approachable to her. He was stunningly handsome, a blend of Gregory Peck and Yves Montand. Every night he and Lucy met for meals, as if not planning to, by showing up in the same Italian restaurant at the same time. At the clubs, they watched each other carefully, approaching and retreating. She liked the way he moved his fingers along her spine when they finally danced, and she liked walking through the slick night streets with him, dodging puddles of neon reflections. They spoke the same amount of each other's language but were mostly silent partners, dancing, exchanging glances and soft laughter as they watched the antics of others.

Eventually, he moved her enough to lie with him. Sharing was certainly the summit, she was reminded, of the joy of happy skin with happy skin. The voluptuousness of kissing. She couldn't believe she was making love again. Then, when she rolled on top of him and looked down into his eyes, his widened, and he asked, "Are you going to rape me?"

Lucy dropped to her side and curled into herself wondering how he could think she would want to do such a thing. Voiceless again, and ashamed of her desire, again. At least she was letting herself enter another's arms, she thought. That seemed like some kind of progress. She wondered if Marcel had ever seen a woman on top, but he was French, and she imagined he had seen women in every position. There they were, two naked human beings, that close, and not talking. He held her, and that felt like enough then. She barely slept before she had to report to work at six.

When Oki saw her the next afternoon, her mouth dropped open and she looked at Lucy as if she were noticing her for the very first time. "Wow, you are so beautiful." Lucy smiled weakly, she imagined it had something to do with the love she was making through the night. It's amazing, she thought, what kissing does for the face, what touching does for one's beauty. As much as her solo raptures satisfied her, they never compared to sharing with another.

When Marcel saw her in Java Jive he came close, then leaned his lips toward her ear. "What happened last night cannot happen again. I have a wife."

The experience felt rounder to Lucy all the time, especially when she looked down and saw he was wearing the same sneakers Julien had. In any case, to maintain her dignity, she asked, "And who was it that stopped what was happening last night?"

Marcel looked at her, both confused and curious. She could see that something in her scared him, and she thought it was her detachment from him. He seemed to her the kind of man who rarely heard *no* from a woman.

Yet, despite his words that night, he didn't stop looking for what he said couldn't happen, to happen again.

Lucy was torn. He was the most fun she was having in Tokyo and she saw the relationship with him as a way out into the world again, a chance for her to love again, but then again, not. In that way, it was both adventurous and safe, because she knew it could only go so far. The fact that he was married bothered her little. It even seemed weirdly fitting, as if it were her turn to experience this, a reversal from her relationship with Julien.

Everything was still too much related to Julien, though, it was almost as if she was trying to be him so she would not miss him.

It was clear to her that Marcel's marriage was his problem, not hers. In any case, it was a pleasant present she was looking for, not a future. She thought about what her grandfather had said to her about not having one, and she wondered, who does? Who can know that they do? What concerned her most was that though Marcel wanted to be close to her, it seemed his only way not to feel guilty about it was if it didn't mean much, and Lucy wanted it to mean a lot. It was her own doing, this sort of bondage to meaning, something she would often question. She had tried the meaningless route, after all, young. Was it that she was looking for the meaning to come from the other, instead of making it for herself?

*

As if he sensed her slipping away, a letter from Julien arrived. When she saw the envelope lying on the agency counter, she passed her fingers over the ink, imagining his hand, writing her name. She had sent a couple of photos and a short letter after her arrival. It had been six months since she had seen him, five since she had heard from him. It surprised her to have news. Once outside the agency, she opened the letter and then walked down the busy street reading. *I have this feeling that I am not basically happy, actually...*

Lucy was glad he had figured out that much. She wondered how much longer it would take until he considered his unhappiness might have something to do with the distance between them. Perhaps he would consider that too attached, she mused. She read his request to present his composite, if she still had it, to her agency, to see if they might need him. This made her wonder if that was the real reason for his interest. She was relieved she had stopped carrying his composite with her, and she was bent on him moving toward her all on his own, *with no help and no private attach*, so she savored the letter, but kept on with her life in Tokyo. She impressed herself by not feeling an urgent need to answer him.

*

Meandering through Ginza on a gloomy afternoon at the beginning of February, Lucy spied a familiar gait and turned to look more closely at a woman in a black bolero. It was the spring in her step and the way she held her head high and light. A fuchsia turtleneck flashed under her black wool cape as she turned to see if traffic was coming. Lucy stopped. The tiny bells around the ankles of Hope's boots jingled as she strode toward Lucy amid the lights, shoppers, and skyscrapers. "You're here! I have been going crazy in Barcelona, everything was delayed for three weeks because of visa papers." Lucy was marveling at the power of imagination. Hope pointed to the female booker, who bowed to Lucy as she waited on the sidewalk. "They brought me from the airport directly to castings." She handed Lucy a piece of paper. "Here is my address. Meet me there in two hours."

Hope's apartment was the one where Lucy had spent the night with Marcel. She knew he had moved in with another model from the agency, which Lucy learned was also Hope's agency. Hope and Lucy lay awake until three, telling stories and laughing.

"You like the French guys," Hope teased.

Lucy rolled her eyes. "I don't know if it is because they are French." But she had to admit nine times out of ten the men that turned her head were speaking that language.

*

Tokyo became more fun with Hope in it. She joined Lucy at the clubs, on weekend excursions, and at the bathhouse in Hiroho. The day after Hope met Marcel, she leaned toward Lucy in the bubbling water of the hot bath, and said, as if she were talking to a child, "He's gorgeous, Lucy. You have to make love with this man."

Lucy sighed into the rising steam then leaned back against the wooden frame. "I have started to, but, you know, I want it to mean something. I think he prefers it to be meaningless."

Hope shook her head in confusion. "Mean what? Just take the pleasure. You deserve it."

"Take it? I want it to be a celebration, a communion, an adventure in intimate ecstasy filled with both of us, all that's in us. I think he wants it to be a stolen relief, a surrender to sex for sex's sake so he can tell himself he was still true to his wife because his heart was not in it."

"You think way too much. Just enjoy it."

This, from a virgin, Lucy thought. Yet, she sensed a point. She, too, saw her quest for meaning as somewhat relentless and perhaps misplaced yet could not ignore it. It seemed as much a part of her as her hair, which she reminded herself she also did her best to shape while allowing for wildness.

*

Then, when she did take the risk to go farther and let him inside of her, she felt first that glorious sensation again for the first time since being with Julien. She also felt a subtle change in Marcel, like a light going out somewhere in his house. His kisses and thrusts became impersonal, as if it no longer mattered who, or even what, was there with him. It was as if she disappeared as a human being under him and became a receptacle. She pressed his chest and whispered, "I do not feel you with me, please stop."

She watched Marcel's confusion turn to anger and insecurity as he moved from her bed to the bathroom and back again, walking through her apartment erect as if searching for a lost object while carrying it. She, too, was confused by the pleasure it brought her to watch him wander this way, part of it was in the beauty of his form, yet she also felt powerful for having stopped what felt wasteful, for having refused, for having said, "Not like that."

Still, he stayed, slept, and they had breakfast together while he watched her like a never-encountered-before specimen, then kissed her and left. *"Ciao, Bella."*

*

That weekend, Felix appeared across the dance floor. He was so tanned he looked black.

Lucy backed away from the scraped skin covering half of his face before kissing him. He frowned and pointed to his wound. "Motorcycle accident in Thailand."

Lucy palmed his back in sympathy.

"I am sad to return to Paris. My father says I really must work with him now."

Lucy still couldn't imagine Felix as a banker, but she liked to. She noticed Marcel was watching them from the other side of the room as Felix lowered his mouth to her ear. "I saw Julien in Paris last fall."

Lucy listened, remembering Julien, as she watched Marcel moving among the crowd. She thought if nothing else, life was beautiful to have given her gorgeous men to love.

Felix continued as if he were trying to tell Lucy something important. "He came to a party at my house."

Lucy, who felt tossed aside by Julien, nodded, acting like any news about him was of little concern to her.

"Alone," Felix added as if to emphasize a point.

This caught Lucy's attention, making her wonder if Felix saw what she sensed, that she and Julien had something to do together, still.

The next morning, when she woke with her nipple in the crux of her second and third fingers as it had rested between Julien's in Paris, she slid open the window to feel the sun in her bed, reached for a piece of beautiful Japanese paper and her fountain pen, then wrote *Dear Julien (who by the way, still remains dearest and deepest in my heart)*. It amazed and pleased her when she realized it had taken her three weeks to respond to his letter. It was some strange proof of his wished-for detachment from him and her wished-for freedom from desire.

*

At the beginning of March, with ten days left on her contract, she sat in her apartment adding up income and deducting expenses: two hundred thousand yen, not enough money to go to Thailand as she had hoped or to set herself up in Europe. She would have to return to Chicago. She thought of the sixty-year-old she had met at a dinner party with Hope the night before, who, when she had told him of her hopes for travel, had exclaimed, "You women don't need husbands." How odd, she thought, this idea that husbands were only for money, for tickets, and expenses.

*

During one of her runs that week, she paused on one of the park's bamboo bridges in the light rain, surrounded by every kind of green. She noticed the buds on the branches and inhaled deeply the smell of damp earth. This all aroused her. As it engulfed her, she closed her eyes. Feeling other eyes on her, she opened her own. Marcel stuck his camera lens in her face with a sly slow smile, clicked the shutter, and walked away. This strengthened her feeling that she was always meeting the right person every time, even if nothing more had happened, or would with him. Little did she know that years later she would be inside an elevator in Paris, and the doors would open to him.

*

The gray and drizzly day before she left, she walked to the phone booth near Roppongi Crossing, the one in front of the bright pink Almond Café. She slid coins into the phone, dialed Julien's number, and her heart both lifted and dropped at the sound of his voice. "Is it you?" she whispered.

His voice, too, was soft, like a voice from bed. "Are you calling me from Japan?"

"Yes, I can't talk long. I'm leaving tomorrow. I wanted to go to Thailand, as I wrote you, but I'm going back to Chicago."

"Problems?"

"I can deal—" she cut herself off as she wondered if she could. She thought about how she had left things with her family, the scant life that remained for her in Chicago, how she wanted to keep traveling but not modeling, and she wondered if she wanted to keep traveling alone.

"You are an optimist," Julien said, in a way that made Lucy think he had not heard one for a while.

She was silent, happy just to hear him breathing, happy they were connected if only by wire and only for moments.

"Lucy."

She closed her eyes at the sound of her name in his voice.

"Are the cherry trees in bloom?"

She nodded as if he could see her.

"You know, I really miss this time," he said.

Lucy was speechless, love in her ear, too far to touch, cars whizzing by.

"Give me a big kiss," Julien said.

Lucy smacked without thinking, then said, "I'm running out of time."

"Don't leave me alone," Julien said.

Now you say it, she thought. She shook all the questions about when, where, why, and how they would see each other again out of her mind and said, "I won't ask."

The line went dead.

Lucy stood for a moment in Roppongi Crossing, remembering the phone booths in Barcelona, Paris, and New York, where she had been in the same position, wondering the same damn thing.

*

"I wonder how long it will be before we are together again," she said as she warmed her cold and trembling hands on the cup of mint tea Hope had poured for her.

Hope raised her brows. "If he is as stubborn as you are, it could be a very long time."

As the thought, me, stubborn? crossed Lucy's face, Hope nodded, and they both laughed.

*

Flights to Paris or Bangkok were both boarding on each side of the flight to Chicago. Lucy sighed as she contemplated slipping onto either of them. She knew she had to go back and face her life again, find her way, and figure out what to make of it all next. There seemed to still be unfinished business, and she was still filled with the notion that she could get it all sorted out once and for all.

When she arrived in Chicago, she went straight to the agency. Angelina threw her arms open. "You look fantastic. I've never seen you in more perfect shape, Lucy."

Lucy imagined she was talking about how thin she was. "I feel like shit," she said, "And I need a place to live."

Angelina picked up the phone and secured a good deal on a studio at The Elms, a small hotel half a block from the lake. She looked at Lucy. "Your mother called here this morning, and says that you should call home collect."

*

Knowing her father hated driving into downtown Chicago, Lucy was impressed when her mother said they were coming to see her.

It didn't take long for Lucy to get to her point, the one she could not let go of. As they looked around her studio apartment, she stabbed her finger into her father's chest and held it there. "Can you imagine how much that hurt me when you told me not to come home last year?"

Viola sighed. "So that is what this has all been about."

Tom squinted at Lucy. "You really take it right to the gut, don't you?"

She pressed her finger deeper into his heart. "That's where I give it from, too."

He lifted his hands to the air, then as quickly shook them out as if to wipe them of this trouble, as if it weren't important, as if once again she was taking it all too hard.

Viola looked Lucy up and down. "Why don't you buy yourself some new clothes? Do you go into the agency looking like that? Why don't you wear a skirt or dress and some heels instead of those flimsy pants and whatever kind of jacket that is?" She slapped Lucy's hand away from the cinnamon rolls she reached for on the kitchen counter. "If this is what you want to do, you can't have those."

Lucy, overwhelmed by all the advice yet strangely pleased that her mother was finally accepting her choice, sighed. "I don't know how much longer I want to do this."

She was thinking of the criticism, her self-confidence, and her insecurity, and she looked at her dad. "You know you never once told me I was beautiful, not once in my whole life."

Tom held her stare. "You are beautiful," he said as if stating an obvious fact. Then he lifted his hands into the air again to add, "And so what?"

Lucy laughed, a little, seeing his point. She was torn between wanting to be seen, and knowing the value of focusing on more than her looks. She turned to her mother. "So are you saying all of these feelings I had of being turned away by my family weren't true?"

Viola narrowed her eyes. "That is what you twist around in that brain of yours."

Lucy wanted to believe her, except for the twisted part.

Viola swept her arm around the circumference of Lucy's studio. "Why would you want to live in a little room like this when you have that nice big bedroom upstairs looking out on the countryside?"

Lucy looked out the window to the brick façade, agreeing that the countryside was a better view. "But what would I do there?"

"Get a real job?" As Lucy was trying to imagine what that might be, Viola lifted a little silver suitcase jewelry box Lucy bought in Tokyo and said, "This is perfect for you." She set it back down and sighed wistfully. "You are rich."

Her admiration surprised Lucy. "Mom, I only have about a thousand dollars in the bank."

Viola swatted the air. "I'm not talking about money, I'm talking about experience."

Lucy wanted to freeze the moment, it was so rare and special to feel this intimacy with her mother. "I wish I knew what to do next. I wanted to see the world, to travel it alone, to prove that I could do it, and I did."

Viola looked confused. "Prove it to who?"

The question gave Lucy pause. There was that proof thing again. Yet, she had wanted something and was afraid to do it, and it did give her some confidence to see that she had. "To me," she said.

Viola still looked puzzled, but Lucy couldn't tell if it was about the need for proof or a sentiment her mother simply didn't share. What moved her most was that her parents were there, giving her all their attention. It made her feel safe.

*

A letter from Julien arrived at the end of the month. *Do what you have to do, if you feel it, even if it hurts...* she read, again, then again.

"He's late again," she said to a bird on the beach.

She also wondered once more why he thought she needed this prompt, this sort of permission to be with someone else. She thought of the motorcycle ride with Beau and the Mediterranean beach, then how she had cried with Mick in New York, at first, before he went wild. How it had hurt to be with another when it was Julien she wanted. She remembered the sweet face she had farted into and the intimacy with Marcel. All beautiful men, all travelers. She liked to think they were all part of her educational journey; she was learning not to squander her desire, push it, fake it, or to play with it. How did people learn about themselves without relationship, she wondered.

That afternoon she was called to the agency to meet a Parisian agent. He looked like a well-dressed ogre to Lucy, and she imagined they were under a Parisian bridge as he flipped through her book. She smiled at the thought of going to Paris more than a meal with him when he looked up and said, "Would you like to have dinner with me tonight? We can talk about you coming to Paris."

Lucy knew they could have talked about it right there, and though she was tired of this game, she accepted his invitation, mostly to observe his methods of entrapment but also because some part of her wanted very much for his proposal of work in Paris to be true. She would consider going to Paris again if work were involved.

After she knocked on the door of the agent's room in the Palmer House Hotel, he opened it and offered her a drink, then lifted a tiny white tablet between his fingers. "Would you like half an ecstasy?"

Lucy smirked. "How about if you give it to me and I take it with somebody else?"

He threw his head back, laughed, and kept his pill for himself.

At the fancy French restaurant near Water Tower Place, she looked across the table at him and had to ask, "Do you know Léon Soinin?"

He wiped his mouth as he nodded. "We have contests together to see who can take off a girl's pantyhose fastest. So tell me, how many guys have you done? Have you tried Japanese? Chinese? French? German? A worldwide tasting?"

Lucy leaned back in the booth, shaking her head. It seemed one way for an ugly, disgusting man to meet and manipulate beautiful women was to become a modeling agent. "People aren't little dolls to be taken off a shelf and tried," she said.

He shrugged, then switched to a new topic as quickly as Léon had in Paris. She wondered if he, too, was doing cocaine. His appetite suggested he was not. She marveled at the way he was relentless, seemingly unaffected by her disinterest in him. "I thought we were going to talk about work in Paris," she said.

He waved a hand to dismiss that as unimportant. "Why don't you come to Vancouver and San Francisco with me? I leave tomorrow."

Lucy shook her head. "Don't think so."

As they walked out of the restaurant, she rejected his invitation to go back to his hotel. He looked at her and said, scornfully, "I bet you are one of those women that don't let anybody touch her then goes home and touches herself."

"I don't even have to touch myself," Lucy said, then left him, his mouth hanging open, looking like he'd missed something.

*

Lucy could hardly bear to stand in front of the camera anymore. She felt like eating it each time it was pointed at her, chewing it up, and spitting it back at the photographer. Perhaps it was about the photographers, it had been too long since one had looked through the lens for her, instead of at her, it seemed. She was a subject being treated like an object and this confused her, made her weary. She worked for a couple of catalogs, then a well-paid whiskey advertisement with a famous photographer she saw as a slob, who became angry with her for not cowering before him.

The next weekend, she slept in her clothes at a Finnish businessman's apartment, after he, too, begged her not to leave him alone. When she woke to his hand on her ass, she sensed there was something she was just not getting and went back to her apartment and called her mother. "Would it be okay for me to come home for a while?"

"When?"

"As soon as you want to come and get me."

That afternoon, she walked over to the agency to tell Angelina her plans. Angelina widened her eyes. "Lucy? Look at you, you are in perfect shape, you are working well. What the hell are you going to do in Iowa?"

"Walk around barefoot in the grass."

Angelina shook her head as she penciled the phone number at the top of her chart.

"Why don't you try a weekend first?" Faith suggested as they ran along the lake. "And what about Julien, you said you wrote and invited him to share your studio. What if he comes?"

"I feel like I need to go there and settle something inside myself. I can't explain it, only that it feels like the right next thing to do. I can always come back. It's not that far. I have some money. More will come. It always does. And who knows when and if I will hear from Julien again?"

*

Her parents drove into the city again, and to the storage place with her, where Lucy wheeled one of the large silver carriers into the elevator. Upstairs, and in the back of the aisle, she opened the wire cage that contained all of her belongings and removed one box after another. Tom looked on in a combination of admiration and disbelief as he helped. "You put this all in here by yourself?"

Lucy nodded. She thought, again, of how everyone in her family seemed to think the divorce had been easy for her. She was happy that her father could see a fraction of it that wasn't. She lifted the last box into the trunk. Her dad handed her the keys to drive out of the city. Before they hit I90, she pulled up alongside a mailbox and dropped a postcard to Paris into it.

[15]

At first, it was great. Lucy walked into the backyard and looked around. The apple trees were full of white blossoms, the grass was so green it made her squint, dandelions were popping bright yellow everywhere, the heady smell of lilacs lulled her into a childlike calm, and every oak unfurling its shiny new leaves looked like it was hoping she would choose to sit underneath it. Robins, cardinals, red-winged blackbirds, blue jays, and chickadees flitted and skeeted over the yard. Goldfinches fed at the feeder outside the kitchen window. Soon horseback, Lucy galloped through the open, rolling fields in the sun. She donned skis, then skimmed over the Mississippi watching for the herons and turtles resting on driftwood along the shore.

She thought of this respite as a time for streamlining her life. In the mornings, she worked whittling away at her piles of possessions, then in the afternoon she drove into town and dumped loads of clothes and household items into the St. Vincent de Paul container, thinking she was becoming cleaner, lighter. In a way, she was stripping herself of all that she owned. She would do this often in her life, a sort of editing out all but the necessary. This made her feel freer, able to move quickly, and easily.

After her trips to town, she lay in the sun on the roof, or in the backyard listening to music. Then, in the evenings she ran up and down the hills along gravel roads, past silver silos, gleaming in the warm and golden sun, and wood barns painted red that looked hot to the touch. Swallowtails fluttered in the tall grass near the fence line where Guernsey cows stopped chewing, looked up, and walked toward her as she approached, their eyes and noses full of flies, tails swishing. She was surprised to like the smell of fresh, grassy manure in the air. She didn't remember liking that. She thought about how she once dreamed of getting away from all this, and it gave her satisfaction to think she had done what she set out to do. It also felt strange to her to be plan-less. She was in an in-between place in her imagination, one both peaceful and tense for her.

Once home from her run, she stretched in the driveway and told her brother Eze the route she ran. He popped a bing cherry in his mouth then spit the pit into his palm and pitched it into the pasture as he said, "You're nuts."

Lucy laughed.

When she walked into the den, her dad dropped the paper on the floor and leaned forward. "Scratch my back, Lulu." She massaged his shoulders. "You know, you look and feel stronger and better than you ever have," he added. She did feel ready for anything.

Fortunately for her, she had no idea what lay just ahead.

When Angelina called, Lucy reluctantly drove the four hours to Chicago for a couple of castings. The closer she came to the city, the higher her stomach rose toward her throat, and her hands quivered on the wheel. She wanted to turn around and escape into the woods, but she parked the car, combed her hair, touched up her makeup, walked into each of those studios on Huron Street, and smiled. She could never quite put her finger on what bothered her so much about this work.

Perhaps it was the pressure of the lid she kept on her bother about so many things like how she constantly wondered what and where was her place in the world, and why she was so insecure about her worth and value in it. Her beauty was where she had received the most recognition from the outside world, yet she knew she had much more to offer. She imagined everyone had more to offer than the world seemed to have room for.

On the way back from Chicago, she sang loudly, with one hand guiding the wheel, wind whipping in the open window. The farther away from people, houses, and buildings she drove the freer she felt, yet she hoped at least one of the jobs would come through so she could add cash to her diminishing bank account.

She was happier back home, though each time she said that word, *home*, or even thought it, she imagined other places in the world as well, and that also made her happy.

Painting the porch swing while her parents planted impatiens, she thought about how much she loved quiet and beautiful work in which she didn't have to pretend to be anyone else. Or was she pretending here, too? She felt quite safe in this home and on this land, yet there was so much of her she did not show here either, so much she did not say, so many things she believed, and ways she was that did not fit the rules, or guilt, of this world.

She pondered whether everyone was pretending all the time, how much anyone knew about anyone else, how necessary it was to know and to pretend, and what would happen if everyone just stopped. Imagining that was exciting to her.

What they all shared was love, Lucy knew, or at least thought, and that was worth keeping quiet for. Yet why did she think she needed to keep quiet to be loved? What kind of love asks for silence?

Whenever she paused from her work and looked up, she glanced at her grandmother's bedroom window, and stood riveted, remembering precious moments and still wanting to protect her.

It was as if Marie's ghost was a vigilant fugitive captive there, watching, pacing, fretting, and looking for a way out.

Ernst was sitting on the lawn chair just outside his door, listening to a ball game on the radio. He and Lucy hadn't talked much since Christmas when he'd told her she had no future, yet she still stopped to sit and listen to the ball game, or garden, or both, with him. When she told him that her parents were getting ready to go out for supper, he looked toward the house. "Are you going to be all alone over there?"

She looked down, at the long blades of grass she was smoothing between her toes. "I like to be alone, Grandpa."

Ernst stood, leaned over the railing, and took her face firmly in his hands. "You know what I'd like to do with you?"

Lucy backed up and looked away.

He twisted her face toward him. "I'd like to open up that head of yours and see what the hell is inside."

She imagined her head split open, and all the people, places, moments, fears, and dreams inside of it blasting out, slamming her grandfather against the limestone wall of his house. When she laughed, he let go. She looked at him, bravado rising with her chin. "What do you think you'd find?"

He shook his head in grumpy frustration. "That is the big question."

"I am as silent as you are. But there's stuff going on in there, you can count on that."

Ernst smirked and turned to go inside, pretending her answer didn't matter.

Lucy would wonder, years after he was gone, how often he thought about what he had done to her, if he ever did, or if in moments like this one, he was trying to figure out if she thought about it and if she remembered. She would wonder, too, if he had been somehow pushing her to start the conversation about it. And she would note that a wound could be old and fresh at the same time.

*

It only took a few weeks for all those values, all those ways she felt different from everyone around her—and all the reminders that she did not measure up—to gain on her and feed her self-doubt. For Lucy, it was like swimming against the current to believe in herself when at least a hundred of her closest relatives seemed as similar to each other as she felt different from them.

Listening to her dad say, "but she does have a college education," when she told people she was a model, seeing one sister's lip curl after Lucy told her she also liked making love with women, hearing another say, "but guys don't want a woman who has been around," when she talked about the lack of attractive men in town, and witnessing the way her brother and dad looked at her as if she were insane when she said, "You can love someone and still not be able to live with them," made her wonder once again what different chemistry had happened the night she was conceived. It also fed a whisper in her mind that she was, perhaps, a weird, superfluous slut.

Yet again, Lucy felt torn by her love for them, and her desire to live otherwise and elsewhere. It occurred to her that perhaps the reason she liked being a foreigner was that she had always felt like one, starting right there in her hometown, and at least being one in another country made sense.

One afternoon while lying topless in the backyard, she was hit with a torrent of cold water. She opened her eyes and saw her father leaning out of the bathroom window above, bucket in hand. "Put some clothes on. We came out of the jungle a long time ago, you know. We're civilized people around here." Lucy looked out over the lush green valley and longed for the Mediterranean. There was a freshly opened letter from Hope lying on the grass next to her, and Lucy wondered how she could have shrugged that life off so easily, how she could have been so impatient. I could still be there, right now, she thought, if I hadn't been running around trying to settle every-thing with Julien and my family. How stupid the thought that she could get her whole life in order once and for all seemed to her now.

That weekend, lounging in the living room after the cele-bration of her parents' anniversary, Tom looked at Lucy in the way he had before telling what he thought would be a funny joke. "You'll be in and out of this thing twenty times or more, by this time, at your rate."

Lucy shook her head to dislodge the stab. She still couldn't believe that people thought she tossed things like marriage around lightly just because she never talked about them. What the hell do they want me to say anyway, she thought, how many times do I need to say I'm sorry and to how many people? She stared at her dad and asked a question she was pondering. "Anyway, how can I promise one man that it will be him, and only him, that I will love all my life? How can I know such a thing?"

"I guess if you want to go hopping in bed with every guy you meet it must be difficult."

Lucy felt her cheeks sting as if slapped. "Not every one, Dad," she said, standing. She faced him, ready to fight for the respectability of the right to make love with whomever she wanted, whenever. Then, she left the room.

*

The problem now was that she didn't know where to go. She still didn't want to go back to city life and modeling, but she was running out of money. She thought about going to graduate school, maybe she could teach art at a university, still have the time to sculpt and draw, and maybe even afford travel. She looked up a list of art galleries in town thinking she might work at one or all three of them, but whatever kind of interesting work she looked for turned out to mean accepting a permanent sort of contract, accepting to live there. Just the thought of that made her chest hurt. Waiting, watching, and believing that work or money would come, as she kept doing what felt like the right next thing to do, still seemed the best plan.

To relax, she read, she drew, she disappeared into the pasture with bottles of water and sat under the same oak trees she had as a girl, muddying the earth, and sculpting pruned bushes like she had seen in Paris in the Tuileries, as well as mini-models of the Arc de Triomf, Le Pont Alexandre III, even the Akasaka Castle, creating little foxes and squirrels to scamper among them.

*

One evening, as she walked along the river with her mother, Viola dropped questions between the two of them like breadcrumbs. "What are your plans, Lucy?"

Lucy sighed. "I'd like to find some work that involves traveling, living, and working in different countries. I miss that."

Her mother snapped her silver head in her direction. "But what do you have to show for it all?"

"What do you mean?"

"I mean you have worked and made money, but—," Viola stopped. "Don't you want to own things? A house? A car? Have a husband?"

"What I want most is an interesting life," Lucy said, then worried that it sounded like she was saying her mother's was not. "Interesting to me, anyway. What did you dream about when you were my age?"

"I dreamed about marrying your dad, having a house, a family."

"So you made your dream come true. Mine's different. Why shouldn't I believe that it could happen?"

Her mother threw a hand in the air in frustration. "I don't know, Luce, I don't know." She pointed at the river bluff where the limestone nunnery sat. "We saw three of the most beautiful deer up there this spring early one morning."

"Mom." Lucy eased into this. "Do you, or did you, ever see things when you make love?"

Viola crinkled her brow. "What kind of things?"

"I have seen different things. Once I saw camels. I just wondered if anything like that ever happened to you."

Her mother shook her head, keeping her pace. "No. But maybe your dad sees things. You could ask him."

Lucy knew she couldn't.

*

Gifts come in such awful packages sometimes. The first Sunday of July, after church and a pancake breakfast, when Ernst pulled into the garage, and Lucy turned to kiss him on the cheek, he lunged forward and forced a kiss deep into her mouth as if he had forgotten who they were. In so doing, his hypocrisy, reiterated, shattered the weight of all of those values she was not living up to. She mistakenly thought she no longer needed to be on her guard. She pushed him off of her, and then sat back horror-struck staring at the spade on the wall. Ernst sputtered his excuse as he crumpled in shame, "I just need some love, honey."

Don't we all, Lucy thought, but I am the wrong leg for you to hump. His desperation was real, and in it, Lucy sensed everyone's. She, too, had been feeling desperate for touch. But not that kind, not from him. She was shaking her head now. She, too, knew the relief that could feel like love in sex, and what a comfort that could be, for a while. But she also knew now that love is love and sex and is sex, and as involved as the two could be, they were not each other.

Years later she would read a French philosopher writing that love is what makes up for sex because sex is all about power and she would think, yes, that's it, but does it have to be that way?

At that moment in her grandfather's garage, she stumbled out of the car and over the lawn mower, shoved open the side door to the bright sky of noon, then tried to bolt across the lawn but felt like she was running against a strong wind in a haze.

She let the screen door slam behind her and then fell across her bed upstairs. It surprised her how vividly the image of Marcel in Tokyo, trying to figure out how to love her, entered her mind and how at that moment, all she wanted was the chance to re-kiss him. Why him? She wondered. Probably because he had been the last one, she imagined, and hence the closest in memory. What she wanted was to erase the kiss that had just been imprinted. She counted. Six months without a kiss and now this. She went to the bathroom and brushed her teeth for a long time.

How terrifically sad that she and her grandfather's desperation had collided in such a way. That was one way to look at it, and easier than thinking that he thought it was normal behavior. Yet this instance of abuse was also fortunate, she would come to see because now she would set herself free. She thought back to the first abuse, and all the work she had done to avoid more while still loving him. She was a woman now, she reminded herself, she could say something, couldn't she? Squeezes, kisses–naming these things made them seem minor. Later, when she would dare to speak about it to certain men in her life, some would shrug it off as minor. Until she asked them how they may have felt if their grandmother touched them, or kissed them, that way.

Lying there in her childhood bed on a hot July afternoon, she thought about the grabs, copped feels, that awful kiss, and Lucy felt like she was back where she began, fourteen again, nothing had changed, and all she wanted to do was run.

Instead, she slept until the next afternoon. When she woke up she asked her father for a thousand dollars. He was standing in the kitchen, his back against the counter. She fidgeted facing him, thinking how she never wanted him to know what his father had done, to spare him the pain or shame. Yet it wasn't his fault, she reminded herself. She was blind to how she had carried and was still carrying, a responsibility that was not hers, protecting the son from the father and the father from himself.

"I'm running out of money. I see there is not much opportunity for me here. I thought I might get a modeling job out of Chicago but that has not happened."

Tom looked at her as if he had known all along that she wouldn't, and was both amazed and relieved she was finally catching on. "You can't get a job there when you're here."

Lucy shifted her balance and held her trembling hands behind her back. "I just need money for one month and once I am there I can make a thousand dollars in a day."

Her father shook his head again. "You can stay in my house and eat my food, but you will have to make your own money."

She imagined he thought she needed some kind of lesson. It was a nice house and good food, she reminded herself, and a generous offer. She wondered if she told him what happened if he would change his mind and help her go. She could hear a distant voice inside her telling her she had to see this thing through another way.

*

Days later, she was downstairs watching a thunderstorm roll in, wondering how long it had been since her grandfather had made love. Or if had ever really made love, perhaps he was just a brute. Her grandparents had different bedrooms for as long as she remembered. She was not looking for excuses, but reasons. His lack of sexual contact, or his lack of love as he put it, did not make it okay for him to try to steal it, especially from her. A girlfriend, she thought, is what he needed. But she knew how second marriages were frowned upon by him and the rest of the community, as much as sex without marriage was. Any female companionship for a widower was gossiped about. This is the extent to which she was searching to remove the burden of shame so unfairly placed on her.

Viola walked down the stairs, and Lucy turned. Her mother stood on the landing with a troubled look on her face. "I've been over at your grandfather's. He is crying in his chair, and wants to know why you don't come and see him anymore."

Lucy followed her mother to the washing machine, where Viola lifted the lid and began to empty a load of whites. Lucy was surprised to feel how ready she was to tell her, yet imagined the impact as brutal. Slowly, she said, "Do you really want to know?"

Viola kept to her task. "I do."

"The last time I was with him, he stuck his tongue in my mouth."

Her mother snapped the wrinkles out of a clean dishtowel as she said, "I knew it was something like that."

Lucy froze, wondered how she knew, or guessed, why nothing had ever been said. She was also struck by the fact that she was listened to, believed, and heard.

Viola looked at her. "Do you want me to go over there and talk to him?"

Lucy was confused by the way she felt like she was three years old again. She felt so small and tall at the same time standing there leaning against the dryer, wanting to wrap herself around her mother's legs. It was something she could not remember ever having done as a child. Yet she did not want to send her mother to do her work. "No, no, I'll handle it. I'm just not ready yet."

Lucy looked down at her tanned thighs, how slim and strong they were. She wondered what it was like for a starved man to see those beautiful legs in front of him daily, at the same time that she asked herself why she should have to cover herself up because he couldn't control himself.

Viola nodded toward Lucy's breasts. "And from now on when you go over there, wear a bra."

Lucy snorted. There it was, the age-old belief that women were responsible for men's desires.

Viola shook her head. "I am not kidding."

Lucy took a deep breath at the insinuation that it was somehow her fault. She knew it didn't matter if she wore a bra or a long flowing skirt. "How about I just wear a suit of armor?"

"Not a bad idea," Viola said.

Lucy lifted the basket of clothes, took them outside, and hung them on the line.

To have her grandparents right next door had been a joy and comfort most of her life, mostly because of her grandmother, and the spirit she left behind. Lucy thought about how Grandma Pilgrim had given her the first glimpses of a wider world from her invalid bed through books, by teaching her to read. Whenever she looked at that window and saw Marie's ghost, she also saw the two of them on those lovely afternoons and she remembered the excitement of learning, the bursting of her curiosity.

Now standing there in the yard she felt watched by a predator, and the house loomed at her like an omen. She had to do something to dispel that heavy darkness but where to start?

She wondered. It seemed her whole life needed rebuilding. She looked toward her parents' house and the previous moments with her mother flashed through her mind like flowers growing out of rubble.

She went back inside and for about an hour, she walked around the house in a daze, wondering what to do next and thinking maybe her mother was onto something with that car, husband, and house idea. Especially the car, and one that was fast, small, and filled with gas, Lucy imagined as she put the recycling in the garage.

When she stepped back inside, Viola called out to her from the living room. "Lucy, please come in here. I want to ask you something."

Lucy looked in and saw her mom sitting in the blue chair that had been her own mother's, snapping her fingernails, one under the other, as she did whenever she was nervous. Viola looked up with a dab of fear in her eyes, something Lucy had never seen in them, and said, "Sit down."

Lucy sat.

Viola kept her gaze on her daughter as she asked, "Did your father ever try anything like that with you?"

Lucy's eyes widened at the horror of the thought. "Mom. No. Never. I have never once felt anything wrong in the way Dad touched me. Why do you ask me that?"

"Because mine did."

Lucy's mouth formed a howl. No sound came out. She swallowed. "What did you do?"

"I slapped him hard, across the face, and told him he had better never do that again."

Lucy stared at her mom in awe, wondering why she had never even thought of belting her grandfather. Her mother's strength encouraged her and made her feel inadequate, and weak, because she had frozen, and run away each time she had been abused. She still had not told her mother about the first time, all those years ago. She thought about it, then, but was not ready to go there, she was still calculating how much it might cost, to tell the truth.

Years later a cousin would tell Lucy that the time to say something about what their grandfather had done to her was at the time he did it and that if she did not tell anyone then, she should not tell anyone ever.

"That's unfair," Lucy would answer, thinking back to that moment in the living room with her mother, wondering if her mother had ever told anyone else that story. "You know, only people who have never been abused have difficulty understanding why it might take a long time to speak of it. Some people never understand the damage done to them, and those who do finally speak, probably do because, like me, they feel their telling might be healing for everyone."

Her cousin was quiet.

*

Later that awful and beautiful summer afternoon in Iowa, while Lucy was sweeping rain puddles out of the hollows in the driveway, Viola walked back across the yard from Ernst's and stood under the maple tree next to her. Lucy could not tell if her mother had said something to her grandfather, but she did notice a certain triumphant glint in her mom's eyes, a look of a mother having done battle for her child. "Your grandpa wants to take us all out to eat at the Hideaway. It's chicken night. If you don't want to go, that's fine."

Lucy snorted, The Hideaway Chicken, she thought, and then immediately felt mean, but decided to face him. The secret she had carried for so long took on a less bruise-like hue now that she had an ally, now that she had told someone else at least part of the story.

They sat at a table in the window, overlooking the winding road and the bank of elms alongside it. Lucy shot glances filled with taunting childish ire at her grandfather throughout the meal, and was either silent or blunt and sarcastic when she spoke to him across the table. Lena, the owner of the restaurant lumbered to the table with a belly full of baby and started chatting with Viola. Viola looked around the supper club. "You need to get some more help here."

"We're looking for waitresses."

Viola turned to Lucy, "Did you hear that?" and then back to Lena. "Lucy has experience and she's looking for a job."

Not that kind of job, Lucy thought as she smiled weakly, and yet, now she felt indebted to Viola. She was so happy to feel her support, but it seemed to already be slipping away, and here she was throwing her back to the lions. Yet, she still wanted to prove to her mother, more than she ever had, that she did not think of herself as "too good" for that kind of job, something her mother had often accused her of whenever she rejected something.

Lucy also agreed to the interview because she did need the money, she told herself it would be temporary, and there was no other way out now.

The next afternoon she drove away from that supper club with a horrid brown cotton dress–with short white puffy sleeves and a front bib that tied around the waist into a large bow at the back–slung over the passenger seat of the car. Each day closer to the day she would have to put it on, panic mounted in her body. Once it was all over, she would say to a friend, "Sometimes I wonder if all that panic and anxiety was just about the dress," and they would laugh.

That moment was still too far in the future for dear Lucy as she pressed it in the laundry room. Then she slumped over when she saw herself in the mirror.

Dawn, her sister-in-law, came downstairs looking for one of the boys' socks and saw her. Lucy looked up. "I look like I belong on a Twisted Swiss Miss canister and I would make a lot more money if I were."

"Lucy, you look great."

Lucy cried out like she'd been stabbed.

Then Dawn said, "I don't think you should do that, though, Lucy, if you don't want to."

"What else am I going to do?"

"I don't know. But if you don't want to, don't. I don't think that's good for you."

Seeing no other way to make money quickly and get out, Lucy did.

*

Her schedule changed to sleeping late, lying in bed dreading to go to work that afternoon, then being driven there by her father, who, as she begged him for a thousand dollars daily, patted her on the thigh, repeating, "You'll find your way. You'll make it through."

Once inside, she moved through the narrow passage between tables with steel trays the size of pigs, loaded with t-bone steaks, baked potatoes, and salads, all balanced on one hand, walking through swinging doors backward praying no one would come around the corner and fly into her.

"Is that Lucy Pilgrim?" she heard and turned to see a high school volleyball rival. "I thought she was modeling in Europe." She often hid in a little cove just outside the kitchen, washing gold plastic glasses, filling them with ice and water, and lining them up on trays, all the while fighting off the thought of becoming the ancient waitress with a graying ponytail who lived upstairs.

Reeking of fried chicken and steak at the end of the night, once home she peeled off the pantyhose and dress, and took long very hot showers. After six or seven hours of hard work, she had thirty-seven dollar bills, maybe. She calculated the months it would take to gather the thousand she needed.

Modeling looked like not such a bad way to make a living after all.

When Lucy's family came in one night, one of the older waitresses perked up and started fluffing her hair, then said, "That grandfather of yours is such a wonderful man," and Lucy thought, now there's someone he can kiss, and wanted to introduce them.

Then, when she came to the table for their order, and her dad said, "Lulu, you are the prettiest waitress in the county," she wanted to cry. But she did appreciate the twenty-dollar tip he left.

She knew he was trying. One afternoon before he drove her to work, he showed her an article in National Geographic about women who worked in National Parks. "There is something I think you would like doing and be good at, Lu."

"I'd love to live in nature and sculpt and draw."

"Then you need to marry a doctor," Tom said as if this were a normal response.

Lucy stared. "You mean be a prostitute?"

She watched the difficulty in his eyes as he registered that, and saw he had never looked at it that way before. "You're right, I guess that is what it would be, like that," he said. Lucy also noticed the way he eyed the title of the novel she had in her hand, *The Magnificent Spinster*. A magnificent spinster slut, she thought. She had not forgotten his opinion of her and imagined those were a few words he might have trouble sitting comfortably next to each other.

*

When the doorbell rang one afternoon, and Lucy said, "Maybe it's Julien," Emmy looked at her sister as if she were further gone than she had thought.

"Um, Lucy, he doesn't even know where this place is."

Lucy took a bite out of one of the chocolate chip cookies Emmy had cooling on the counter. She remembered that she had not known where his apartment was, either. She shrugged. "There are maps."

Emmy shook her head. "Oooookaaay," she sang as walked out of the kitchen.

Lucy had an inkling then that perhaps she was only pretending not to be attached all this time. Or that all of her efforts at detachment had not worked. The way her sister thought it ludicrous that Julien might reappear in Lucy's life made her once again question the feeling deep inside of her that he would.

That night she tore apart all of the photos she had of them together in Japan, and then she ripped the sheets that had been a wedding present off her bed. She wanted to forget all the men she had ever known and start again, fresh. She went downstairs and looked in the encyclopedia for random orgasms, hoping for some explanation. Nothing. She questioned her sanity.

"Do you think it means I'm crazy that I tore apart all those pictures?" She asked Emmy the next morning.

Emmy shrugged. "Just sounds like a waste of money to me."

*

She took on another waitress job in the afternoons on a yacht, for a luncheon cruise. That way she could ride up and down the river and make money, too. Every morning she deposited all of her cash in the bank doing her best not to think of the minutes it had taken her to make similar quantities posing as someone else, which she was doing now, too, anyway. She thought life was punishing her, yet she could see she was the one who couldn't seem to stop beating up on herself, because, after all, it was herself she had followed here, to this place of pain. It was her instinct that brought her to what she considered this awful mess. Everyone close to her simply shied away or told her she was overreacting, or that she was being too hard on herself. The way she figured it, she'd rather be the one with the whip than anyone else.

Faith had warned her about coming back here. She did not feel like talking to her now or making contact with anyone outside of Iowa, either. Forlorn was the word that came to her, often. To the point that she asked Eze if one of those shotguns on the wall downstairs could kill her if she shot herself in the head. He looked at her as if he had no idea she was such an idiot and said, "Quit talking so fucking stupid."

Then, when Gina, the wild bartender Lucy worked with on the luncheon cruise listened as Lucy asked, "If I jump in the river, will I drown?" and answered, simply, "Can you swim?" Lucy knew she was surrounded by the right folks.

Her brother Blaze confirmed that hunch when he took her for a drive and she lamented, "What are people going to think of me when they find out all of this?"

He looked at her and shrugged. "Just don't tell 'em."

"Your whole trouble is that you've tasted the good life," was Gina's assessment of the situation. Lucy couldn't argue.

Finally, she sent what she considered a last letter to Julien, like a flare into the sky one night in mid-July. *I thought I was so smart, I thought I had it all figured out, but now I see I know nothing. I'm back at the beginning. I must have missed a step. I only want you to know that I am not the person I appeared to be. I wanted to be a "hero" but am facing the reality that I am not strong enough. At least now. I am truly frightened.*

*

After she hung up the phone, having apologized to Vic in a pathetic attempt at the forgiveness she could not yet give herself, her mother barreled into the room, and looked at Lucy as if she might bite her head off. "If I ever hear you talking like that again, I am coming in here and taking the phone out of your hands and hanging it up."

"You have to get a grip," her sister Ruby said over the phone from Iowa City. "I set up an appointment for you to see some people down here who I think could help you."

"What did you tell them?"

"I told them, for one thing, that you are someone who doesn't even understand the meaning of the word compromise."

"I know what it means. I just don't like it."

"Whatever. Just come and talk to them, please. Maybe they can help."

So Lucy did. She sat across from a young male psychiatry intern in a white coat, who had that detached impartial expression that she hated. She told her story from divorce onward, except for the part about Ernst. Not a flinch, blink or twitch crossed his face.

"The fact that you weren't spending all of your money staying in four-star hotels, for example, while you were traveling in Europe, shows that you still maintained your reason."

Lucy waited for more.

He scratched some words on his clipboard. "I'll be right back."

He then ushered her into a large clinical room and offered her a seat in front of four other doctors in white coats. They all stared at her. One small woman, the only female other than her in the room, spoke. "We have talked this over and we think that you may have a slight manic-depressive condition. We'd like to put you on lithium to see if that helps."

"I know I have my ups and downs, and I am working on that. But what I am most curious about," Lucy opened her hands in front of her, "are these spontaneous orgasms. Where do they come from?"

The woman looked down, seemingly embarrassed to have no answer. "We think the lithium will stabilize that." She leaned over the table, scribbled something on paper, tore the prescription off the pad, and handed it to Lucy.

Lucy stared at her. "Stabilize?"

Now the woman looked ashamed. She couldn't look Lucy in the eye. She looked out the window. "We don't know. We think it will stop them. Try it and come back to see us in a month."

Lucy shook her head, then left. She crumpled the prescription into a ball and tossed it in the tall aluminum wastebasket in the hallway. She did a similar thing with the bill for their services when it arrived.

*

August rolled in, hot and white, and Lucy kept on with her routine. The days seemed eternal. One morning, Viola slid a large manila envelope, covered in Julien's handwriting and French stamps, across the table. Lucy stared at it, felt its thickness, then took a knife from the drawer to open it. She skimmed through three pages, thinking how strange it was that she could no longer imagine being with him, it was like searching for a hole that was no longer there. How had this happened? She wondered, then glanced through the photocopies he'd also sent. Viola looked at them out of the corner of her eye. "Why is he sending you all those pictures?"

"He wants me to introduce him to my agency in Chicago. He would like to work in America."

"When?"

"He says October."

"I thought you were tired of modeling."

"It beats waiting tables."

Her mother glanced back at the pictures. "That one there, where he's in the suit. Twenty years and twenty pounds ago I would have given you a run for your money."

Lucy laughed but she was shifting her weight, shaking her leg, squinting as she tried to concentrate on what Julien was telling her. She couldn't believe that he wanted to live with her now after she had told him how frightened and lost she was. Instead of telling her to find her way, he was telling her to stop punishing herself, telling her that she had not missed any step but had stepped right on it. That she was a hero, that she was strong enough, that all she needed to do was keep on, and that wherever she was he would like to come and share her space, and in fact, her spirit.

A wave of gentleness moved through her. It seemed that perhaps he did love her. Even the weakness in her. She thought of all the ways she had let herself crumble, all the theatrics she had allowed herself. Had she let herself fall apart in front of her family for proof of their love? Now that she had found that all of the people she loved would accept the pathetic in her, would the need for proof stop?

Yet, it was confusing to get more attention from them for being pathetic than for being smart and beautiful. That could create a weird pattern. She thought of the Wisconsin professor who had listened to her Asian and European adventure story on the boat the night before. She could still see the riveted look in his eyes. Maybe her life could be inspiring to others, she thought, maybe it wasn't all over.

*

She wrote more than eighteen pages in response to Julien, different letters that she never sent, in which she circled what was going on, asking and answering herself until she got to the end of her line, and realized she had formed a spiral. Rereading them on the swing in the wind, she saw what lay beneath it all was the open wound of her relationship with Ernst. She could feel him in the house at her back, moving around, not knowing what to do either, but she still didn't want to deal with it. She just wanted out. And though she was close, she was still churning, filled with self-centered fear.

She looked for more help. Her dad wouldn't even look at her as he dropped her off at the outpatient service of the local hospital because he disliked what she was doing. She imagined he thought it weak and unnecessary. She was charged for therapy on a sliding scale and as far as Lucy was concerned, she'd venture three bucks on talking to a supposed professional, at least someone other than her family who didn't know her family, which was hard to come by in that town. She tried to explain to the ex-nun psychoanalyst that getting out of town was the key to solving all her problems. It was the talking that seemed to help, even to this woman who was like a stone with blinking eyes. She insisted what Lucy needed to do was write a five-year plan, and was unamused when Lucy explained that she was more interested in the five-minute variety.

Her father hardly spoke to her now and this made Lucy angry even if she understood him partially. She knew that he knew what had happened with Ernst because her mother had told her that she had told him. And though Lucy wished he would just say something, anything to show that he recognized it was difficult for her, she also believed he stayed away because he could not stand to see the way she'd caved in. Her breaking down made sense to her when so little else did. Her father's recipe of "pulling herself up by her bootstraps" had some sense to it as well, she thought.

She also knew that her mother, who prodded, yet comforted, was right. One morning Lucy came downstairs distraught after dreaming that all of her teeth had fallen out, and her mother reached over the table, pried her mouth open, looked in, and proclaimed, "They're all there."

That afternoon as she rode to the bank with her mom, Lucy was thinking about not answering Julien's letter and the detachment that represented to her, and about the rising balance in her bank account. It occurred to her that her situation was improving, and then her next thought was of the only obstacle to continued amelioration she saw. As Viola parked, Lucy looked at her and blurted, "I feel like Dad is never going to respect me again."

Viola snapped her head to face her, her hands tightened around the wheel and her eyes were fiery. "So what? Is he God of the universe?"

And that's how Lucy realized he wasn't. Once again, her mother, in a matter of seconds, gave her the gift of freedom.

*

Then Faith called, and Lucy lay back on her bed, twirling her hair in her fingers as she listened. "The thing is, I would like Julien to just show up on his own without asking anything of me."

"Why?"

"I guess because it would prove that he loved me."

"What do you want—love or proof?"

There it was again, out in the open, giving Lucy pause. "It seems I need both."

It would take her a long time to learn that it was not necessarily proof, but something more than love was necessary from a partner.

*

And then, Marky Spark, an old boyfriend from grade school, came back to town and took Lucy out for dinner and drinks. He had grown into a handsome and successful businessman, and Lucy wondered yet again, about the mystery of magnetism. Nevertheless, she listened to the quiet inside as they enjoyed a cocktail, a steak, and the view of the Mississippi while telling their stories.

On the way home, Lucy asked, "Do you still play the harmonica?" and Marky pulled into a park and played for her.

Once they were back in the car, he handed Lucy his car phone. "Now would you please call this man in Paris and let him know what is going on?"

Lucy leaned back and shook her head. "I don't know what to say."

"How about I miss you, I want you to come here?"

"I can't say that."

"Why not? It's the truth."

Lucy looked Marky in the eye. "It's not exactly the truth," she said. She was not even sure she wanted Julien to come anymore. She did not want him to see her like this, nor was she ready to live with him. She did want to see him again one day. That much, she knew.

"Call him," Marky insisted.

She was both touched by his genuine concern and bothered that she seemed so much in need. "It's too expensive."

"What you are doing to yourself is too expensive, Luce. You're like that frog they put in warm water and keep turning up the heat."

"Frog?"

"If you put a frog in very hot water, it will jump right out, which you would have done had you jumped straight into this situation. But if you put a frog in warm water, it gets comfortable, and then you can slowly turn up the heat and kill it before it realizes it is dying. That's like you, now, here. So call now. I'm not saying it's him or being with him that will save your life but maybe it will move you. I'll pay for it just so I don't have to see you like this anymore."

Julien was there. His voice sounded like background music to Lucy's thoughts. She thanked him for the letter, mumbled about having tried to answer, and still wanting to see him, but how it wasn't the right time. "I am going back to Chicago soon, but am not sure when yet or what I want to do."

She couldn't hear half of what he said because his voice only made her ache. She set the phone on the dashboard and wanted to disappear. There was so much Julien did not know that she did not want to tell him that could explain so much. So much Marky did not know, either. She thought it might have been confusing to Julien to receive so much enthusiasm from her for over a year and to now receive a depressed call from her, filled with uncertainty about him.

"What did he say?"

"He said, 'Lucy, I think you should decide the moon is where you want to be and then you can spend your life saying, but I have to get to the moon.'"

"That's not very supportive."

"I told you it wasn't a good idea to call."

Sitting in her parents' driveway with the motor running, Spark, as she liked to call him, looked at her, and she hoped he wasn't going to try to kiss her. It had become her sort of Pavlov response when alone with men, trying to gauge when they might dive in for the kill. He kept his hands on the wheel. "Lucy, what would it take for me to persuade you to leave?"

"I have nine hundred and thirty-seven dollars, as soon as I have a thousand I'll go." She sounded ridiculous even to herself.

Marky leaned forward and slipped his wallet from his back pocket, then plucked three crisp one hundred dollar bills from it. One by one he dropped them on Lucy's lap. "Get out of here, Lucy."

She looked at Ben Franklin's face fanned out on her lap. It was the first time she had ever had hundred-dollar bills, any bills, dropped on her lap. She liked it. "I can't take that, Spark."

"You will take that. That is my gift to you."

She stared, considered. "I will take it but I will pay you back."

"It's a gift, Lucy."

He let out a sigh of relief as she lifted the bills one by one to her nose and said, "I love the smell."

*

Lucy and her parents were eating hash browns and fried eggs at the Busy Bee diner when Lucy announced her decision to leave. It was the end of September. Viola carefully set her fork down. "I don't think you should go."

Lucy thought of all the trouble of the summer. "I don't think I should have come here."

Viola looked into her eyes. "I'm glad you did. Imagine if this had happened to you somewhere else."

Lucy wondered if she would have fallen apart like this anywhere else. She would not have minded erasing the entire summer from her memory. Wasn't it because she was there that it had happened? she wondered. She would never know.

As much as she wanted to leave, she was now afraid to go. In her childhood home, there was still some sense of security.

Yet, she carried through with her plan day by day in that last week. She was determined to go before, or on, the first day of October, to start a new month in a new place. She withdrew cash from the bank, called Angelina who set up an apartment, and she quit the luncheon cruise and the Hideaway job. And then, she woke early the day she felt ready. She dressed and paced back and forth from bathroom to bedroom gathering courage. She even called Marky to hear him say, "Go."

Then she walked downstairs into her parents' room. Tom's eyes blinked open when Lucy touched his shoulder. "Will you please take me to the bus station?"

"When?"

"Right now."

He was out of bed and dressed in the five minutes it took her to kiss her worried mother goodbye and put her bags in the car. They pulled out of the driveway with no time to spare. Lucy glanced at her grandfather's house and felt cruel and right for not saying goodbye. This, too, was hard for Lucy, this learning that doing the right thing for herself could feel awful. She was learning to take care of herself without realizing it, as she learned to give herself the space and time she needed.

Three minutes before departure, Lucy lifted her luggage into the bus. Tom stood by the door, an expression she could not read on his face. Lucy was speechless and grateful. She hugged his limp body. It pained her to think she had lost the enthusiasm of her father. He could hardly look at her. She kissed his cheek. "Thanks, Dad."

"You take care now," he said to the bus, "and call. Your mother will be worried about you."

From her back window seat, she watched him walk toward the car, turn, and stand there. The two of them watched each other until they were out of sight.

If only she had known then what it would take him years to tell her—that helping her leave that morning was one of the hardest things he had ever done in his life.

[16]

Inside the Greyhound Terminal in Chicago, a strap from Lucy's suitcase caught in the escalator, sending her legs into the air and people stepping over her. This so flustered her she rode back down to buy a ticket for the next bus back to Iowa. The man behind the window shook his head. "No more buses headed there today, Miss."

So she took a cab to the brick residence on Goethe Street where, when asked how long she would be staying, she again hesitated, until a lovely young woman walked into the lobby, as if coming out of hiding, and surveyed Lucy with her cinnamon eyes while smoothing a palm over her cheek the color of café au lait. "Are you Lucy Pilgrim?"

Lucy nodded.

"I'm Claire, your roommate."

The kindness in her presence spun Lucy back to the concierge to confirm her stay. "At least a month."

*

There in that stark studio apartment with twin beds, Lucy sorted through things out loud, in snippets, always asking Claire, "Does that make any sense to you?"

Claire always studied her thoughtfully, with some fear in her eyes, too, wondering out loud, too, if her decision to take a semester off university in the East to model in the Midwest had been a good idea.

"Go back to school, Claire," Lucy often said. "I'm glad I did."

To soothe Lucy's anxiety, Claire told her a story. "My mom says there is a divine order to things, and we have to bear what comes to us to find out what it is. Whenever I have had a hard time, she tells me about when she was a girl in Alabama, and how the white children threw rocks and spit at her when she stepped off the bus to come to their school."

Lucy covered her face. "And here I am distraught over the flimsy fact that I can't stop fretting over what people might be thinking of me."

Claire was sitting at the edge of her bed now, dangling her feet as if on a riverbank. "My dad would say that is very conceited of you to think that people are even paying that much attention to you."

Those words entered Lucy like slants of light through a deep, dark mine. How had she missed the arrogance, the self-centeredness, and the conceit of her fear? It was difficult for her to discern between her pain and her fear. The wounded girl inside was still calling for her attention, wanting to be loved and admired, waiting for Lucy to give voice to her, and sad to see Lucy, instead, wishing and worrying whether others would.

*

Within a Chicago week, Lucy modeled for a poster for running shoes and made more money in three hours than she had all summer. Regular work for *Land's End* catalog followed, as did bartending in a chic hotel in the Gold Coast at night. Lucy was thrilled to pile cash in her drawer.

One night, as she poured another martini for a British advertising executive, he nodded toward the copy of *Scientology* she was reading in between shaking cocktails for customers. "Save yourself the time," he said, "and just do whatever it is you want to do."

Lucy knew he was right, but some small part of her was still hoping for a clear-cut formula to eliminate self-doubt and fear. It continued to amaze her how much guts it took to suit herself. The summer extravaganza of freaking out had left her more gun-shy of her instincts and intuition than ever, as they had guided her into hell, and even if she could see the benefits of that trip, she wasn't interested in going back.

She ran again and took long walks along the lake. She spent time at the Art Institute studying the light in Renoir's *Near the Lake* and *Seascape* and was fascinated by La Touche's *Pardon in Brittany*. She liked to sit near Columbus Fountain drawing and reading and to go to foreign films with Claire. Lucy struck up chats with strangers, and with the waiters, bartenders, and customers around her at 3rd Coast Café, which became a home away from home. She liked to have her meals there and hang out in the evening, sketching people. She even went out on dates.

Theo invited her on bike rides through the fall leaves, to his swank office parties, to the theater, and dinner at interesting restaurants. He played the guitar and sang to her in his West Side loft overlooking the city. His gentleness and the way he did not coax her to come to his bed, or bother her when she slept on his couch, comforted her. She wondered why she felt no desire to kiss such a fine man. It just wasn't in the chemistry, she supposed. With Theo, friendship seemed possible though it also seemed like he hoped for something more, which made her feel like a disappointment to him. This, of course, was also in her self-centered fear mind, rather than spoken by him, or her.

*

"I feel like I lost my balls," Lucy lamented one morning at 3rd Coast, to Sheldon, a middle-aged Jewish journalist who often sat nearby.

He peered over the top of half-glasses. "Darling, you never had them."

Lucy laughed. "Okay, guts, then, my guts."

He shook his head. "It's none of that. What you have been doing, I imagine, is watching yourself as a character, and enjoying the drama of it. Consider it your Holly Golightly phase, you'll get tired of it."

Lucy shook her head. "Me? Holly? I think not." She had never read or seen *Breakfast at Tiffany's*. She imagined Holly as a somewhat flighty and frivolous character and she certainly was not that. She did like a quote about never falling in love with a wild thing she'd read that Holly supposedly said. In any case, Sheldon was getting her gander up, telling her what he thought of her like that, and that was a good thing. She knew he was right in some way. She had been sort of watching a movie of her life in her mind, seeing herself doing all she had done, especially what she considered the awful and embarrassing parts, and she was tired of it.

An Italian-Austrian young man sat down on the banquette next to her one evening and began raving about the Giacometti exhibition he had seen at the Art Institute. He asked about her life, and she told him some of her stories. He took a breath and a swallow of his wine, then studied her like an unfinished sculpture, as if something was not quite right. He seemed to be looking for the right words, then just blurted, "Why is someone like you insecure? It doesn't make sense."

Lucy swallowed, unsettled at how quickly obvious it was. She shrugged and began shrinking back into the banquette.

He picked up the matchbox on the table. "Imagine you are this matchbox, and it is like you have a lot of dust on you, and all you have to do is wipe the dust off."

Lucy wondered if people had seen through her long before what she was beginning to think of as "that awful summer" and if she, perhaps, was the only one who had believed her former charade of invincibility.

When Yoichi, the Japanese journalist she had worked for, asked over lunch how her summer had been, Lucy covered her face in shame and said, "I was so bad."

He looked at her with loving eyes as he stroked his salt-and-peppered mustache in concern. "You should not think of yourself as a bad person, Lucy. You are a lovely person, growing."

All of these people moved her back into herself. Or more deeply into herself. At least she was not beside herself anymore. Yet, had she ever left herself, after all? Did it matter? All these thoughts, all these questions, seemed both unanswerable and wonderfully superfluous to Lucy. What was clear to her was that people did help. Maybe she did need them, after all, she pondered, though the idea still made her squirm. She remembered crying out to Ruby that summer, "I'm just trying to figure out who I am," and Ruby rolling her eyes and saying, "You are who you are. Don't sweat it. You just need to get out of that house."

Perhaps it was that simple, Lucy mused, walking through Lincoln Park, winding south along the paths on her way home from the health club. She stopped to look up at the pure and vivid intensity of the November blue sky, and the sight of a bare branch against it struck her. Something about its outline, its separateness. She thought of the generations of leaves it had sprouted, and would again, and how its resting fruitfulness appeared barren.

Joy rose in her as she noticed the edges of things again, the clear line where branch was branch and sky, sky, and spring a kept promise between them. She felt alive again. Maybe happiness did simply boil down to physical exercise, she mused. She had stopped running after that afternoon in the garage with her grandfather, and now that she was working out again, the endorphins were back at work, too.

The spontaneous combustions reappeared, as well, with Lucy's coming out from under the dust. They had gone quiet since that afternoon when she'd sunk into gloom. She celebrated their return. She would wonder for decades, perhaps the rest of her life, about the mystery of them.

She would read a French psychoanalyst say that women had a sort of *jouissance* that had nothing to do with men (and she would love the word *jouissance*, a French one meaning the enjoyment of rights, property, and/or sexual pleasure). Lucy would read his lament on a sunny rooftop terrace in Spain. When he mentioned that he was begging women, especially the women psychoanalysts, to talk about it, even getting down on his knees, and still they would not, Lucy would imagine herself at his lecture, waving her hand to get his attention.

And, eventually, she would talk about it with a French psychoanalyst, one she suspected had been begged by this very man, and this woman would scoff at Lucy's understanding of *jouissance*, telling her that he was not talking about "that" *jouissance* but something broader and more abstract. Lucy would point to the way he cited The Ecstasy of Saint Teresa, asking what she was getting off on. She would wish that the man was still alive so she could tell and ask him things.

As winter approached Chicago, all of this was in Lucy's unknown future, the one she was afraid of, which would turn out even more beautiful and exciting than she imagined.

*

New opportunities presented themselves as the year ended: Angelina called to say an agency in Barcelona was interested in her return. Lucy called Hope.

"You have to come first to Bonica, and stay with me. We'll celebrate the New Year together!"

Lucy looked at the stack of graduate school applications, want ads, and resumé drafts on the kitchen table and couldn't decide if going back to Europe would make her happy or not. It seemed time to build something new in America. Yet she could feel the Mediterranean lifestyle lapping around her ankles and if modeling could buy her more time there, she'd do it.

And then, Leif walked in. He stood at the top of the three red carpeted stairs, just inside the door of the 3rd Coast, looking very much like a young president. He moved a hand through his deep red hair as he cased the open room for a place to sit. His eyes stopped at Lucy, seated on the far banquette. She had looked up when the door opened, and thought, now there is a man I might love.

Leif held her gaze as if saying, Do we maybe know each other? I hope so, and Lucy smiled as he walked toward her.

"Will I interrupt your sketching?" he asked as he looked at the banquette next to her. There was a foot of space between the tables. She shook her head.

She listened to him order lamb chops and a glass of wine, ordered another herself, and then closed her sketchbook. "Do you live in the neighborhood?" she asked, then when he looked at her, she saw that his eyes were the same color as hers.

"No. I've just come from an interview. I'm only in town for a night and have never been to Chicago. I'd like to listen to some blues. Do you know a place?"

She nodded, noticing that a door in her heart seemed to already have his name on it, so she opened it.

While watching Koko Taylor sing the blues in a smoky club uptown, Lucy enjoyed the feeling of his lips and the warmth of his breath near her ear as he said, "I'd be up for breakfast."

They met at 9 at Artist's Cafe, and after a visit to the Art Institute, he changed the time of his return flight to D.C. After lunch at the Billy Goat they spent hours on a walking tour of Chicago, paying attention, storytelling, asking, answering, their gestures and movements filled with mutual attraction. Lucy felt stoned with a fearless happiness she had never known with a man. Later, when he surprised her with a deep goodbye kiss at her door, her entire body blushed.

And then his letters overcame her, giving her a vision of herself that she liked better than her own. It was a celebration of her she had never known and it lifted her.

*

Days later, while Lucy was dancing alone in the apartment, Viola called. "You have a letter here. Well, it's a postcard. From France. What do you want me to do with it?"

Lucy never had answered Julien's July letter, nor had she contacted him since that embarrassing call from Marky's car. "What does it say?"

"This postcard is only a candy before I write you a real letter. I wish I make enough money to spend time in USA very soon and give you kisses you deserve. I'm boring, need to move. I'm missing fun, action, craziness." Viola paused. "What does he mean by craziness?"

Kisses you deserve, hmm, Lucy thought, and wondered what had changed and if it had anything to do with her. "Fun, Mom, he just means fun. Is that all?"

"He says, 'I hope life is still a big adventure for you. I send you my best kisses, love and hugs. I'll write you very soon. With all my love, Julien.'"

Lucy was silent.

Viola waited. "What do you want me to do with it? What are you going to do?"

No one had ever talked to Lucy about what she deserved. She thought about Leif, who'd also written that she deserved so much. She was still thinking about his kiss and was interested in more. It was easy to imagine happiness with him. She tasted Julien's kiss, then Leif's, like two ice cream flavors that were very difficult to choose between. Then she remembered

Viola was still waiting for an answer. "Just send it to me, please. And, for now, Mom, I'm just going to enjoy it."

"Whatever that means," Viola mumbled, and then smooched kisses before hanging up.

Rain pattered against the windows. Lucy cranked Katrina and the Waves singing "I'm Walking on Sunshine" and danced around the apartment.

She decided to allow herself everything.

*

Lucy booked a room at The Elms for Leif when he came for a visit and she was elated to find herself having the most delicious time she had ever had there. She was elated to make love in love, elated to be elated.

Angelina pulled her aside at the Christmas party. "Lucy? Harvard Law? Marry that man."

Lucy shook her head and rolled her eyes. Her body tingled. Angelina stared at her like she was insane. Lucy raised a shoulder. "I think I have to go to Barcelona first."

"Oh, now I get it. You are one of those people who like what is not good for them."

Lucy crinkled her face in confusion and hurt, thinking of all the good-for-her things she liked. She guessed Angelina had translated Harvard Law into money into a good husband, which made her think of that man in Tokyo who had suggested that women needed husbands for money. Lucy was interested in equal partnership. Yet, it was obvious to all who saw that she and Leif enjoyed each other very much.

She turned, then, to look for him, he was laughing with Claire on the other side of the room, and he looked at her as if he'd felt her search. She had found communion. It was possible. Here was proof when she was no longer looking for it. It felt like money in the bank of love to Lucy. The future was opening with her heart, and more importantly, she was joy-filled in the present.

*

She decided to go to Spain, if only for the winter. She knew that she had to go see what it would feel like to be in Julien's presence again, she wanted to know before she invested in more of the life she was thinking about in America, which included going deeper with Leif. She knew how rare, at least in her short life, the connection she felt with Julien was. She also felt a precious rareness with Leif. Yet she still had that odd, uncanny feeling that, with Julien, she could live the life she meant to, the open one she most wanted to live.

This sensation confused her, but there it was, and instead of exploring more with Leif and wondering about Julien, she would explore more about Julien and wonder about Leif.

Lucy wouldn't go directly to Julien, though. "I'm not showing up on his doorstep again," as she put it to Faith, who had told her the year before "if I felt like you did, I'd have been back on the guy's doorstep with all my suitcases long ago," but then during the summer had suggested another sort of appearance there. "If you are going to kill yourself, go slit your wrists on his doorstep, please. I don't want to see it."

That doorstep had haunted Lucy's mind, along with those upstairs curtains moving in the Parisian breeze, Julien behind them somewhere doing whatever it was he needed to do, she imagined. It was a lonely doorstep to Lucy, one that did not call her back.

*

As she prepared to leave America again, she wanted to leave as clean as possible. First, she found the courage and will to write to her grandfather to tell him what she never had.

One could say she held her own younger hand and urged that girl she was to say, "What you did to me was wrong."

It was a start.

She wondered how to improve communication with her father and did not know, she hoped time and distance would help.

She fretted over telling her mother she was going and wished her mother would not see her decision to leave as a rejection, but rather would see Lucy as a bird that loved resting in the nest as much as she loved to fly.

Lucy told Viola by phone in the interest of it being passing news. "After Christmas, I'm going to stay with Claire and her family in Virginia and see a friend in Washington, D.C., and then go to Barcelona to work, to see how it goes, I don't know for how long."

After a pause, Viola spoke. "You see, you are working a lot and everything is going well and now you are leaving. What kind of sense does that make?"

Lucy kept her main mission—to enjoy herself with Claire, and then Leif, and then to find out if what she felt for and from Julien was real, all while traveling—to herself. "I'll leave money in the bank, Mom, and I can always come back if it does not go well there. Spain will be more comfortable than Chicago in the winter. How's that for sense?"

"That makes a bit more. Who is this friend in Washington?"

"A kind man I met."

"Is he American?"

"Yes."

"Good."

Lucy laughed.

"I just hope what happened to you here this summer doesn't happen to you over there."

"I hope not, too, Mom." Lucy smooched and hung up.

Faith scolded her at the 3rd Coast that evening. "It won't, that is what you say to your mom when she says things like that, Lucy, you say, 'it won't.'"

And Lucy realized Faith was right.

*

"Maybe you can help me with this." She opened up at a Sunday breakfast with Theo. She wanted to ask a man about what had happened with her grandfather. "What bothers me is that my dad never said anything to me about it."

"Maybe your dad thought you could handle it just fine on your own."

It would take him a long time, long after she had given up on hearing it, to say, "I am sorry that happened to you." And he would never know what his father had done to his daughter that first time, at that tender age. He would understand one day, though, that his father had known what he was doing when he did it the second time. She would see the knowledge change her father's face–how it tightened his jaw, stopped his breath, and turned his vision inward.

There, with Theo, she sipped her cappuccino and went on to her other recurring question. "What do you think about this idea that we all need people? I hate the idea of being dependent, yet I can see the way we help each other. It just drives me nuts when people talk as if they are setting up some sort of needy network. When people tell me I am too independent, it sounds insane to me. What do you think about that?"

Theo finished chewing his bite of blueberry pancake and wiped his mouth. "I think in being independent, we are all interdependent."

"That's exactly it. Why could I never say it like that?"

"You didn't need to say it. You live it, Lucy."

What a gift, Lucy thought, to hear that, to be seen like that. This, too, lifted her.

She kissed Theo on the cheek before getting out of his car. "When I come back, we have to continue this conversation."

He looked through her, his eyes smiling. "Do tell about this mythical return of yours, Lucy."

She smiled, speechless again.

*

It was a gray afternoon on Goethe Street and midnight in Paris as Lucy looked out the window while listening to Julien's phone ring. "It's for engineering, I'm working on a, I don't know how you call it—"

Lucy pictured him on a stool, stenciling a plan. "Perspective?" she said, then smiled to herself thinking of all the layers to that word and their situation.

"Yes, that's it."

"Well, listen," she said, "what's your perspective on this? I'm flying to Spain on the twenty-ninth of December and was thinking of passing through Paris."

"Why don't you come another day?"

Lucy's body tightened. That adolescent, defensive girl in her came to the forefront and she couldn't believe, all things considered, he was now going to get picky about the day. "Because I am coming on the twenty-ninth," she said.

"Of course. Right."

Listening to him speak in that vulnerable voice she had not heard since she'd called from Tokyo, she became quiet, softened for a moment.

"It's just that I won't be here that day, but if you come in January—"

"I have a party to go to in Barcelona on New Year's Eve."

"Please call from Barcelona. It would be perfect if I come, no?"

Lucy closed her eyes. "Incredible," was all she could say, before "goodbye".

Claire walked into the apartment and saw Lucy in front of the window, staring at the phone she'd just hung up. She shook her head, smiling. "I'm going to miss you and your nakedness, Lucy."

*

A few days before Christmas, Lucy was back in her Iowa home, all of her belongings stored in the attic and a couple of suitcases packed. She felt buoyant again and ready to see her grandfather.

Viola jerked her head in the direction of Ernst's house and said, "He's over there," when Lucy asked how he was.

"I wrote to him. Here's a copy of the letter, if you want to read it." Lucy laid it on the table.

Viola read it. "Why would you even want to save a copy of that?" she said, looking at it as if it were moldy vegetables.

Emmy came into the kitchen, then, and stood watching the conversation.

"I don't know," Lucy said. "Maybe it just felt good to write it out once before I sent it. I'm going to go over and talk to him."

"Do you want me to go with you?" Emmy asked.

"No, I'll be fine. Thanks."

The house was dark as Lucy walked across the frozen yard and up the back stairs. The door was unlocked. "I'm in here." His voice came from his bedroom. Lucy paused at his open door, the light from the moon shone through the two corner windows. She saw movement under the covers. "Come in, honey, come in and sit down."

She sat at the far edge of the bed. "Did you get my letter?"

She stiffened as he lifted his arm out from under the sheet. He laid it across his forehead. He looked so white in the moonlight. "I don't know how a girl could think such terrible things about her grandfather," he said.

Lucy had not expected him to take this tack. She had never once felt that he didn't know what he was doing. "You know damn well how I could. Where is the letter?"

"I burned it like you told me to."

"So you know. And I didn't tell you to, I just said you could."

She'd suggested the burning to keep the secret as if the shame were both of theirs instead of just his. Yet, it was a private matter, and at least, and at last, they were talking about it. How had it come to this, she wondered, why did this have to be? Why did she have to be there even having this conversation? Why couldn't he be like those grandfathers in movies and storybooks? Perhaps they were all lies.

Anyway, sex was the answer. Sex. If it hadn't been for that, she thought, but knew, too, that if it hadn't been for that none of us would be here.

She wondered, too, why our source is so rarely exalted as a sacred art of communication and so blatantly degraded in public.

Lucy looked at her grandfather, ashamed in his bed.

If she didn't love him, they wouldn't be there either.

350

"I don't think you are a terrible man. You are a man, just a man. All I know is that I never want it to happen again. Just tell me you understand."

Ernst stared at the ceiling, rubbing his hand back and forth on his forehead, and biting his lip. She thought about how he would soon be alone in his bed in the dark again. Either he couldn't speak, or wouldn't.

In any case, Lucy was not going to make him. She stood, leaned forward, kissed his cheek then walked away.

When she reached the threshold of his bedroom door, Ernst gurgled, "I love you, honey, I do," and Lucy paused. She looked toward her grandmother's room. She saw her rocking back and forth on the edge of her bed, looking worried.

Lucy froze, then whispered, "I didn't want you to know anything about all of that."

Grandma Pilgrim shook her head and opened her arms, motioning for Lucy to come.

Lucy went.

Marie gathered her granddaughter into her and rocked gently. As their breathing slowed, she began humming, then singing, "Be Not Afraid" while she stroked her granddaughter's hair, caressed her face, and lulled her into restoration.

*

Christmas morning, Lucy could feel her mother watching her as she opened one of her gifts, the package wrapped in gold paper, which was filled with what seemed to her like a mile of tissue paper. She unraveled it until she reached an ivory porcelain camel, its saddle trimmed in gold. She looked up at Viola, who smiled at her as if to say, See? I was listening.

The doorbell rang, and Ernst was visible through the window, upright again. Lucy answered it. She stood back as she ushered him in. "Merry Christmas, Grandpa."

He raised his chin and looked down at her. "Well, can I kiss ya?"

Lucy pointed to her cheek. "Right there you can." And he did.

Red napkins flowered out of glasses over a green tablecloth on the dining room table, set in front of the picture window overlooking the snow-covered valley. They drank sweet wine and ate Viola's special pheasant, wild rice, cranberries, green bean casserole, and warm bread from the oven. There was ease and laughter around the table set for fifteen. Lucy was coming to accept that she might not be able to have the kind of relationships she wanted with everyone. What mattered most was to have a good one with herself, and she still had a lot to learn about that.

Her send-off crew from the small regional airport, just over the hill from home, was Tom, Viola, Emmy, Dawn, and the grandkids. Ernst said he needed a nap and stayed home.

"Always be thinking," Viola warned with a raised index finger.

"I always am, Mom," Lucy said, as she hugged her. "It's my blessing and my curse." She backed away to get a look at everyone then, and added, "I just wish I could get to the point where I don't worry about anything anymore."

Her father, who had been quiet throughout the day, spoke up. "That's when you're dead."

And Lucy laughed as she hugged him.

After she climbed the ten stairs up into that tiny plane, she looked back once more, to see all their hopeful faces from the window. From her front row seat, she watched them waving at her while the plane taxied, then rose above the rolling hills, gleaming white.

Marianne Maili is an author and professor. She has a PhD in *The Construction and Representation of Cultural Identities* from the University of Barcelona. She has been a Spanish Ministry International Mobility Scholar, a Visiting Scholar at the International Writing Program at the University of Iowa, and an Erasmus Distinguished Foreign Visitor at the Josef Skvorecky Literary Academy in Prague. She lives between Los Angeles, Barcelona, and Paris.

www.ingramcontent.com/pod-product-compliance
Lightning Source LLC
Chambersburg PA
CBHW020320140726
47905CB00013B/1288